By
ABBY MCCARTHY

Copyright © 2017 by **Abby McCarthy**

All rights reserved. No part of this publication may be reproduced, distributed or transmitted in any form or by any means, without prior written permission.

Abby McCarthy
www.abbymccarthyauthor.com

Publisher's Note: This is a work of fiction. Names, characters, places, and incidents are a product of the author's imagination. Locales and public names are sometimes used for atmospheric purposes. Any resemblance to actual people, living or dead, or to businesses, companies, events, institutions, or locales is completely coincidental.

Cover Design by Hang Le
http://www.byhangle.com

Cut Wide Open Abby McCarthy
ISBN-13:
978-1544015385

ISBN-10:
1544015380

•Dedication:

To Emily Smith-Kidman an amazing blogger, publicist and friend, who always has my back, and who pushed me to not hold back with going dark. Welcome to my dark side.

CONTENTS

Part One

Prologue Gunner

Sometimes, after I'd park my bike at whatever shitty motel I was staying at, in whatever shit hole town I stopped in, I'd walk searching for her. Another crowded street with nameless faces. None of their names mattered, because none of them were her. Each day that passed without my Mouse was another day where I lost more of myself.

Sure, I knew those fucking Hades bastards were after me, but I'd be ready for them. I'd be ready for anything, as long as I knew she was out there somewhere.

Another street, another day. I thought I saw her once. A flash of dark hair moved as a woman rounded a corner. I was on my bike. I gripped my bars and pulled back on the throttle. I needed to go faster. I needed to see if it was her. It wasn't.

I was losing hope.

I was in a bar drinking until the dark liquid made me numb. I pictured her walking through the door and even pictured the woman who dropped to her knees outside of the bar in the dirty, dark alleyway as her. I hated myself for giving in to the liquor and the women. The guilt ate away at me. My life was in a constant state of fighting, fucking and getting wasted. I preferred getting wasted. It made it easier. She was out there somewhere, but maybe I'd never find her. Maybe this road, I was meant to walk alone.

8 years old Charlie

I see you through the dark dirty glass. You're kicking a ball laughing with an older man. I wonder if he's your grandpa. You smile at him. I think that's what love looks like. You have sandy hair. You look like you're my age, maybe a little older. I wonder if we can be friends. I laugh at myself. It's not really funny. No one would want to be friends with me.

I'm invisible.

I watch you until another man opens the door to the little white house and calls you inside. You wave to the old man as he gets into his car, and run without a care in the world into your home.

Home.

I wonder what that's like.

I am here as a paycheck. I eat alone. I sit in my room. Alone. I walk to school. Alone. I barely talk. I am alone in my thoughts. I am alone in life. I have no one.

I see your mom through the window. Her blonde hair blows in the wind. She gets in her car. She's smiling and even from the distance, I can see how beautiful her face is when she smiles. If I had to choose a word to describe her, it would be alive. Everything about her screams, "I'm alive."

Your daddy bends into the window and kisses her. You run from the house with your backpack slung over your shoulder and hop into the backseat. Your daddy ruffles your hair before closing the door.

I see you at school, but only for a few seconds. I am in line on my way to the library. You're wearing gym shorts heading towards the gym. I recognize the boys you're with. I think you're in the fourth grade.

You don't see me.

I read a book in the library and get lost in it for thirty minutes. I'm reading Harry Potter. I love the fictional world.

No one sits by me.

It's okay. They might want to talk, and I don't want to talk.

I hope to see you in the hall, but I don't.

I watch for you every day through my thick, stained glass. I watch you grab a basketball, get on your BMX and head toward the park. I see your friends knock on your door, and you come outside and sit on the stairs.

You don't see me, but I watch you. I wonder what it's like to be happy.

"Take out the trash," Mitchell yells. Claire is sitting on the couch smoking a cigarette with a can of beer in her hand.

I do as he says and quickly grab the red ties and pull the garbage out, and go outside to the can. You're outside. I keep my head down. I wonder if you'll notice me. The metal trash can lid falls to curb and clatters. I jump. Loud noises make me nervous.

I look up and see you staring.

Right.

At.

Me.

I run inside to my room. Alone.

9 years old

Muted red and blue lights flash across my room. I was sleeping, but the noise and the light woke me. I hear your momma wailing, and I know it's bad. I watch through my dark stained glass as she cradles you in her arms. I don't see your dad.

Two days pass. You wear a black suit, holding your momma up as a black stretch limo pulls up in front of your house. I see you later in the day. People enter your house. You sit on the side of the house with your head hung low. You're alone.

10 years old

You're not at the same school this year. You're getting older. I don't see you playing basketball or riding your bike anymore. You don't laugh like you used too.

I'm walking home from school. You're in your mom's car.

I see you and I think for the first time, you see me.

I make it home and you're sitting on your front steps. You're wearing a light blue t-shirt and shorts. I can feel you staring at me.

"Hey!" you shout, but I'm afraid. I don't know what to say, so I run inside to the window. I watch you through the dirt stained glass, and for the first time ever, you're looking at the house. I swear, I think you can see through the hazy glass and look directly at me.

11 years old

I'm home from school today. I don't feel well.

I hear a loud rumble and stare out to see what the noise is. A shiny, black motorcycle pulls into your drive. Your mom's changed. She no longer has the same smile. She is still pretty, but she's different. She's no longer life. She's existing. She's like me.

She grabs the man's hand and walks him inside. He is there for hours, but is gone before you get home.

You don't know this man visits your mom, at least I don't think you do, because he's never there when you are.

You're outside and another boy says something to you. You don't like it. You punch the boy. Your mom comes out of the house and yells. The boy grabs his face and rides away. I don't know what he says to you. I want to ask. I've been watching you for so long, I feel like I know you. You're angry and storm off down the street.

I don't know why, but I slip my shoes on and walk to the park. I hope that you're there. I want to see you, but I don't want you to see me. I hide in the shadows along the edge of the park and watch. I see a few kids I recognize from school on the swings. There is an old pavilion, part of the roof is caving in.

That's where I spot you.

You're smoking a cigarette. I didn't know you smoked.

I am fascinated by you.

You're so young, yet you pull the smoke into your lungs like you've been doing it for years. You've changed some. Your hair is a tiny bit darker than when I first saw you through the glass. You're taller too. You have a black T-shirt on, black jeans and black boots.

You look around the park. Your eyes roam and then finally still.

On me.

You're staring at me and I can't look away.

I watch as you pull the smoke into your lungs again. You exhale. The haze clouds your face hiding your eyes. Normally I'd run but I can't today, I'm too frozen by your stare. You take another puff, then stomp out your cigarette. Your boot moves back and forth extinguishing the red glow.

You stare at me for another moment and then someone calls your name. You look up to greet your friend and our connection is lost.

I become invisible.

Twelve years old

I am changing.

I got my period.

I'm suddenly sadder than normal. I let my thoughts drift to all that I've lost and all that I'll never have. I wonder why I exist. I wonder what's the point. I try to dream, but dreams are for girls with futures. I don't see tomorrows, I can barely see today. Sometimes I wonder if I should just end it, but then I see you and you give me a reason. I don't understand it since I don't know you, but you've become a beacon I hold onto. Even through your loss, you have light. I want that.

Mitchell and Claire are fighting. Claire throws a dish. Mitchell calls her a drunk. They're yelling about money. They're always yelling about money. Mitchell threatens to leave. I wonder what will happen to me.

Mitchell slaps Claire. Something crashes. I need to leave this room. The four walls are suffocating. I stay in my bedroom when I can, but today, I need air. This is all too much.

I tiptoe out of the house and quickly walk down the street towards the playground. I don't look around. I'm trying to be fast. I don't want to be seen. I don't hear you approach.

"You okay, Mouse?" you ask me. *Mouse?* I look up at you quizzically, but don't say a word. I can't, I'm too shocked that you're here... talking to me. I slow my pace as we enter the park. It's empty. I imagine children are at home sitting at dining room tables, sharing their day with their parents.

I move to the picnic table under the pavilion. I do this without saying anything, but my hand is trembling slightly because you're near. I'm nervous. I'm always nervous around people, but you, who I've been watching for so long, especially make me nervous.

I sit at the picnic table and you sit down next to me. You're close. I can feel your body heat and your leg brushes against mine. I stare at you, directly in your eyes. Flecks of green that I never noticed before contrast against the brown in your eyes. You're bigger this year. I wonder how tall you'll get.

"Cat got your tongue, Mouse? You don't say much, do you?" You stare at me. Your eyes penetrate me. I feel like you *SEE* me. Not the me that hides, or the me that can walk through a crowded room and not be seen. You. See. Me.

"I can talk." My voice comes out quiet and meek.

You close your eyes like you're savoring something, but I'm uncertain as to what could make you do that.

Your eyes open, "What's your name, Mouse."

"Why do you keep calling me Mouse?"

"'Cause you're quiet and sneaky like one. Now, what's your name?"

"Charlie, short for Charlotte," I shrug.

"Well, Charlie short for Charlotte, I'm Gunner Reed."

I nod because I know this already. It does something to me to hear you say my name. I can't remember the last time someone said it with any type of inflection.

"How long have you lived across the street from me?" You're curious about me. This shocks me.

"Since I was eight," I answer honestly.

"How old are you now?"

"Twelve," I answer and I swear it feels like you're doing a perusal of me.

"Damn, four years you've been across the street from me," you say and take a cigarette from your pocket. Your fingers move to flick a wooden match against the table. You bring it to the tobacco-- a red glow and then a puff of smoke. I smell you, a mixture of smoke and soap.

"Your parents fight like that a lot?"

I shake my head. "Not my parents."

You look at me like you're trying to figure me out.

"Foster care. I bring them a whopping twenty-one dollars a day." I'm startled by my openness with you. I've never admitted this much to anyone so freely.

You nod your head as if you can understand. I know that you don't because I know you were happy once. But you do know pain. I see this too. Maybe you see the same in me and that's why you're sitting here. You exhale smoke then ask, "They hurt you?"

I shake my head. "They don't put their hands on me, but does it hurt me to know that I am only a check? I do what I'm told and in return, I have shelter and food. I shouldn't complain. I know what it's like to not have both of those things. But the loneliness hurts."

"You want to talk about it?" You ask inhaling your smoke.

"I don't talk much," I say simply.

"Maybe that's 'cause no one was listening."

Thirteen years old

We talk. Not much, but you catch me when I'm walking and you try to make me smile. I don't know why you do this, but you do, and it matters. I look forward to it and walk more than I used too. Every once and awhile, you'll pry. Slowly finding out more about me.

"What happened to your parents?" It's a question I don't want to answer. You catch my chin as I try to look away. "Don't do that, Mouse. Don't hide from me."

So, I tell you what I remember of my Mom. How we lived in crack houses where people sold themselves. I tell you how I didn't know who my dad was, but that my Mom cared more about her next fix than my next meal. I tell you how I woke to find her with a needle in her arm, her skin a bluish gray. I didn't know what to do. I was only five years old. I stayed with her until a police officer eventually stumbled upon us. They took me and I didn't understand, but they fed me and at least it was food. They put a blanket on my shoulders and took me in the opposite direction than my mother's body. I didn't see her again.

You cuss at my story. You're angry for me. I put a hand on your shoulder to calm the rage coming off of you and it works. "No one deserves the start you got Charlie," you tell me like I'm important. I want to believe you.

Mitchell and Claire are on vacation visiting his mom for the week. I'm home alone. So incredibly sick of being alone. I watched you minutes before, as you walked out of your house. I hope you're going to the park. I want to see you. I want to talk to you. You have become my only friend.

I look for you through the branches. I don't like to approach you in case you're with friends. I don't want their attention. Today, you're not with the guys. You're with a girl. She's beautiful; a year older than you. She has long blonde hair, the complete opposite of my dark locks and her breasts are fuller than mine. She has curves. I have none. I know I'm staring, but she presses herself against you.

Your hand goes into the back pocket of her jean shorts and she laughs then slaps your arm. You say something low, and I don't hear it. But she does. She leans into you, presses close and her lips are against yours.

I watch.

I see you.

It doesn't feel good to see you like this. A pit forms in my belly and I want to throw up at the sight of you with her. I let out a gasp.

She freezes, pulls away from you and looks around until her eyes land directly on ME.

I'm caught.

"What are you doing? You little freak," she yells.

You try to tell her to calm down--that it's just me. Mouse.

She argues with you and starts to come towards the bushes where I've been watching you. I'm frozen in place. My heart screams for me to run, but my feet won't move.

"You like to watch, you nasty little bitch," she sneers.

And you lose it. You grab her arm and move her away from me. Then, you pull me from the bushes and stand protectively in front of me.

"You don't talk to her like that!" you yell.

"Mouse, look at me. You're not a freak. You did nothing wrong." I don't meet your eyes. I'm embarrassed and afraid. My insecurities feel suffocating.

"What do you mean, she did nothing wrong? She was watching us make out through the bushes."

"Heather, stop. Go home."

"But what about us?" she whines. You look at her and say without emotion, "There is no us. It wasn't even a good kiss. You don't talk to Mouse again. Yeah?"

"Whatever, asshole," she yells and walks away.

"Mouse, look at me."

I know I should lift my eyes. It's not that I care what she said. People have called me worse. It was your lips on hers. The way my heart aches. I don't want you to see that on my face. My legs finally kick in and decide to work. I run. You chase me, but I'm fast. By the time I reach my front door, you're winded, but close behind me.

"I'm sorry," I say and close myself behind the door.

"Charlie, don't." Your fist hits the door once in defeat.

You see me after that and pretend it didn't happen. You never mention it again. You meet me as I walk to the park. You don't mention Heather or why I ran.

Fourteen years old

I am a freshman and at the same school as you. This year feels different. I see you in the halls and you always stop to say hi.

You look at me differently. I'm not sure what it means. You seem like a loner; like me. You don't hang with the jocks. You get into fights sometimes. I hate when that happens, because then you're not at school. Even when I see you angry, I see the fuel behind your eyes. You have so much inside of you. Sometimes, I'm envious of the spark behind your eyes.

I hear your mom yell at you for getting into another fight. Her boyfriend has made an appearance in your life. I don't think you like him, but you don't fight with him.

He has friends who ride motorcycles that often come over. They hang out in the front yard. They smoke their cigarettes and drink their beers. I watch as you stand in the shadows watching them.

The man who dates your mom brings you a motorcycle. It's not as big or as fancy as his, but you get on it and he helps teach you to ride it. He's over your house often now. You work on your bike together. You no longer ride the bus with me.

Fifteen years old

Boys are starting to notice me no matter how invisible I try to be. They all want to talk to me, but I only see you. You date and have girlfriends. I hate this, but I understand. After all, I am me. I sometimes feel your eyes on me but they never linger.

I'm walking home from school today. I stayed after to work in the computer lab. It's a few mile walk, but it isn't bad. I work hard at school and you tease me from time to time. I know I'm a bookworm, but it's my only outlet. It's not that Mitchell and Claire are bad, it's just they are not really there. They don't talk to me. We exist. They fight with each other and I stay out of their way. I try to be as invisible as I can around them. I don't want them to send me to a group home where I'll no longer be able to see you.

Today, as I walk, a group of boys in a jeep pulls up alongside me. I cling my books to my chest. They holler things at me from their open jeep. They slow to almost a stop and a boy I recognize jumps out. "Charlotte, right?" he asks.

I don't say anything. I continue to walk.

"I'm Fitch," he says and stands in front of me, so I can't continue to walk forward. I take a step to the side, but he sidesteps too.

I'm so focused on what is happening that I don't hear you approach. I should've.

"Get the hell away from her," you say, hooking an arm around my waist and pulling me back towards you. You're bigger now. You look like a man. You have hair on your chin and your hazel eyes stand out against your dirty blonde hair. You're dressed in black all the way down to your motorcycle boots. You're bigger than the guys at school.

"Gunner. Isn't it enough you're fucking half the cheer-leading team. You gotta fuck this one too?" Fitch says.

I flinch and you notice. You probably think it's because of his terse words. It's not. It's because he said you're fucking so many women. I know your reputation. I hate it.

Your nostrils flare, I've seen that look before.

"Mouse, go to my bike." I look at you, not wanting you to do anything drastic. The guys in the jeep jump out. There are three more of them. I look at the guys and then to you. "Mouse, now!"

I move to your bike. You're quick to throw a punch and then another. They try to hit you, but you're fast and they are weak.

One screams, "My nose."

Another, "Let's go."

You stalk towards me. There's a power about you that's unmistakable. The look on your face is raw. Primal. "Get on!" you order, then take my books from me and throw them in a side bag.

I've never been on your bike, but I've never seen you with anyone else on it either. I get on. Your hands reach behind you and you pull my arms around your waist. "Hang on," you tell me and the bike roars to life.

Adrenaline pumps through me as you go faster and faster. I don't feel invisible. I feel like I'm part of the wind, part of the road. My sole purpose is to move, and I'm moving holding on to YOU. I feel alive in a way I've been missing.

You pull into your driveway and I'm disappointed with how quickly the ride is over. You help me down and then ask me to come in. I've never been in your house before. I'm nervous.

It's simple in decor inside. It's clean, but feels empty. There is a nice, newer couch and a large TV. There are no pictures on the walls. The warmth that I've imagined through the window isn't here. Maybe it once was, but not anymore.

You take me by the hand and guide me to your room. I follow you without hesitation. Your room is simple. A nice dresser against a wall. A window with black curtains. A bed, large with black blankets. A large T.V. mounted across from that with a gaming system on the floor. You close the door after you. We're close. You get closer.

"That shit happen to you a lot, Mouse?" you ask with anger in your voice. I don't know why you're mad, but your nose is still flaring. I look down and see your knuckles are split open.

You don't like when I look away from you, so as my eyes turn down, you grab my chin to make sure my eyes meet yours. "Answer me."

"I guess so. Last week it was outside of the girl's locker room. Different guy. It happens. It's not a big deal. I don't talk to them, and they eventually go away."

"It's a big fucking deal, Mouse. Nobody gets to talk to you like that. No one." I shrug because it's not really a big deal. I wish they didn't see me, and I wonder if that's why he's mad.

"It's a big fucking deal. You're young and innocent and have already been dealt a shitty blow. You don't deal with any more blows. Not now. Not ever. One day Mouse, I swear to God, I'm taking you out of here."

My heart beats wildly in my chest.

I look up at you and bat my lashes. It's not intentional. You make me feel vulnerable. You're making promises to me, and I want to believe you. I have a bravery that I only feel when I'm with you, so in an uncharacteristic move, I grab your hand.

"Why would it bother you if boys start to notice me?" I gulp wanting the answer and being afraid of it all at once.

"You want that, Mouse? Boys in your space? Their eyes on you? Their hands on you?" You step closer to me. I should shy away, but I don't. I look you in the eyes, loving the amber, browns and greens.

"I don't want boys in my space." My eyes say what my mouth doesn't. *Only yours.*

"Then yeah, it bothers me. You been looking at me with those fucking doe eyes for far too fucking long. Been waiting for you to be okay enough in your skin that when I touch you, you won't shrivel from me."

"You're the only person that makes me feel safe, Gunner."

You stalk to me. It's predatory. I think you do it on purpose to see if I'll flinch. You cup my face and pull me close. That's when my world shifts.

Lips brush against my own. Gently at first. You test me. I've never been kissed before, you know this. You give me soft kisses, parting my lips and letting your tongue skim along the seam. For the first time, I feel right in my own skin. I feel bolder than I ever have. I dart my tongue out meeting yours. It's soft, fleshy, sweet, a hint of tobacco. My boldness spurs you on. You take my mouth fully, twining your tongue alongside mine, then nipping at my lip. You tug my hair back and I moan into the kiss. It's intoxicating. Raw. Everything I never knew I wanted.

You push me up against the bed and you lay down next to me. You never break the kiss. We kiss for hours.

Sixteen years old

4 months later

You've been busy lately, but you always make time for me. You were kicked out of school, but you try to be around as much as possible. You wait outside the school gates and pick me up from time to time. This makes me happy. I love when you surprise me.

We ride and then stop to make out. You're careful not to go too far. You've slipped your fingers inside of me and I've used my hands on you. I love the way you make me feel. When we're together, I come alive, maybe that's what it's been like watching you; a glimpse at living.

The boys at school stay clear of me. I often wonder if you've scared them all away and I secretly am thrilled with the idea that you have.

Today is different. Today, you're in a mood when you pick me up and I notice blood on your knuckles. We drive for a while, on a trek I'm familiar with. You pull the bike up to an abandoned junkyard. We've been here before. You like finding things you can use to build bikes. It's something you're good at. I tell you this and you shrug off my compliments, but I think you like that I love what you can build.

You hop off the bike and pace. I'm not sure what's going on, but you seem like you need to collect yourself. I give you a minute, then another.

"Gunner?" I finally say.

You look at me. "Fuck, I got charges for assault. Hades says he'll pull some strings if I join the club, or I'm facing time."

Okay, I'm a bit confused at your reaction to this. "Assault? I ask looking at your hand. "Are you okay?"

You shake your hand and stretch out your fingers like you're just now noticing they're bloody. "This is nothing. I'm pissed because both of those options will mean less time with you."

My gut sinks, and I get it.

"I'm not going anywhere. I'll always be yours," I reassure you. "So, what are you going to do?"

You shrug, "Not much choice. Joining Hades Runners, I guess."

"I'll be here. I'll always be here." I rub your back trying to calm your frayed nerves.

You pause and then mumble, "Thank fuck." you come to me with such force. You slam your lips against mine and lift me up by my ass so that my legs move around your hips. You lean me against the hood of a car. We kiss, but it's more than that. We are a frenzy of groping hands and labored breaths. I claw at your back wanting you as close to me as you can be. I hitch my leg up and you grind your hard length against me. It's the first time I feel you and I don't want to wait anymore. I want you inside of me.

"Gunner," I whimper.

You search my eyes, understanding my plea,"You sure?"

I nod.

"Give me your words, Mouse."

"Yes. Yes, Gunner. I want you."

Your eyes darken, and then everything becomes more frantic. You whip my shirt over my head, and take my breast into your mouth. Your tongue swirls and then you nip. Already this feeling is new to me. My nipples harden in response and I arch into your touch.

Next, goes your shirt and my hands explore. You're in complete control, guiding how you want everything to go. I'm glad since I have no experience. I want to please you, but deep down I wish you didn't have so much experience. I wish I was your first like you're mine, but I can't change that. I'm just glad that you're taking me there.

You rid me of my pants and panties next, the white cotton discarded on the dirt ground. The metal beneath my back is warm, that added with the late sun beating on my face, makes a trickle of sweat run along my hairline.

You trail kisses along my hip bone and I run my fingers through your hair.

Down you go.

Further.

I'm exposed.

You're mouth presses hard on my clit. It's shocking but it feels good. I trust you. You slide your tongue up and down my slit and then you push a finger inside of me. Your tongue moves fast and your finger hooks deep inside of me. You stroke me. Then you suck me.

I'm withering, experiencing feelings I've never felt before. I thrash my hips back and forth. "Be still, Charlie. Relax."

I see moisture dripping from your lip onto your chin. I'm fascinated by it. I want to memorize the way you look coated in my wetness.

You place your arm over my stomach holding me in place. Another flick of your tongue and I feel your finger curl inside and then I'm exploding. My hips are shaking and I'm having an orgasm like you've never given me before.

"It's gonna hurt, Charlie. You know that, right?" I like hearing you call me Charlie as much as I like Mouse.

I nod giving you the okay because I want the pain. I want everything from you. The good, the bad. The pleasure, the pain. I want it all. You're the only one that takes away the loneliness.

You kiss me and I taste me, but I taste you too.

"You don't know how long I've dreamt of being inside of you. You're the only good thing I have and I can't wait to sink into your slick pussy. You ready for me?"

"Yes."

"Yes, what? Words, Charlie."

"Want you inside of me. Take me."

Your dick presses against me and then slowly you push inside. It hurts. I close my eyes and revel in the burn. You're doing it to me, so I'll cherish it. You go slowly until you're all the way seated. My eyes flash open in surprise. you're deep. So. Very. Deep. You stare in my eyes. You see me.

Every.

Single.

Part.

Of.

Me.

I want to be a good lover to you. I move my hips up and you still, making sure you have the go ahead.

"So fucking tight. Ain't nothing sweeter than this, baby. I'm gonna move more now. You good?"

"So good," I say and commit to memory the look of bliss that covers your face. It's a look I'll never forget. You look at me with so much feeling in your eyes.

You rock forward and out again. I'm hanging on to you and moving my hips in time with yours. It hurts, but it doesn't matter. It's you and it's right. You back up so you're not completely on top of me, and then you're out of me.

You stand and I watch as your cock glistens. You pull my feet so I'm at the edge of the car and then you push into me again. My tits that feel so full and heavy bounce with each thrust. It's a different sting, but it doesn't hurt the same way. You move fast and your eyes burn with lust.

"So fucking sexy. Grab your titties."

I do as you say and grab my breasts. It feels good.

"Good. Now, use your fingers and roll your nipples."

I do that too and it makes me quiver tight in my pussy.

"Fuck, I want to go deeper. Can you take more?"

"Everything. Give me it all," I pant.

You grab my ankles lifting my legs high on your shoulders. You lean forward, nearly bending me in half and you slam hard. You hit so deep, I scream. Your hair falls in your eyes and you lean my head close to my legs. You pump in and out of my body and my eyes start to roll in the back of my head.

"Gunner," I cry out, experiencing all of you and all of the ways your body can fill mine. Pleasure ripples through me. "Oh, God! I think I'm going to come again."

"Don't fight it. I can't wait to feel your tight little cunt clench around me."

I couldn't fight it if I tried. You push and pull back and push and pull back and then I'm clenching all around you.

"Fuck," you roar and slam down on me again and again. Then, your thrusts change. You slam down hard once, then pause. Twice, pause and again, until you groan loudly. Your eyes are fierce and your face is beautiful. I've never seen you look so happy. I've never seen you so pleased. I'm happy. I gave that to you and you gave me so much more in return. You kiss me and kiss me again and again until you slowly pull out of me. I feel the loss, but I'm not alone because you cradle me in your arms and whisper promises about a future. I tell you I'm yours and I want more from you. I want this again. Today and tomorrow.

"I promise, Mouse. I'll give you the world."

I look at you like you hung the moon, because in my world, you do. You're it for me, and have been since I was eight years old.

Part Two

Chapter One

Charlie

I wasn't sure what was going on, but I hadn't seen Gunner for a week. He hadn't been home. He hadn't picked me up from school. We slept together and then poof; nothing. I had seen bikes at his place when we returned that day. I watched through my window as Gunner looked back at my house a few times, and then he was gone.

I felt horrible. I didn't know where he was or how to reach him. I missed him and it was like all of the loneliness that I had before was only intensified. Once you know what it feels like to be loved, it only hurts more when it's gone.

A month passed and then another. His mom hadn't been to his house either and a fearful part of me wondered if I'd ever see him again.

I threw up today in Home Economics. The smell of grated cheese made me immediately sick. I couldn't even make it to the bathroom. I was grateful there was a sink nearby, but nonetheless, I felt horrible.

Everything seemed to be making me sick lately. I was sent to the nurse's office, where they called Mitchell to come and get me. He didn't answer, so they called Claire. I'd rather deal with Mitchell than Claire. She dragged her hungover ass into the school and gave me a death glare when she saw me laying down in the office. I watched her stumble a bit when she signed me out, I wondered if anyone else would pick up on the fact that she was probably still drunk.

I got into the car with her, cringing at the overwhelming smell of smoke. Her blonde hair was brittle and her skin looked older than she actually was. "You gonna get sick again?" Her voice was raspy from years of smoking making her sound a lot like Marge Simpson's sister.

"No, it was the strangest thing. One minute I felt fine, and the next minute, I felt so nauseous. But I'm feeling much better."

"Fuck, you 'ain't pregnant, is you?" she spoke in broken English and it made her seem all the more ignorant to me.

My eyes bulged and I feared that it was a real possibility. "Nnn...o," I stuttered.

Claire looked at me as we pulled into the driveway. I must have looked guilty. How could I be pregnant? It was only the one time, and I didn't think you could get pregnant on your first time. That's what I overheard Misty Wellington telling Izzy in the bathroom anyways, but what if they were wrong? I felt like the world was spinning around me.

"You dumb little shit. You got yourself knocked up, didn't you? Go to your room."

I got out of the car and did like she said. I was shocked, but deep down I thought that she was right. It fit with everything I'd ever heard about being pregnant. Holy shit. I was sixteen and pregnant. I just became a reality show on MTV.

I stared out the window through the dirt stained glass and wished Gunner was there. I wondered why he left me and what I was going to do. All of his promises seemed broken. I needed him and he was gone. I berated myself for needing him. It wasn't his fault, it was mine. I should've known that I'd be alone again. I should've expected it.

I heard the door slam as Mitchell entered the house. There was arguing and more door slamming. Mitchell yelled, "We wouldn't even need her here, if you would just lay off the fucking booze."

I had heard it before. I was only a way for her to get more booze. You'd think that the money she got for me wouldn't even be worth it, but she was a master at working the system and getting as many things for free as she could. Because she had me she got almost double in food stamps and just about every other benefit gave her extras because of me.

I didn't have many things. My clothes were hand-me-downs or things I had gotten when it was Christmas time and the United Way threw their annual event that helped clothe foster kids.

I stayed in my room as they argued. It was so drab in here. My blanket was covered in holes, but it didn't bother me. It was the same one I had since I was eight years old. I pulled it up tightly over my head. I felt lost. Gunner was gone and I was most likely having his baby. I had no idea what I'd do.

My door opened and Mitchell shoved a brown paper bag at me. "Take this," I'll be waiting by the door.

I walked into the bathroom and opened the bag. The paper crinkled as it moved and I found a pregnancy test. I sat with my pants around my ankles while I read the directions. There was a knock at the door, "C'mon, hurry up."

"It says it'll be five minutes." I moved the stick between my legs as I let the stream coat it. It didn't even take five minutes. The little window showed double lines almost instantly. Pregnant. I was pregnant.

I didn't know what to say or do so, I opened the door, handed Mitchell the stick and went to my bed where I threw my blanket over my head and sobbed.

"Fucking shit. You're fucking right," Mitchell yelled from the hallway.

I stayed in bed until I fell asleep which took forever since I was scared out of my mind.

The next day I went to school and when I got home there was an unfamiliar white sedan in the driveway. I walked in the door and saw a nicely dressed black woman. She had braids in her hair that were twisted into a bun. She wore an iridescent floral printed blouse with navy colored slacks.

"Hello, Charlotte. I'm Mrs. Jackson. I'll be your new case worker. Your foster parents contacted me and informed me of your situation." Her eyes traveled to my stomach and I instantly felt protective. "They've packed your bag, but please take a minute and see if we missed anything." Her tone held finality to it. I knew that the decision was final and that there was no arguing with it. I walked to my room and as I passed the living room I saw Claire and Mitchell starring at the TV. It was like I didn't exist.

I know there was nothing here of any real value except for the one thing that I couldn't take with me. I looked at the window that I spent so much time watching Gunner. I wondered why he left me. I wondered what he'd think if he knew I had his baby in my belly. I put my head to the cold glass and closed my eyes, wishing that when I opened them he'd be there staring back at me.

But when I opened my eyes he wasn't there. I wanted to cry and scream that the only person I'd ever loved left me.

A knock at the door startled me.

"It's time," Mrs. Jackson's voice was calm and reassuring. It didn't matter. I was in a tumultuous sea. No reassurance would settle this storm.

I pressed my hand to the glass one more time, then followed Mrs. Jackson out of the house. There was no long goodbye from Mitchell or Claire. Not that I'd expected there to be. For eight years I'd been invisible to them, why would now be any different?

Gunner

Crack. Hades' fist connected with my jaw. Um-pf. A swift kick from Radar to my ribs.

Another hit to my kidney and I wondered if I'd black out.

"Hades! Enough! He's just a kid!" I heard my Momma shout through tears.

"A kid? He's six-three and besides Jake, he's one of the biggest motherfuckers in here. He's gotta learn if he wants to be a Hades Runner, he's gotta follow the rules."

Another hit to my body. I wasn't sure by whom this time. My vision was going black. I had tried to leave the clubhouse. I'd been here for months, and I needed to see Mouse. I hated that I had disappeared on her right after we fucked. And it was the sweetest fucking gift that girl could've ever given me. I've been craving it like you wouldn't believe, that's why I told these fuckers to fuck off. I was going to see my girl. They didn't take to kindly to the disrespect.

I heard my Mom yell again. "Hades!"

Fuck, she was crying. I hated when she cried.

Another hit, then finally, "Enough," Hades shouted. I couldn't move or get up if I'd wanted too. My vision was spotty. I'm not sure how long I laid there until a few of the brother's dragged me across the street to one of the houses the Hades Runner's owned.

Days had passed since my beat down. I could finally get up from my bed without crawling. Good thing it was close to the bathroom. Between throwing up from my concussion and needing water from the faucet, I was glad it was near. Today I could walk, not well, but enough that I was going to walk into the clubhouse, grab a bottle of whiskey and hold my head up high. I would not show weakness to these guys, because, well, fuck 'em.

I was only three houses away from the clubhouse, but my vision was still spotty. I had to do this without passing out. My hand was reaching for the door when my vision really started to spin. I closed my eyes for a moment and thought of Mouse. I'd get through this and I'd be the strongest fucking man for her. With thoughts of her, my mind steadied enough that I was able to walk through those doors. I got a look from a few of the guys and I gave some equally pissed glares as best as I could muster to the guys that I knew hit me the hardest.

What I didn't expect to see when I walked in, was my Ma, snorting a line of coke off Hades's dick. "Ma!" I roared. Hades just grinned at me as he pushed her head down. She wasn't the woman I knew anymore. No, she might've been in there somewhere, but it became obvious to me she was Hades's coke whore. I was pissed I didn't see it sooner. Sometimes, as a boy, you see shit how you need to see it. Heck, even as a man, your eyes could play tricks on you, but it was painfully obvious I was missing this vital piece. Hades wasn't my brother, he was the devil that took a grieving widow and turned her out. She used to bake apple pies and now she was between that motherfucker's thighs. My old man would be rolling over in his grave.

Disgusted with the scene, I grabbed a bottle of whiskey. I don't remember how I made it back to my bed. I barely remembered the weeks that followed, but one thing I knew for sure, was that this wasn't a club of solidarity and brotherhood. This club was the place keeping me from my woman and the place that turned my Ma into a whore. I'd do what I'd need to do to get by. Isn't that what life was teaching me, to keep on getting by. Mouse was out there, I just needed to hang on.

It's been six months since I'd left the clubhouse. The first month, we were on lock down and then after that, I was prospecting. Prospects were expected to be here twenty-four-seven. The one time I told them I was leaving and to fuck off, cost me a near month of being in bed, which just made my prospecting even longer.

Today, I rode away from these fuckers for the first time. I was going to get Mouse. I didn't give a fuck that she was underage. She was mine and she was no longer going to live with those fuckwit foster parents of hers. They could keep their foster money for all I cared. I was taking care of her.

I practically sped through every light on my way to her house. Six months was a long time, and I cringed when I thought of any of those high school fucks getting near her. I know she wouldn't go there. But they would try and that thought drove me nuts.

I pulled up in front of her house and the breath left my lungs. It was condemned with boards over the windows and the door. You could tell there was a fire from the black soot covering the siding. My gut turned. *No God, please no.* I shut the bike off noticing the demolition sign stating that it would be torn down in just four short days. I walked up the broken cement walkway and kicked in the plywood covering the door. The couch was burned and it looked like a fucking crime scene. *No. No. No.* I stepped over fallen beams. Thick black soot coated everything. The smell of smoke was so heavy in the air that I lifted my t-shirt over my nose so I could breathe. I walked back to her room, not sure of what I'd find. I knew she wouldn't be there.

"Fuck!" I cursed under my breath when I walked in and saw her room nearly burned down to the studs. If she were asleep in here there is no way she would've survived. I just prayed that she wasn't home when the fire started.

I needed answers. I knocked on Mrs. Ellerson's door. She was an older lady who had lived there all my life. She was a nosy old hag, she'd know. No one fucking answered.

I walked across the street and banged on another door. Nothing. Where the fuck was everyone? Since when do these people go to work?

One more house and finally Mr. Barker answered. "What is it, boy?" I was breathing hard adrenaline was coursing through my veins.

"What happened to the house across the street?"

His voice cracked. Years of smoking left Mr. Barker with tumors on his voice-box. "Tragic, really. Left her cigarette burning. Killed her and her old man too. Real shame. Happened about a month ago. Whole neighborhood was lit up. You couldn't have missed it. Where you been under a rock or something boy?"

I growled at the old man. He was pissing me off, and I was scared shitless that Mouse was gone. "What about the girl?"

"I don't know nothin' 'bout no girl."

I stormed away. I needed answers, but wasn't sure where to get them. For a month Mitchell and Claire had been dead, and I had to hold onto some kind of hope that Mouse was still alive.

The pit in my stomach grew even bigger. I got back on my bike, went to the school and sat on my bike for nearly an hour watching the only entrance at the school that was left unlocked, hoping like fuck I'd see her and this would all be some cruel fucking joke. Nothing.

I drove to the library and searched inside. Nothing there either. I tried to ask the librarian if they'd seen her, but no one seemed to know who I was talking about. I pulled out my phone and did a google search for the fire and there it was in black and white. Two dead in an accidental fire. Two. I had fucking hope, now, where was Charlie?

I waited outside of the school hoping I'd see her or someone who might be able to tell me where the hell she went. The chilly morning air heightened my senses. I watched every single person as they arrived for school, but still I didn't see her. I saw those tools whose asses I handed to them pull up in their Jeep. They were blasting Timberlake. I wanted to punch them again for being such pussies. Their eyes widened as I approached. Sure, my down time at the club had a lot to do with me lifting weights. I built so much muscle that if someone hit me again, they'd have a lot to get through until they could crack ribs. Cracked ribs sucked.

I was also pretty sure the leather vest I now wore that sported the Hades Runners insignia had a lot to do with the scared shitless looks on their face.

"You guys seen Charlie?"

"Who?" The weaselly guy who talked to her the last time I kicked his ass asked.

"Charlotte," I gritted out because I was damn sure they knew who I was talking about.

"Nah, man. She hasn't been to this school in months," A guy said from the back seat.

"Yeah, one day she was here, and the next she was gone," the fucking little dick weasel answered.

Blood rushed to my head. The empty pit in my stomach intensified. I was pissed. I hit the fucker who delivered the news. He went down screaming. I didn't give a fuck. I had to find my Mouse.

My heart thumped. I was so angry. Angry at my brotherhood for taking me away from her. Angry at myself for not coming back sooner. "Fuck!" I bellowed. This couldn't be happening.

I went back to her house and searched her room for any sign. Her dresser was empty. I knocked it over because I was pissed off. Her mattress was mostly melted and in my anger, I picked it up and threw that too. Against the corner of the wall was a blanket. I lifted it. No sign that it was melted. It had holes throughout it and I wondered if that's all she had? Was I so caught up in my own shit, that I couldn't see how bad she actually had it? I headed out to my bike, grabbed a couple small bungee cords from the small leather bag tucked under my headlight and rolled the blanket tight strapping it to my back seat. I had hoped she would be on the back, not this worthless rag, but it was all I had left of her.

I reached the clubhouse, which was an old store that the club had bought. We also owned the eight houses on the street. Each house had three or four bedrooms and a few of the houses were duplexes. The clubhouse wasn't the traditional bar that you might think an MC would have. Inside, there were leather couches that lined two walls. In the middle of the room was a dance floor with a stripper pole. On the opposite side of that, there were large industrial-sized stainless steel refrigerators that were stocked with tons of food. Next to those, were coolers that you might find at your local Seven-Eleven. Some were stocked with soda, while others were filled with beer.

Once inside, I ignored the hellos from my brothers and went straight for the beer. I grabbed the first one I saw, tilted my head back and chugged the entire thing, then I grabbed another. I searched the room until my eyes landed on the man I needed to speak with; Dirk.

Dirk had mad computer skills, and was usually really good at finding out information.

"Brother," I tilted my beer towards him as I approached.

"What's got your panties all twisted? Your little girl find some football player, while you been hanging with the big boys?"

"Fuck off," I growled ready to throw down.

"Cool it, just giving you a hard time. What gives?"

"What gives is she's gone. House burned to the ground. Foster parents dead. I got no clue where she went and I really am curious as fuck to find out how come no one told me the house next to mine burned down. The house my girl lives in. You guys are supposed to be my brothers, but that shit was kept from me. Fuck, I need to find her man."

Dirk's eyes changed. No longer was he my ball busting brother, sympathy instantly flashed in his eyes. He saw me practically clawing at the walls to get out of here. They thought it was funny. Their new prospect, the president's new old lady's son, pining over a teen-aged girl--but they didn't know. How could they? That girl was the only fucking saving grace for me. All those years, she watched me. And I don't give a fuck if it sounds like I'm a pussy, but I wasn't alone. Even if she wouldn't talk she was always right there, and I left her... alone. And now, she's gone.

"I'll find her. Let me get some paper, so I can write down what you know about her."

While he walked away I thought about the details I knew about her. I knew her last name. That was a start. But I didn't know Mitchell and Claire's. I knew her biological mom was dead, but I didn't know her name. When she told me the heartbreaking story about her piece of shit junky mom, I was beside myself. I wished I could bring that piece of shit back to life and kill her myself for doing that to Charlie. No one should be raised like that.

What else could I tell him? I could tell him how she was the prettiest girl I'd ever seen, and how she had no idea. Or how when she'd get nervous, she'd bite her lip and try to hide behind her long dark hair. I could tell him how she was the sweetest pussy I'd ever had and that even though she was a virgin, she greedily took my cock. But no, those things were not for my brother's ears. They were mine and I was holding them close. She was my fucking Mouse, and I didn't want to share that with anyone.

So, I told him the facts I knew. Her name is Charlotte Morris. She sometimes goes by Charlie. Her birthday is December fourth and she's sixteen years old. She lived with her foster parents Claire and Mitchell since she was eight. Mitchell worked various jobs. Claire was a drunk. That's it. That's all I had to go on. As I recalled the details, I wanted to hit something or someone. I had so much rage.

"This is good info. I'll make some calls, see what I can find out. I'll find your girl," Dirk put his hand to mine and leaned in bumping his chest with my own.

"Reece," I called out. "I need to fight. Set something up, will you?"

Reece had a devilish grin even under his dark beard. He rubbed his beard in contemplation as his smirk grew bigger. The woman on his side pressed her phony-ass breasts against him. He always had a chick hanging on him, in some way or another, and he had connections. "You hear that, everyone? Gunner's going to fight. Max has a guy he's been dying to have fight one of ours. Big motherfucker, too. I got a hundred on Gun."

And just like that, I had a fight set.

I rode my bike with my brothers behind me. We met at a warehouse on neutral ground. It was one of three places illegal fights took place. It wasn't my first match, but it was the first time I needed the release.

My opponent's name was Jeremiah. Reece didn't lie. He was a big ass dude. Had at least half a foot on me, and I was a beast. I bet that stupid motherfucker, Reece, actually bet on the other guy. That'd be his mistake. I had so much rage to fuel my fight. Jeremiah barely lasted a round.

Knockout.

I wasn't done, though. "You got anyone else?" I asked Reece. Reece nodded to Max and Max returned his nod with a chin lift.

A new fighter was brought out. This guy wasn't as big, but he was fast. He had full tat sleeves and a back piece that was fucking incredible. Maybe after I beat his ass, I'd find out who did his ink.

It didn't end as quickly as the first fight. Make no mistake, though, I did end it. He got a few good hits on me. I couldn't help but feel that I deserved them. I wanted to hurt physically. I needed to distract myself from the pain in my chest. I'd find my Mouse and I'd stop at nothing until I did.

6 months later

"Still nothing?" I balled my fist to stop from hitting Dirk. He didn't have any news for me. He never did. It'd been nearly a year since I saw her last. Who knew that finding out records on juveniles in the system was so hard? She had a change in caseworkers and no one seemed to be able to give me any clear answers.

"I don't know, man. It's like she vanished. I can find her going to a temporary house, and then nothing. Those foster parents said she was quiet and that she was only there for a week."

Of course, she was quiet. I didn't start calling her Mouse because she was fucking boisterous.

"Screw this. I've given you time to find her. I'm hitting the streets on my own."

"Brother, you know you can't just leave. There's so much going down. Hades will never be cool with that."

49

"Then, I'll leave my fucking patch at the door."

"You don't mean that. She's a kid. You'd turn your back on your brothers for some pussy?"

Whack.

I couldn't help it. My fist was connecting to Dirk's jaw as soon as he called Mouse pussy. I was over all of these assholes. In the year I'd been with them, I'd seen more fucked up shit than I could stand. My mother was no longer a woman I recognized. I also kept thinking that even if I did find Mouse, I'd die before I let her live among these pigs. I'd seen a few guys gang rape one of the whores. Granted she was a whore, but if a woman said no, then even if you fucked her willingly an hour ago, no still meant no. I would've killed them then, if Hades didn't see me getting all pissed off and held a gun to the back of my head. The longer I was with these men, the more I had wished I'd chosen jail. I couldn't take another minute of this.

I tore my patch from my shoulders and stormed out of the clubhouse. "Don't do it, man. Hades will hunt you," Dirk hollered after me.

I got a few looks from some of the guys, but that was it. This club was bullshit. No one was my brother here. They made me lose the only woman, besides my Ma who had ever mattered to me.

So, I got on my bike and rode away. If they weren't all too caught up in their own bullshit maybe they'd have come after me right then. As it was, Hades was on a run, and half the club was either coked out, or doing their own thing. Fuck this piece of shit life. Hades made it seem glorious, but there was no brotherhood here. I didn't even flinch at the loss as I rode away.

I'd made a plan to find Mouse. I took the info Dirk had given me and went over it again starting with the caseworker. I rode to her last caseworker's house. The house was a dump and there was at least five kids running around her yard. She was hard, not a soft bone in her body. I asked about Mouse. The bitch didn't remember her. "I have dozens of kids cross my desk each month. You think I can remember one from a year ago?"

I pleaded with her to remember, I had a picture from the fucking yearbook that I showed her, but she didn't know and she wasn't her case worker anymore. She gave me group homes to check, but after that meeting, I felt lost. It seemed that my Mouse just disappeared. I rode from one nothing town to the next, searching out group homes, but the truth was, she could be anywhere.

After a year of scouring the entire state of Ohio, I lost hope. So, I lost myself in a hole in the wall bar until I needed money, then I'd find a fight or do what I needed to do to get by. I wasn't always proud of how I was surviving, but I'd do what I had too.

Old Crow and any other cheap whiskey I could find became my Breakfast of Champions. I fucked occasionally, but it wasn't the same. Nothing felt like the sweet I remembered. I let down the one person I'd made promises too, and fuck if I didn't hate myself a little for it.

So, I fought, and I fucked, and I found myself so deep in the gutter I didn't recognize myself any longer. I blamed Hades Runners. I blamed my Ma. But mostly, I blamed myself. Hate was a feeling I let build around my heart. I got a reputation for being cruel. I never let up on my opponents in the ring, and if you looked at me twice, I didn't hesitate to show you who the fuck I was.

Except, the whiskey not only made me numb, at times, it made me dumb. I was set to fight a new guy. A guy, that in the past I'd do my research on, but tonight I was too blitzed and my ego was too big, that I didn't care.

Shane Dunaway with his blonde hair that fell over his eyes, wasn't quite as big as me, but he was faster. I should've been able to beat him, but the three-day bender I'd been on had me slower than normal. I hadn't had my ass handed to me by someone so quickly in a long time. When the fight was over, instead of leaving me on the concrete floor, he took me by the hand and helped me up.

"You gotta get your head on straight. Saw you fight at a barn in Hinkley, you were a lot quicker then."

"Fuck off," I slurred, the room spinning overhead.

He ignored me and made sure I wasn't going to topple over. I don't know what it was that he saw in me that made him take the time, but he threw me in a motel room for days until I was finally dry and all that booze was out of my system. During withdrawal, I went between wanting to kill him and begging him for a drink. In the end, I was glad for his help.

To this day, I watched how much I drank, afraid that I'd fall over the edge.

Shane Dunaway became a brother. A real one. Not like the fake bond that Hades Runners promised me. We rode when we wanted and we fought when we wanted, and eventually our brotherhood of two became four, and then it was eight. Six years later, we started a club that grew to be one of the biggest clubs in all of Ohio. We'd run into Hades Runners and there was always a fight. They were my enemies, so they were my brothers' enemies. That's how we rolled. You messed with one of us, you took on all of us.

I never did see my Ma again, as far as I was concerned she was dead to me.

I kept my eyes open for Mouse, but she was a ghost. My life had hardened and I was no longer delusional enough to think that I'd actually see her again. That flicker of hope had long since burned out.

Chapter Three

Charlie

Twenty-Four years old

The lights dimmed as I took my spot center stage. For the next four minutes, I was not a quiet woman. I was a woman with a purpose. I was strong and sexy. I didn't feel like this on the inside, but up here, I was fierce. I'd been doing this long enough now that my reputation not only made me money, but it drew the crowds.

The boom boom boom of the baseline told me I was close to my cue. I pointed my five-inch stiletto. My calf arched. My hips tilted forward and my ass pushed out. The pole in front of me was cold in my grip. I threw my head forward. My long, sleek, dark trusses covered my face. The moment the next thump hit, the lights flashed on me and I thrust my head backward ignoring the cheers, hoots, and hollers. My hair whipped over my head as I began to move. I swayed my hips back and forth. This was me at least four nights a week. Slowly and seductively, I moved around the pole not giving them too much yet. The round curve of my fleshy ass just barely peeked out from under the small, black skirt. I gave them what they wanted, and they were hungry tonight. So many eyes on me. I turned on the pole, put it to my back, lowered myself slowly and flashed open my legs.

A tease.

I lifted my hands overhead and gripped. With my legs spread, hand over hand, I lifted my entire body higher until I was near the top of the pole where I hooked one leg around the metal and twisted my body. Around and around I went until I neared the bottom of the pole where I arched backward, put my palms to the ground, and flipped my legs off of the pole, all while letting the crowd glimpse the small black fabric between my legs.

I raised up to my knees and undid the first button on my skirt and then another. It was all about anticipation. Boom. Boom. I made them wait two beats before I undid the last of the buttons. As my skirt fell away, the small black triangle revealed almost everything. I crawled to the edge of the stage and collected money. It disappeared in between my breasts and into the string of my thong until I could discreetly drop it into my black satchel I left on stage.

I seductively climbed the pole again, swiveled then turned on it until my muscles burned, and I was upside down. The men were absolutely wild as I righted myself and flung my hair as part of the dance. When every eye was completely transfixed, I went for it. I unzipped the small fabric that covered my breasts. Their fullness, strangled by the top, finally sprang free. Two very small, blue stars covered my nipples, but who was I kidding? The stickers were a requirement, but they did nothing to really hide the fact that I was practically nude.

Green littered the stage. Frank, one of the bouncers, collected my loot while all eyes were on my dance. No one noticed him. This was my show, and he was invisible. I was the only thing they could see. And boy, did I let them see. Modesty was something I gave up a long time ago. Once, I cared about hiding, but you do what you need to do to survive, and then you get on with owning it.

And I owned this fucking stage.

I cupped my breast and gyrated my hips against the stage and I gave these men their fantasy. They wanted to pretend they knew what it was like to be inside of me so, I filled their imagination. Their spank banks would be well fueled. There was power in this seduction. I threw my head back as I pumped my hips against the ground and just as it looked like I was going to come, the lights went dark.

"Damn, girl! I might need to finish myself off after that one." Marjorie smacked my ass as she sauntered past me on my way to the dressing area. I shook my head as her wild red hair flashed one last time before she turned the corner.

Grabbing my floral printed, Asian style robe from the hook, I quickly slipped it on, then downed a bottle of water, and chased it with a few Excedrin. My head was killing me, and I didn't really want to go out on the floor, but I knew that I didn't have much choice. I slipped on a pair of black Lycra shorts that the bottom of my ass hung out of and a silver bikini top with long dangly silver tassels that caught the lights and reflected them, like my tits were a goddamn disco ball.

"Char," Dick the owner of *The Select Club,* whose name was, in fact, Dick-- which was fitting because he was actually a dick, walked into the dressing room. "Got a request for you on table five." I gave him an irritated look. I hated getting on tables after my dance. They were always too handsy and still way too turned on. The girls' loved it because they made money, but I did well on stage where I was far away from grabby hands. What I did not do well with was when they pawed me. Dick knew this. He caught my glare and looked at me sternly. "I let you get away with a lot, Char, because you shake your tits like no other, but you need to get your ass out there. Table number five. No excuses. They requested you specifically, and these are not men you fuck around with."

I nodded because he was right. He usually was good about not making me do shit I didn't want to do, but occasionally he had to remind me of that, and I knew that even though Dick was a dick, he wouldn't be making me unless it was important. So I strapped on a pair of heels that were an inch shorter than the stilettos I wore on stage and followed Dick out. He moved into the shadows, but I trusted he'd be close by.

The club was nicer than a lot of clubs, and although Dick was a dick, he did take care of his club. He hired experienced dancers, and kept the drinks expensive enough that the clientele ended up being more upscale. I did not mind this, seeing as though I'd worked at other clubs and I didn't make as much money and too many times people got handsy with me. I either had to quit, or my refusal to do certain things made it so I didn't last long.

There were two rows of chairs around the stage, followed by free standing circular tables with four chairs around each of them. Beyond those were large posh booths with black suede backs. The lighting was low, but there was enough light that men could easily see each other. Lights rimmed the inside of the table to illuminate the dancer.

57

On the edge of the table was a pole and in the center of the tables, hanging overhead, was a pair of gymnast rings.

Depending on the number of men at the table and the amount of drinks that littered it changed what I would use to perform.

As I approached the table, I put on my biggest faux smile. They were businessmen that reeked of money. Tailored suits, fresh pressed shirts and a mix of expensive cologne radiated off of the men.

Frank approached the table just as I did. He took my hand and assisted me as I climbed on the table. His presence reassured me that he'd be nearby. I made a note to tip him extra tonight. He knows how much I hate these.

The men at clubs like this tend to become just a sea of faces. No matter their size or their dress, they typically are all the same. They like tits, and don't give a damn about fidelity.

I began to rock my hips, swaying back and forth. There was small rocks glasses on the table, filled with expensive Scotch. The Maker's Mark bottle was half empty on the table. I was careful to avoid the glasses. A few men sat back in their chairs to watch my show while one man didn't look at me. He was engaged in a conversation. His body was tight and it seemed that at any second, he could break the man he was talking to. One thing we learn as dancers is that if you sense a situation arising, you make sure you're safe first, and second to that, you see if you can defuse the situation by distracting the men. This is what I choose to do. I increased my movement, used the rings to swing myself in a circle and bent forward in front of the man so that my feet were planted on each side of his Scotch, ankles and ass to him. I grabbed the pole to steady myself and then very slowly began to rock my hips forward and backward, all while arching my back. It was incredibly sexy and incredibly stupid. I had no idea that catching this man's attention would be a critical mistake.

Chapter Four

Charlie

"Don't move!" A thickly accented voice commanded as he grabbed hold of my ankle stilling me. His hand was firm. I turned my body and made eye contact. To some, he'd be an attractive man. Dark hair slicked back, narrow nose, strong jawline, tanned skin, those were nice features that would've made him attractive, but his eyes, they were black and they were evil. I'd seen a few glimpses of raw, primal, evil in my life, and none of that matched the pure hate I saw. I sucked in an audible breath, as I heard him repeat through gritted teeth, "I said, don't move."

I tried to dart my eyes to Frank, but I couldn't see him without moving again. I tightened my hand on the pole and didn't move. The man kept his hand on my ankle, not moving, just gripping me tightly. It didn't feel warm, it felt powerful, and not in a good way. I didn't feel like I had much choice and that was something I hated, but it was only an ankle. He wasn't touching me otherwise. My ass was perched out and I was bending forward grabbing the pole. The good news was this man no longer looked like he was going to murder the man next to him. The bad news was that I was in his grip, and being in the grip of a monster sent shivers to my soul. It was something I was familiar with. Better the devil you know, right? Well, I didn't know him, and as he made me stand there, my self-preservation screamed run. I couldn't run though, not with my foot planted in place.

Dick was going to owe me for this shit.

The song ended and another began.

"Hands off the dancers," I heard Frank who was easily two hundred and fifty pounds, and although rumor has it that 'roids were a major contributor, it didn't matter because he was a wall of muscle and at that moment, I didn't care how he got big, only that he was there to save my ass.

"No harm. Just making sure she didn't tip my drink. The harlot was very close."

"Yeah well, she's a professional. Hands off."

"I'd like her in a room in five minutes."

My body stiffened. I don't do rooms, and I could tell he wasn't going to like no. He released his grip from my ankle, and I looked to Frank to help me down.

"Jewel is available for a room, or Angie. This one doesn't do rooms."

Frank grabbed my hand as I started to descend, but the man shot his hand out again and grabbed my ankle. "Surely you have a price. Every whore has her number."

I saw Frank's nostrils flare.

"You move your hand, or I remove it. She doesn't do rooms."

"Is that so? Is there nothing I could offer that would make you change your mind?"

I took a deep breath, "I'm not for sale."

His eyes glinted. I hated the way they looked at me, but he released my ankle. A moment later, I was on the ground. Frank positioned me in front of him as we walked to the back.

"I didn't like that fuck. You alright?" he asked as I grabbed my robe.

I breathed in and then out. I needed to calm myself. I loathed when men touched me, and everything about that man made me fearful.

"I'm okay. I mean he didn't hurt me, but he creeped me the fuck out."

Dick stormed through the dressing room. A robe that was on the hook next to the doorway fell to the ground as he moved past. "Why the fuck are you in here? You should be on that table where I told your ass to be."

Frank stepped slightly in front of me. "No fucking way. I shut that shit down. He was grabbing her and making her just stand there with her ass in the air."

"Do you know who he is? If Enrico Santos tells you to stand there with your ass in the air, then you fucking do it. What you do not fucking do is tell that man no."

"Boss," Frank warned. That was too much and we all knew it, Dick just didn't care.

I stood there through this exchange, but I didn't say anything. I slipped out of my heels, knowing there was nothing Dick could say that would make me go out there. I pulled a pair of black sweatpants from my bag and pulled them up and over my shorts. Next, I grabbed a t-shirt donned it over my head and then under my shirt I slipped off the flashy top and pulled it out of a sleeve. He could bitch all he wanted, but I was done for the night. The headache in the back of my skull began thumping. I don't even think Dick noticed I was getting dressed until I flung my bag over my shoulder.

"I'm going home," I stated.

Dick's eyes hardened on me. "The fuck you are."

Frank ignored Dick, "I'll walk you out, Char."

Marjorie walked back from her set, "Oh, my girl! What was that? Your ass was perched my entire routine."

"Just some ass who gets off on calling women whores and trying to humiliate them."

This was the first time Dick heard me talk about what happened out there. He might be a dick, but he was also human and he did have some compassion.

"First a harlot, then a whore. Ordered me not to move, and I swear to Christ the only reason I did it was because I thought he was going to kill the man next to him. I'm done for the night."

"Oh, honey." Marjorie ran her hand down my hair. She was the touchy feely type and normally I would move away from someone's touch, but Marjorie grew on you.

"I'm alright, a little shaken up, but I'm calling it a night."

I got a look from Dick that said he wasn't pleased as he walked out of the dressing room.

"You ready?" Frank asked grabbing my bag off my shoulder.

We went out the employee exit. Frank stood beside me as I fished out my keys, and then got in my car. It was nice to know he had my back and even if Dick was an ass, at least he employed good people who looked out for you.

"Mrs. Warner, I'm here." I shook her shoulder and watched as her eyes peeked open. She mumbled in her sleepy haze, "Gun's in my bed."

I slipped a few twenties under her coffee cup with a shiny gold tea bag tag hanging off the side. Then, I opened her bedroom door and stood stock still. Gun was asleep. For a moment, he took my breath away with how much he looked like his daddy. The older he got, the more the uncanny resemblance unsettled me. His hair that started off so blonde was already getting darker, and as his face changed from a baby boy to a kid, he looked more and more like the Gunner from my memories. Lord knows, I had his face burned into my brain.

I watched him for a minute. It's something I always did. He'd catch me sometimes and get a goofy grin on his face, but I didn't care. He was the single most important thing to me. We had some incredibly hard years. When I first left Mitchell and Claire's care, Mrs. Jackson had to bring me to a temporary foster home until a spot opened up at a group home although, I never made it there.

The foster home I was placed in didn't just have two insanely Christian parents who were so over the top they believed they would beat the devil out of their twin seventeen-year-old sons with a "switch". These parents were more or less creating twin devils in their hope to crucify one. I was there only two nights when the boys came to my room. It only happened once. Once was one too many times.

Those parents knew what happened, and they had the audacity to say I was a temptress sent from the devil himself. I hated them. All of them.

They underestimated me. Years of being quiet had given me an edge. When everyone was sleeping, I got a hold of one of their pistols, that they left right out in the open, along with a handful of bullets. Money was the next easiest thing. Shelby, the evil twins' mom, had a huge vase over her mantel, right next to the two three foot statues of Jesus, that she filled with change and any spare dollars. No one was around when I reached in and grabbed every bill I could find.

The next time the boys came to my room, I was prepared. Gabriel, the meaner of the two, clicked on the light hoping to take me off guard. I barely knew what I was doing with a gun, but I didn't wait to pull the trigger. I shot him, hitting him in the thigh. He screamed and cried as Abel tried to come to his aide.

"You bitch, I'll kill you," he roared just as Shelby and her husband entered the room. No one was prepared for me to aim a gun at them. I pulled the trigger and shot Abel too. This was also in the leg. I didn't want to kill them, but I wouldn't let them touch me. I had Gunner's baby inside of me and these two violated me. I was helpless, but wouldn't fall victim to them twice. Shelby screamed and I aimed the gun at her. "Get me your keys, now." Her husband was a weak man, who seemed to bend at Shelby's will. "Don't shoot her," he begged.

I took the rest of their money in their wallets, their cell phones, and high-tailed it out of there as fast as I could. I thanked the heavens Gunner taught me how to drive. It was a ten-minute drive to the nearest house and a twenty-five minute drive to the nearest Walmart. They were truly in the middle of nowhere.

I drove their car to a truck stop and waited until I found the only female truck driver I could find, then paid her twenty dollars to ride with her south to West Virginia.

I bounced around several homeless shelters, and eventually stole an ID from a woman who looked similar enough to me. I went to a free clinic that helped me fill out paperwork to start receiving services. It was easy to become someone else, they thought I was a few years older than I was, and eventually I moved into a low-income apartment building. I slept on an air mattress for the first year, with little Gunner tucked close to me. A part of me was always afraid that the cops would come after me for shooting the twins, so I lived in fear and did the best I could to stay under the radar. I didn't know the first thing about taking care of a baby, but I did the best I could. I was incredibly grateful for the Medicaid. It helped me feed Gun. Organizations like Catholic Charities, which helped clothe me as a child, also helped me clothe him. Talk about the past repeating itself. I don't know what I would've done without the help.

Eventually, I met Mrs. Warner, who was nice enough. She didn't ask questions, and she needed the extra cash as much as I needed help with Gun.

I sighed and looked at my boy again. I hated waking him. I lifted him and held him close. God, this boy was heavy. I knew I shouldn't be lifting him any more, he was much too big. Even though I worked out, I knew carrying a seven-year old was not something I should be doing. "Mom," he mumbled sleepily.

"Yeah, baby it's me. Go to sleep." I cooed, and made my way across the hall, fishing my key out of my bag, while balancing him on my hip and shoulder.

Just a little while longer, I thought. I'd been saving for years now. I almost had enough saved to move. My plan was to move into a house, stop "entertaining" and have enough bank that I could be comfortable while I opened a studio. I had one skill and that was dancing. I loved that pole dancing had become the new workout craze. I was going to teach suburban women how to pole dance and from everything I've read, I'd make a killing.

I smiled thinking about my dream as I laid Gun down in his bed. I kissed him on his head and was about to walk out of his room when I heard, "Momma," in a sleepy voice.

"Gun."

"Missed you," he yawned.

I climbed into bed beside him and wrapped him close to me. "Missed you too, Gun," I whispered as my eyes fluttered closed.

"Mom, I just have to get one more power up." Gun hit the controls fast and furiously. This kid's addiction to video games was out of this world.

"Alright, five more minutes, and we have to go." I got a grunt in response and finished doing the dishes leftover from dinner while I waited.

"Gun. Time's up."

"Mom," he whined.

"Sorry, bud." He reluctantly put the remote control down and I clicked off the TV.

"I wasn't done saving it yet."

I gave my son a look that said enough and he reluctantly followed me across the hall. Mrs. Warner's apartment was a one bedroom, where mine was a two. Her worn couch and recliner had towels over the armrest to hide where the material had frayed. She had a small coffee table in the living room in front of her old box style TV.

She was a black woman with gray hair and a round belly. There was a softness to her eyes that instantly made me trust her, and the easy way Gun took to her made it an easy choice to have her watch him.

"Hey, sugar. I made cookies," Mrs. Warner called as soon as we walked in.

"You're going to spoil him too much!" I joked.

"There is no such thing with this boy. Gun, get over here and kiss your Momma goodbye."

A few minutes and a nice long hug later, I was on my way to work. After last night, I wasn't looking forward to going in. Not that I usually looked forward to it, but tonight, I wanted nothing to do with it.

The night was going okay. I went on to do my set. Tonight, I wore a black frayed top with black star pasties under it and lace cheeky panties. The music cued and the lights dimmed. I thumped my five-inch stiletto on the stage and waited until the perfect beat when the spotlight shone brightly on me.

I moved my hips fast as Shakira's voice echoed in the room. I had a few songs tonight and I usually started off with something sexy and fast, then finished the night off with an intense number.

My ass was to the crowd and my hips were shaking, when I turned around and my eyes landed on Enrico Santos. He was sitting in the chairs that surrounded the stage. One of his business associates was seated next to him trying to get his attention, but his eyes were trained directly on me. I tried not to look in his direction, but I could feel his steely gaze. It wasn't a warm touch either, no this felt like a vice grip.

I did my best to get through my song, even though his presence had shaken me. By the end of the song, I was wearing only my pasties and panties. I shook my hips and my full tits for the crowd, and then the lights dimmed.

I rushed to collect my money. Frank was nearby, but the darkness, with this monster so near, made me nervous. The lights flicked back on and the DJ announced that Sky would be on in ten minutes and to give it up for me one more time. The crowd was hooting and cheering as I was about to round the corner to the dressing room. Enrico's hand caught my wrist in a firm grip.

"You tease me," his thick-accented voice snarled.

My eyes darted and I saw Frank in my peripheral talking to one of Enrico's goons. I steadied my shaky voice, "I'm sorry, it's my job to dance. Please let me go. I don't want any trouble."

"I want you to do your job and dance for me."

"I don't do private dances. I'm on the stage, that's all."

"You'll dance for me, and when I get you alone, I'll sink my fingers into that tight pussy and you'll gag on my cock until I let you up for air."

"Hands off the dancer," Frank ordered.

Enrico wasn't the type of guy to be ordered around. He released my wrist, and in the same movement, grabbed my long dark locks in a tight fist.

"Certainly, you can tell I'm a man who gets what I want. You resist me, I might just keep you." He let me go, turned, then walked away as if he didn't just scare the shit out of me.

"You alright, Char?" Frank asked handing me a robe as we walked into the dressing area.

"No. That guy gives me the creeps."

"I talked to Dick when I saw him come in. Dick's scared shitless of him. Said he's one powerful motherfucker and if we all knew what was good for us, we'd do whatever the fuck the guy wanted and try to keep our heads down and our mouths closed.

"I can't go in that room with that guy."

"I know, Char. Why don't you leave for the night? I'll tell Dick you weren't feeling good."

"Thanks, Frank." I quickly shimmied on some sweats and threw a sweatshirt on top. I always dressed in sweats. After being on stage I would do whatever it took to stay out of the limelight.

In a hurry, as if not to be caught by Dick, Frank ushered me out.

Mrs. Warner was still up when I arrived. "You're here early? Bad night?" she asked.

"You could say that."

"Everything okay, darling?" Concern laced her voice.

"Just some creep," I shook my head, willing away any thoughts of Enrico. "How was Gun tonight?"

"Oh you know that boy, he's no trouble." I smiled at Mrs. Warner. She took good care of my boy. "I'm going to grab him, okay?"

"Yeah, honey. You sure you're okay, though?"

I nodded and opened Mrs. Warner's bedroom door." Gunner's face didn't look quite right. There were small creases by the sides of his eyes and when I stepped even closer I could see that there was a slight grin he was holding back. "Busted little dude. I know you're totally faking."

"How'd you know?" He sat up laughing.

"Can't fool me, bugger." I walked over and kissed his head. "Let's go." He hopped out of bed and raced towards the door.

"Jesus, he's wide awake. How many cookies did he have?" I asked Mrs. Warner and was met with a smirk before walking across the hall.

The hallway looked like it always did, but for some reason, I felt protective of Gunner. While I unlocked my door, I held him close to my body. I looked over my shoulder before closing the door behind me and I could've sworn I saw a shadow move. I looked again and saw nothing. As I locked the door and tucked Gunner to my side, I felt fear. I laid with Gunner while he fell asleep but couldn't help the sick feeling deep in the pit of my belly that I hadn't seen the last of Enrico.

I was able to get Marjorie to cover my shift the next night and I seriously considered just leaving the club. I had money saved. I wanted more, and I was so close to my dream I could taste it. I wondered at what cost, though?

I had just dropped Gunner off at school, when my car started to act up. It wasn't a new car, but so far I hadn't had any issues with it. I wasn't in a great neighborhood, considering I lived in a not so great neighborhood, when it started to overheat.

"Fuck," I hit the steering wheel as I pulled to the side of the road. This couldn't be happening. White steam billowed from under the hood. I shut the car off, stepped out, saw more steam and let off another string of expletives.

An hour and a half later, I was at Junior's Garage where Junior, who wasn't so Junior, told me, I needed a new water pump and a whole list of other things. It was going to cost me just under eight hundred dollars.

That was a hit I really couldn't take. I walked home from the garage. It took me an hour and twenty minutes. I wished like hell I didn't give up my shift the other night to Marjorie. With this hit, I was going to have to dance my ass off to make up for it.

"Is he out there?" I asked Sky who had just returned backstage.

"Relax, I haven't seen that fine piece of ass since the weekend. I don't know why you're all strung up. That man is fine. If he wanted me in a room, I would drop to my knees. I bet he's hung like a fucking rocket ship."

"It's not like that. He's scary. And you know I don't do rooms."

"That's right! Miss, I'm too good to go behind closed doors."

Jesus, I knew I shouldn't have asked Sky. She was a total bitch. Usually, Marjorie had my back, but Marjorie was in a room of her own and I really wanted to know before I went out there if he was watching.

"Char. You're on." Frank saved me from Sky's tirade.

The lights were dimmed. I counted the beats. I danced and was relieved when I didn't see Enrico. My set finished and I actually was feeling pretty good about tonight.

I did a table dance for a bunch of suits. It wasn't half bad either. They tipped generously and for the most part kept their hands and crude comments to themselves.

I finished two more dances on the stage and was getting ready to call it a night when Dick walked in. "This is for you," he said and handed me a note.

I changed into my sweats and waited for Frank to finish up. He was going to give me a ride home since my car was in the shop.

While I waited, I poured a drink from Marjorie's stash. I sat in a black folding chair and stared at the note. It reminded me of a birthday invitation that I would receive in Gunner's backpack. The small white envelope had my name scrawled on the front and not just Char or Charlie, but Charlotte.

I opened it and the chilling words made me want to vomit.

I'm sorry I couldn't be there tonight, my pet. I'll see you soon, and when I do you'll give me what I want. You'll beg like the good little pet you are. -E

Behind the letter, was a picture. It was from this morning outside of my apartment. I was handing Gunner his backpack as he was getting in the backseat of my car.

Shit.

Fucking hell.

If that wasn't a threat, I didn't know what was.

Chapter Five

Charlie

I was scared out of my damn mind when my next shift started. Part of me wanted to run away, but my car was still in the shop. That same part of me didn't care. I thought, maybe I should just pack a bag with Gunner, get on a bus and disappear. It was an appealing thought, but then the idea of an enraged Enrico finding me and hurting Gunner made me stay.

It also didn't help matters that Frank did not answer his phone tonight to give me a lift. Which was odd all by itself since he always answered and even odder since he offered last night when he dropped me off to come and get me. I was stuck taking the bus to work and that always sucked.

I was resigned to giving Enrico a night and prayed that he would let me be. I'd been used before. This wouldn't be new to me. I just had to suck it up and figure a way out of this mess.

I was applying thick black liner with a trembling hand when I made a mistake smearing black onto my lid. "Shit," I cursed.

"What's gotten into you?" Marjorie asked pressing her lips together to even out her plum lips and then smacking them together. I watched her reflection in the mirror and wondered how much I could tell her. ...

"You know that guy that's been messing with me?"

Her eyes flashed sympathy and she nodded. I knew the gossip-mill had been going haywire. I'd heard a few snickers from girls, wondering what made me special. Why would he want me? I wondered the same thing. Sure I had looks and could dance, but so what. All the girls here were hot. I wouldn't even say I was in the top three.

"He sent me a pic of Gunner and me yesterday. Said he's going to have his way and I just know that picture was a threat. I can't let him hurt my boy."

"Fuck, honey. Did you tell Dick?"

"Dick's scared shitless of him, which only adds to my fear. I've never seen him back down so much." That was the absolute truth. Dick, for the most part, had our backs, so this uncharacteristic behavior of his only made me realize that I didn't have much choice.

"What are you going to do?" Her hand settled on my shoulder to offer me comfort.

"What choice do I have? I'm going to do my set and then I'll go in the room with him." Just saying that made me sick.

"Fuck."

"Yeah, fuck."

"Marjorie, you're on," Dick called from the doorway just as Sky moved from behind a large row of clothes. I didn't know she was back there and I wondered how much she'd heard. I fixed the smear of my makeup and then finished fastening my thigh high black plastic boots.

My first set tonight was a newer routine. I'd only done it a few times and every time the crowd went nuts. I usually loved it, but with the knowledge of what tonight had in store for me, I wasn't nearly as pumped as I should be.

I fixed my half cat mask and checked my bodice on my Cat-girl suit. Everything fit perfectly.

"Damn, girl. You look hot." Sky appraised me.

"Thanks," I sighed wishing I wasn't the object of any man's dreams. Gone were the days I was invisible and I'd have done anything to become the girl no one saw again.

"Heard you talking to Marjorie. Looks like you could use a drink." She handed me a flask. Normally, Sky wasn't nice to me, so I had no idea why she was handing me her drink, but to hell with it. She was right. I needed to calm my nerves. I took a swig and attempted to hand the cold silver flask back to her.

She tilted her head, "Finish it. Sounds like you need it more than me," then she grabbed a drink tray and left me there.

A minute later, Marjorie walked back in. My routine was next. "How was it out there?"

"Rowdier than usual. Your guy's at table six, but it's pretty full out there and it looks like he's doing business. Maybe you'll get lucky and he'll be too occupied?"

I could only hope that was the case.

"Char," Dick called and I knew it was my time.

77

The lights were dimmed and I had a long black whip that I flicked against the stage in tune with the beat. My heel tapped in rhythm against the stage and the crowd quieted in anticipation. Christina Aguilera's "Dirty" thrummed and I pranced to the end of the stage while shaking my hips. The whip was an extension of me as I turned and swayed. My left leg crossed with my right. I spun so my back was to the crowd and bent as seductively low as I could. They were getting a show, that was for sure. More than half of my cheeks stuck out from my barely-there pleather shorts.

When I was vertical again I snapped the whip and for a second I felt powerful as if the single most vile man wasn't behind me plotting what he'd do to me. I hadn't looked in his direction yet, I was too afraid. I danced. My mind started to feel a little fuzzy but I shook it off. I put the whip in my mouth and climbed the pole. Arm over arm, I realized they felt a little jelly like.

Shit, whatever Sky gave me to drink was stronger than I anticipated. From the top of the pole, I bent backward facing the crowd and when Christina belted out Dirty I unzipped my corset letting my breasts fall free. I moved in fast circles around the pole until I reached the bottom then freed myself from my top the rest of the way. Only black plastic stars covered my nipples.

I took the whip from my mouth and moved the handle between my legs. I rubbed it up and down teasing the crowd. As I did this my mouth popped open like I was in ecstasy. My tongue swept out and over my red lips. My eyes finally moved to table six and my steps faltered. Not because I was feeling a little woozy, which I was, and not because the devil Enrico was staring at me like he wanted to eat me. No, it was the man who was seated across from Enrico. A man I'd prayed to see one day, but never here. Never under these circumstances. For a brief moment, I stared transfixed in my place, missing my cue. I knew I needed to get on with the show. He wouldn't know it was me, half of my face was covered and my body had definitely changed since I was sixteen.

I knew it was him. I'd know him anywhere. I'd been staring at his eyes for the last seven years. He was the man who both saved me and broke me and there he was; drinking with the enemy.

I finished my set in a haze, not even sure how I made it off stage. I was definitely fucked up from whatever was in Sky's drink, but I also was completely fucked up from seeing Gunner.

I had to get ready for my next set and I was even more afraid knowing that I didn't wear a mask for the next dance. Maybe he wouldn't even recognize me? Gone was the mousy girl whose virginity he took before leaving her and never looking back. Hell, I'd barely recognized me. On the other hand, maybe he could help me? And maybe he could save me one more time?

Chapter Six

Gunner

The last thing I wanted to do was meet with this piece of shit in this piece of shit town, but we needed him. Enrico Santos was a fucking Colombian God, or so he proclaimed. Two reasons I was here. One, he was going to sell guns to either myself or to Hades. We were at war with Hades and couldn't let more guns fall into his hands. And two, we had a big fucking problem with the Mexicans. We needed this meeting with Enrico to go well tonight. I hated the fucker. Every time I'd been around him, I wanted to slit his throat because of his arrogance.

His men cowered to him. They feared him. I saw this as his biggest weakness. Better to have the loyalty of your men out of respect than fear.

I swirled the ice in the amber liquid and only partially listened as Enrico retold a story about killing a guy while getting a blow-job from a whore. Filthy fucker.

Shane was sitting across from me. I could tell he wasn't amused either, but he was a far better actor than me. He smirked at the appropriate time, while I just wanted to rip the guy's throat out. We also had two of our guys, Knuckles and Donny with us. Both of them were big ass dudes, and I was glad to know they had our backs. They left their cuts at home to blend in. I about busted a nut laughing when I saw the redneck Duck Dynasty shirts they had on, courtesy of Walmart's clearance rack.

Movement on the stage caught my attention. Hell, it caught every man's attention. A woman dressed in a cat suit worked the stage. She didn't just dance, she fucking prowled and pranced. She was sexy as hell. I was drawn to her. She had curves. And when her breasts poured from her top I had an overwhelming desire to cover her up. I felt protective and felt like they should only be for me, which was absurd--I was in a fucking strip club.

Enrico even stopped running his mouth, so he could watch her. I swear I saw his hand go under the table to rub his dick.

Briefly, it looked like the cat recognized me. She paused on stage and for a small second her steps faltered. For all I knew, it could've been the slime ball next to me, though.

A scantily dressed waitress walked by and I watched Enrico grab her arm, pull her close, whisper in her ear, and then pat her ass sticking a Benjamin in her panties.

"Damn, she's fine," one of Enrico's goons said, breaking the mesmerized silence I'd been in.

"That she is. She's one of mine." Enrico threw back his drink and then got down to business just as the cat walked off the stage. "So, gentlemen, what is that you want from me?"

He damn well knew why we were here. He just wanted to hear us say it again. Shane was the better talker of the two of us. That's why he was president of our club.

"A hundred-seventy-five," Shane said cutting to the chase. He was low balling Enrico and we both knew it.

"Now, now, you know that's not a fair price. I know you need me way more than I need you. I know about your problems with Hades."

We knew he was aware of this, so Shane and I spent the next fifteen minutes bargaining with the devil.

We just agreed on a price of two hundred and seventy thousand dollars when they called out a new dancer. Her back was to us and I saw that it was the same beautifully curved ass of cat girl. She wore a schoolgirl outfit and her dark hair was in pigtails. A plaid skirt barely covered her tight ass and her legs went on for miles landing in delicious red fuck me heels.

Enrico saying this girl was his made me want to hurt him even more.

"Porn Star" by My Darkest Days blared and the dark haired vixen bent over grabbed her ankles and peaked between her thighs. I couldn't see her face completely there were shadows and lights covering it. She moved to the pole and worked it, although, she did miss a few steps. She turned in circles, climbed it and threw her head back. It was then that my life was completely fucking altered.

My eyes met hers and there was no doubt that I was staring at those beautiful blue doe eyes. She had changed so much. She had filled out in all the ways I knew she would someday. Her hips were fuller. Her ass more curved, and her tits were so goddamned full and beautiful. If I thought I had a hard on for her when she was sixteen, it was nothing like what I felt right now. Rage started to build deep in my chest. What the fuck was she doing on a stage fucking taking her clothes off?

I wanted her. I had always wanted her, but I also wanted to take her over my knee and spank her ass for letting anyone other than me look at her. With even less grace, she landed at the bottom of the pole, then crawled and almost stumbled to the front of the stage. Her eyes, even through the dark lighting and strobing stage lights, looked glassed over.

Fuck! She wasn't just a stripper, she was blitzed out of her ever-loving mind. Every instinct in me wanted to pull her off of the stage, but Enrico's words echoed through my head. *She's one of mine.* I had to be smart about this. With all my willpower, I took my eyes off of her. I listened to Enrico talk for another minute. He made a few comments about how the whore on stage would have his dick in her mouth before the night was over. I saw red and wanted to kill him, but knew I couldn't do a damn thing right then. Our club had worked hard to get this meeting with Enrico, and he had agreed to everything we needed from him. If I went off half cocked, there would be war with not just Enrico, but the Mexicans and Hades Runners too. My brothers' lives were at stake.

I finished my drink and tilted the glass to Shane, who had been watching me curiously. He could tell something was up with me. He always had that insight. "Gonna hit the john," I said and stalked down the dark hallway towards the bathroom.

83

I didn't waste time. I hurried into the dressing room. Robes hung by the door. A blonde was in front of a mirror adjusting her tits in her teddy. Make-up covered the table in front of the mirror and clothes were everywhere. The room stunk of cheap oil and bad perfume.

"You can't be in here," she said with little emotion in her voice.

I handed her a fifty, "I can do whatever the fuck I want. Now leave and tell no one you saw me." Her eyes narrowed on me, but she took the fifty from me and left.

I stood in the back of the room hidden in the shadows. A moment later, the owner of the club stalked in with Charlie's arm in his grip. "You're trashed. You know you can't be trashed at my club. What the fuck, Char?"

"Dick?" she asked confused as he sat her down in a chair. He shook his head at her and stormed out of the dressing room.

I was alone with her. At. Fucking. Last.

The second the door clicked I stalked her. She was waving her fingers in front of her face in wonderment. "What the hell are you doing, Charlie?"

It was like she didn't hear me, which pissed me off even more. I moved her chair, crouched in front of her and stilled her hands. Her eyes were unfocused. "Charlie, look at me."

"Gunner," she sighed dreamily. Her voice was music to my ears. It was my favorite song. From the very first moment I ever heard her speak, it was a balm to my uneasy soul.

She blinked a few times as if trying to bring me into focus.

Rage, uninhibited rage, filled me. I had searched for her for years and here she was; stoned stupid in a fucking strip club. Her tits were hanging out and the only thing keeping her from being fully naked was a barely there black strip of silk between her legs and some fucking smiley face pasties glaring at me. The cheesy grin was a taunt.

I wanted to rip the stickers off and pull her dark nipple into my mouth. I still remembered how she'd react when I'd pull on them with my teeth. I remembered how her cheeks would flush when I'd sink my fingers into her tight pussy. Fuck, I'd jerked off to the memory of her milking my cock more than once.

I was so pissed at her. All this time, I'd searched. I wanted to hurt her for hurting me, but I could never hurt my Mouse, so I did the only thing my brain would let me do. I grabbed her shoulders almost violently, pulled her to me, and crushed my lips against hers.

Chapter Seven

Charlie

My limbs were heavy and I was stumbling. The stage lights swirled in a dancing prism of colors. Dick grabbed me by the arm and threw me into the dressing room.

Nothing felt right.

And then I see you. You're magnificent. I couldn't have dreamed up a more beautiful version of you. You're big and ominous. Dark blonde, shaggy hair falls over your hazel eyes. A leather vest sits on your shoulders that have gotten even wider. You have tattoos on your arms. The colors swirl. I want to run my fingers over them.

You're kissing me. It's different than any kiss we've shared. Hungry, but angry. My lips feel bruised from the punishing way your lips connect with mine. I want to ask you where you went and why you're here, but that would stop this moment. This moment feels good. Then, your lips pull away from mine.

I'm stunned.

What was happening?

Everything was a blur.

What was happening to me? Why didn't I feel right?

My pulse sped up. I could feel the thump, thump, thump in my head. My vision was spotty. You're talking to me, but I don't hear you. Something catches my eyes behind you. On the dressing table in front of my mirror is a vase filled with dark purple roses. I know these are not from you. Flowers were never your speed. I know who these are from because behind it is the picture of Gun and me. Even in my haze of confusion, I knew.

I was panicking inside. I wanted to scream and ask you to save me, but my lips are barely working. So, I say the one word that I hope will convey my fear, "Enrico."

Chapter Eight

Gunner

Christ! Who was this woman in front of me? I broke from our kiss even more confused. She was so high. I wasn't even sure she knew it was me, and then as I stared at her, and asked her what the hell she was on, she called me Enrico.

Fucking Enrico.

If I was pissed before, I was even more so now. I wanted to hit something, and I wanted to kill Enrico. I needed to get away from Charlie before I did something seriously fucked up.

I started to move away from her when she slurred, "Gun, slys yours."

What the fuck did that even mean?

My temper couldn't take it. "Jesus fucking Christ, Charlie! You're fucking stoned," I yelled. My blood boiled.

"'Rico, dance," she mumbled, not making any sense. She looked afraid, but I didn't know what to make of any of it. All I heard was Enrico saying she was his and she kept repeating Enrico's name. I'd loved her and held her on a pedestal for so long, and she was a fucking drug lord's tweaked out pussy.

I ripped my gaze from her. I couldn't look at her. Everything I'd ever thought about and dreamed about pertaining to Charlie was being crushed. I'd thought of finding her one day, and making her mine like it was always meant to be. Hell, near every time I got my dick wet since we'd been apart, all I thought about was Charlie. On nights when I'd had to do unthinkable shit, it was the memories of Charlie that got me through, but now I could see that my Mouse was gone. I couldn't fucking handle it. So, I did the only thing I could do without losing my shit. I left, but not before delivering one final blow, "I can't believe you're his fucking whore."

I returned to the table and Enrico's eyes latched onto me. "You were gone a long time. Everything alright?"

"Bad tacos," I rebutted and watched as both Shane, knowing I was lying, and Enrico, believing I was lying, narrowed their eyes at me. I sat down, not looking back at the stage. I needed to get the fuck out of there.

I threw back a shot of whiskey, still rattled from seeing Charlie, and listened to the plan with Enrico. It was a sound plan, and I had to admit, as much as I didn't like the guy, he didn't get to be a king without being able to knock down some pawns.

"What the fuck was that?" Shane asked me as we were mounting our bikes, leaving the strip club behind.

"Not now, brother." My nose flared, but I knew now wasn't the time for me to lose my shit. Donny and Knuckles spotted us, gave us a chin lift, and got into their truck. I started my Harley Street Glide, let it warm up for a minute since it had been sitting, and pulled out, but not before wondering if I'd ever see Charlie again, and how she could've gotten to the place she was in.

"Let's celebrate!" Shane slammed his fist down as church ended. We had just finished going over the deal with Enrico and the guys were more than pleased.

Twenty of us filed out of church down a corridor and into a large area that had a makeshift bar on one side that was surrounded by tables, mismatched chairs and leather couches. There was a large flat screen behind the bar and the Browns were getting their asses handed to them A-fucking-gain. Lachlan and Anthony moved to one of the machines in the back of the building and powered it on. They had a piece they were machining for a custom bike they were working on. Our clubhouse was an old machine shop that was close to the highway and surrounded by other businesses. We machined several pieces for big corporations on a contractual basis. That was our main source of income.

I grabbed a beer from the glass cooler, took it to the head, and finished it in near one gulp.

"Jesus, man. What's gotten into you?" Shane asked, "And what the fuck was that shit about bad tacos?"

I shook my head at him and grabbed another beer. I didn't want to talk. I wanted to get fucked up. It'd been years since I felt as out of control as I did right now.

I grabbed another beer and slammed that one back too. Shane's eyes were boring into me. I finished that beer and said, "Need to fight. Any of you fuckers got balls enough to spar with me?" I took off my shirt. The Bleeding Scars MC tattoo, with the words written across my back and a Celtic cross with a motorcycle handlebar going through it to make the cross, covered my back. Every man in the room had the same tattoo, except the hang-arounds and the prospects that were always just here.

I grabbed a cigarette, lit it, and rolled my neck.

"I'll fight you," Shane pulled his shirt off too and headed to the ring. Yes, we had an actual boxing ring.

"Figures you'd be the only one with balls," I mumbled.

"Nah, I'm just the only one who doesn't give a fuck what crawled up your ass. I'll still lay you out."

I laughed and shook my head, "Keep dreaming."

We rounded each other in the ring. Our men flanked all sides of the ropes. Ace, the other original member who barely ever spoke, sat in the corner of the room silently observing. Ace was a Marine. His hair was dark and was always cut short. He was a big motherfucker. He always wore his vest, and the only time I'd ever seen him without a shirt, he was covered in scars. He kept his story close to him, not really ever letting anyone in. I knew, Shane knew, but no one else did. He pulled smoke into his lungs, and gave a subtle shake of his head. I know my brothers didn't understand the turmoil going through my heart right now, but it was clear that I needed to expunge my rage.

Shane bounced on his heels and held his fist high, elbows in, protecting his ribs. I waited. I always waited, never striking first. It was more fun for me that way. Shane threw a jab, clipping my chin. I smirked and the motherfucker smirked back. A three punch combo to his ribs, then a head butt to my nose. It stunned me for a moment, and he was able to get another hit in. I ducked his next blow, then released my fury. He was waiting for me to explode. That quick fucker dodged half my hits. I swung-- he took it. He swung-- I savored it. I needed the blow. Physical pain took away everything else. All I could feel was the bite of his throws, and that was better than the ache in my gut.

I split his lip. He cut my eye. I wasn't even trying to win.

"Enough," Ace shouted. The entire room turned to look at him, our fight forgotten. He nodded his head toward one of the backrooms, and Shane and I left the ring, neither of us in pristine condition. Men handed us our cuts as we passed by.

We walked into a room that was filled with tools. Some in working condition and some not, but the room had become a catch all for anything that needed a place.

"He's not even trying, Shane," Ace said closing the door behind us. It was like we were being called to the principal's office.

"Right here, motherfucker. Right here."

"You're being stupid," Ace said calmly. He was always so fucking calm.

"Nah, he's got something to work out. Better he works it out in the ring, then make some stupid fucked up decision." Shane tore a smoke from his jeans and his lighter from his vest. He lit his smoke, and continued to flip open and close the Zippo.

"Stop talking about me like I'm not in the room. I'm fine."

"Really? You don't seem fine," Shane's blew his smoke at me.

"If I wanted a bitch, I'd call your mother."

He flipped me off and Ace shook his head.

"You know what? Fuck this. I need to ride." I started to walk out of the room when Ace put his hand on my shoulder.

"Then, we ride."

I didn't glance back. I threw my leg over my bike and rode east. Nine of my brothers were with me, with Ace to my right and Shane on my left. We took the highway until there was no more highway. There was no more of anything. It was just me and my thoughts, and the road. My mind tried to make sense of everything that happened tonight, and I decided on one thing. It didn't matter if she thought she was Enrico's, or if she was a druggie. For all I knew, that piece of shit made her that way. What I did know is that none of that really mattered. The only thing that mattered was that she was safe and I knew where she was. I wasn't going to let her slip away again. If I had to dry her ass out and hide her from the fucker I would. Deep down, she was still my Mouse, and I realized earlier I'd reacted in rage. What I should've done was waited until her shift was over, and taken her home with me. I shouldn't have called her a whore, and I shouldn't have jumped to conclusions. I didn't know what lead her to that stage. I was just so angry.

It was well past dark. My hands cramped a little. We rode so long that eventually the roar of the pipes behind me started to lessen, as little by little, my brothers dropped off.

Hues of pink, orange and purple started to fill the sky, and I knew it was time to turn back. I had a plan. I decided I was going to find out where she lived, and I was going to figure out her shit whether she liked it or not.

Only Ace and Shane were left with me. We pulled into a gas station. The open sign was half lit, and it almost looked abandoned except for the twentyish kid headbanging to metal inside the store. I grabbed a pack of smokes and paid. The kid looked up at me like I was a fucking God when he saw my MC vest.

"Are you, like, in a real MC?"

I glared.

"Have you met Jax Teller? That dude is so cool. You kind of look like him, only your way fucking bigger."

I glared again, then an idea struck me. "Kid, you ever seen a real MC before?" Considering we were in the middle of nowhere I wasn't sure that he would have.

"Only Sons! That shit was dope, but I hated how Teller went out."

"I'll tell you what, kid. You want to be an insider for me? Do something real special for the club?"

"Are you kidding me? That'd be rock 'n roll." He moved his thumbs to his two middle fingers and made the traditional rock n roll sign then banged his head like Beavis and Butthead. This kid was never getting laid.

"What's your name, kid?"

"Joshua."

"Well, Joshua. I'll tell you what. If you ever see any big bad bikers with a different cut on than ours, you text me."

"You want me to like give you intel? That's so rad, dude!" I leaned into him and grabbed his orange and white striped standard issued shirt fisting it. The kid's face became even paler than it was.

"Don't fuck with me. You cross me and....," I took my finger and ran it across my throat pretending to slit it. The kid's shaking knees rattled the counter.

"I...I...I,"

"Spit it out, kid."

"I understand."

"Good. Now, tell no one of this meeting."

His voice shook as he asked, "How will I reach you?"

I smirked, and pulled from my wallet one of the shop's cards and left it on the counter, then turned and walked out. The door creaked as it closed behind me.

"What the fuck was that in there?" Shane asked as he flicked his smoke towards the road, the red glow sparking in different directions as it collided with the ground.

I smirked, "A little Sons hero worship, that's all."

Ace shook his head. He was always getting the Sons reference.

"So, what's the plan?" Shane asked, knowing I finally had my head on straight.

"That dancer from last night, the one in the cat suit? That's my Charlie. She was all kinds of fucked up when I talked to her last night, and I totally lost my shit. Plus, she has ties to Enrico and that makes me insane. I went in blazing. I was beyond pissed. Said things." I shook my head in disgust with myself. "Shane, need you to get her address from the club." His hand was already on his phone texting as I asked.

"What else?" Ace questioned.

"Need you guys to have my back, once we get to her place. Make sure none of Enrico's guys are around. I don't want to fuck anything up with him, but I need to see her."

Ace put his hand on my shoulder and nodded while Shane started his bike and yelled, "Let's ride."

Chapter Nine

Gunner

The apartment was in a shit neighborhood. Even shittier than that was the lack of any type of security at the large brick building. I spotted two guys dealing and a tweaker near a large green dumpster. Trash lined the fenced in parking lot that was wide open for anyone to come in and jack your car. No way were we leaving our bikes unattended. Ace gave a nod with his head to say he was staying, and that Shane and I should go. So far, there had been no sign of Enrico, or his men.

The entryway had a few broken mailboxes hanging open. I double-checked to make sure the apartment number Shane was given matched up. Paint peeled from the walls. It made me want to get a lead check just standing there.

"What a dump," Shane murmured under his breath. We walked to the elevator. Our motorcycle boots echoed with loud thumps down the deserted hall. Out of service. Shouldn't even be surprised. The stairway door was propped open, and a giant sign that hung on the door read, DO NOT PISS IN THE STAIRWELL.

"Christ," I mumbled when I took a whiff of the rank air.

We reached our desired floor. The stairwell door slammed behind us making a loud bang as we stomped down the hallway. The walls were too thin in this place. A door at the end of the hall sprung open and I heard a kid shout, "It's her, Mrs. Warner. It has to be." A kid raced out of an apartment wearing Ninja Turtle pajamas. His sandy blonde hair hung over his face.

A woman yelled, "Gun, get your butt back in this apartment."

I froze and swore, "The fuck?"

The kid looked up at me. His eyes connected with mine. The air left my lungs, and I dropped to my knees. It was like looking in the damn mirror. He was me, only a version of me from eighteen years earlier.

"You okay, mister?" The boy asked and my heart thumped.

"Did she call you Gun?" I asked and the older black woman halted her steps.

"Yeah, that's my name. I'm Gunner. Gunner Reed. Do you know where my mom is?"

"Boy," the woman called in a warning tone.

Shane sucked in a breath. I wanted to cry out in agony and in joy. I had a son. I had a fucking son, with my name. I had a son that I'd missed years of his life with. I had a son, living and breathing, a few hours away from me.

"Holy shit," Shane muttered.

"Gun, you get back here, boy. That ain't your Momma. I don't know where she is, but she'll be here."

"I ain't his momma, but my name's Gunner Reed."

I couldn't read the woman. She seemed apprehensive, where Gunner looked shocked. "But, that's my name," he said searching my face.

"Yeah, kid. Your momma named you after your daddy."

"But, I don't have a dad."

"Yeah, you do. I just didn't know about you until right now. Why don't we go on into your apartment and wait for that mom of yours." I had so many questions for her.

Mrs. Warner, the woman who apparently babysat my kid while his mom was out whoring, still wasn't sure. "I don't know if that's a good idea, Gun."

I flashed her a look, then pulled out my ID showing her my name. "Look, I saw Charlie for the first time in eight years last night, and this is the first time I'm finding out that we got a kid. Swear to you, don't even know the kid, but I'd lay my life down for him."

What more could she say to my more than honest declaration?

"She should've been home last night. I have to get to work, anyways. Here's the key to her place. It's not like her to not be here. You take care of that boy."

I unlocked the apartment door and held it open as my son walked under my arm and into his space. Shane followed behind me. I took in the place. Clean. A blue and white afghan hung over the back of a brown suede couch. In front of that, there was a coffee table with a stack of coloring books and crayons on it. There was a TV with an X-box and a stack of games to the side. On the walls, there were a few

99

pictures of Gunner and Charlie. Gunner was younger in the pictures. There were also several pictures of dinosaurs in bright green and blue crayons that were taped up amongst the frames.

Seeing her with him as a toddler made a place in my heart ache. My heart, which I just now realized, was fragmented. I could see the puzzle pieces, Gun, Charlie and me, but we were a bunch of square pegs trying to fit into round holes.

I eyed her apartment again, then Gun broke my silence.

"So, you're really my dad?"

I ruffled the kid's hair, "Yep, you look identical to me. Your mom gave you my name and everything."

"Where you been then?" He was a little defensive, and I couldn't blame him. I actually liked that he wasn't afraid to speak up and ask. He was gutsy. Here he was with two large bikers he never met before in his apartment, and he was questioning me like I owed him answers, and boy did I ever. I wished I had more to give him, though.

"I gotta tell you, kid. I briefly saw your mom last night for the first time since I was eighteen. I lost touch with her, and then when I could, I tried to find her. Searched for a long time. Had no idea she was here, and no idea that you were born. Swear to you, I'd known, you'd both have been with me for a long time."

He nodded his head at me like he got it. I had to find out what my kid had seen and how much Enrico was in their life. I also had this twisting feeling in my gut,because Charlie wasn't home yet. It didn't feel like it was Gun's normal.

Shane sat on the sofa. I imagined it was to try to make himself look less intimidating. His long legs stretched out wide taking in my interaction with my son. *My Son.*

"So, do you know where Mom is?"

"Nah, kid. She ever not come home like this?"

He shook his head, then walked into the tiny kitchen, pulled up a stool and climbed up on the counter grabbing himself a bowl. I watched in fascination as he opened another cupboard and grabbed a box of cereal, poured it into the bowl, then opened the fridge and grabbed the milk. He was so young, but so independent. God, he reminded me of me. He poured the milk into the cereal and then he grinned, "I love Fruity Pebbles. Want some?"

"Fruity pebbles are the shit! I'll take a bowl." Shane said from the couch. The kid gave him a chin lift and said, "Help yourself." This kid was seriously cool. Shane grabbed a bowl, then sat back down, and put cartoons on.

I took a minute to look around more closely. I opened the first door in the hallway. It was a small bathroom with a rubber ducky shower curtain and a lime green rug. There was a hamper half-filled with dirty laundry, a few towels were haphazardly hung over a towel rack. I opened the medicine cabinet. Tampons, toothpaste, deodorant, but nothing that gave me any cause for concern. It was normal. I was expecting to find a bunch of pill bottles, but sometimes junkies are clever.

I moved to the bedroom. A black comforter with small yellow stitched flowers covered the bed and a blue, silk robe laid across the end of the bed. I couldn't help it. I grabbed it and brought it up to my face. I imagined her silky, soft skin coming out of a shower. How her large, round breasts must've pressed against the silk and how it would've cinched at the waist then flowed over her supple ass and hips.

Shaking my head, I set it down and continued going through her things. I didn't care if she would be pissed. She'd left our kid, and wasn't here. I needed some clues as to how bad she was. I searched through her drawers, and then under the bed. I found a lock box, and thought I'd hit the jackpot, after breaking the flimsy lock, I found thousands of dollars. What in the actual fuck? Enrico must be supplying her drugs? Or maybe she just wasn't that bad yet, but where in the hell was she?

Nothing in her apartment told me much about anything. I had no idea where she was, and as time ticked by, I became more and more worried. Shane called the strip joint and was told she left with Enrico last night, and that she was three sheets to the wind.

We waited for a few hours. I called in a favor. Someone came by with a truck and trailer for my bike. There was no way I was leaving Gunner here. In those couple of hours, I played video games with Gunner and got to know him. Damn, the kid was cool.

"Kid, not sure when your Mom is going to be back, and I don't feel comfortable leaving you here. I want you to pack a bag. Bring plenty of your toys and whatever else you want. I got a truck downstairs.

"But, what if I'm not here when she gets home? She'll be so worried." He was unsure, so I got down to his level and tried the best I could.

"How about we wait until your neighbor gets home, and we leave all my info for your Mom to call me, okay?"

He considered this for a few minutes and asked, "Can I bring my Xbox?"

"You don't need to. I have one. But why don't you bring your games?"

"Yeah, okay. Are you really sure we should leave?"

I put my hand on Gunner's shoulder, "Yeah, kid. We'll find her, though. Promise."

Chapter Ten

Charlie

I was gagging. I had no air. I had no breath. Something was being shoved down my throat. Vomit was threatening to come up, the acidic bile burned my esophagus. Just when I thought I'd pass back out again from lack of oxygen, it let up. I regained consciousness, but had no idea where I was, or what was happening. My eyes squinted open, the bright lights hurt. Then, it was happening again, only this time I knew what it was.

Black slacks came at me, and I realized what I was being gagged with. A hard cock hit my lips. I refused to open my mouth and was met with a hard slap to my cheek, and my nose being squeezed shut. After a minute, I had no choice, but to gasp for air.

"Swear, you bite me, and you'll regret it." He thrust forward. I knew exactly whose voice that was, even though I hadn't seen him yet. I coughed as he hit the back of my throat. He held his cock there and still held my nose closed. I couldn't breathe, but then his dick slid out again, only enough for me to gasp for air. Then, it was right back in there, choking me.

"Do you know how beautiful your lips look wrapped around my cock? I told you I would have you." He reached down and twisted my nipple. It wasn't sexy, it hurt. Everything hurt. Tears leaked out of my eyes as I gasped for air again. "No? What's the matter? Cat got your tongue?" He slid deep into the back of my throat again and began to just thrust in and out. A quick slap to my breast and then another. I was being abused in such a vile way. "You're my plaything, now. You'll be here for as long as I like to use and play with as much as I want."

This couldn't be happening. There was so much pain. My entire body hurt.

I squeezed my eyes shut, wishing I could just pretend this all away. His dick pulled out and he slapped my face again, hard, so hard it felt like my brain slammed against my skull.

"No, you keep those eyes open, and open your mouth again. I'm not done fucking it." It was then that I realized that my hands were restrained behind my back. I complied, because what choice did I have? My mouth opened and he slid inside my mouth again. "Good girl."

I saw his face for the first time. His eyes, they were evil. So cold and calculating. They watched me with mirth. He enjoyed every second of this. I knew I was, in fact, his toy.

He continued thrusting in and out, sometimes taking his time. It felt like he was delaying his own orgasm just to make this last longer. My throat burned. I gagged again, and I couldn't breathe. My vision was spotty. I thought I was going to pass out. I prayed that I would.

He released me again, then pumped three times hard and fast until I was choking on his semen. The warm hot liquid filled the back of my throat. I coughed and coughed, but his dick was still jammed inside my mouth. Cum came up over my lips. He eased up just enough and ordered, "Swallow."

I swallowed as much as I could as he pumped gently on the edge of my lips. My jaw ached. My throat burned. My face felt like it was on fire. I could only imagine that it was swelling up fairly good. His dick left my mouth. I breathed in and out deeply, grateful to be able to pull air into my lungs. I was glad the assault was over.

"You did well. Maybe I'll reward you. Yeah?" Enrico asked. He sat me up, his hands sliding all over my body. It felt repulsive. It was like the devil was touching me and leaving his evil all over my body.

I looked around, trying to see if there was any way out. I was on a bed. It was large with black satin surrounding me. There was a large armoire and dresser in the room and a few doors. There was one window with heavy black curtains drapes covering it. A large decorative rug with oriental swirls of reds and blacks covered the hardwood floor. There was a painting on a wall that scared me. It was black with shades of reds, and reminded me of blood dripping.

He had a distinct cologne that I'd smelled before, something rich by Armani. I couldn't place the name, but I remembered smelling it at the department store once and took a sample, thinking I'd like the smell on a man one day. It was instantly my most hated scent. It was everywhere, surrounding me.

My arms were restrained behind my back and I was naked. I moved my legs and pulled my knees up to my chest. It wasn't easy, since I didn't have use of my arms.

I faced him. He tucked his dick back in his pants. His white dress shirt was still sharply creased. I watched as he effortlessly took off his cuff-links and set them down on a nightstand, then proceeded to roll his sleeves up past his elbows. His dark hair hung over his forehead and he had a look that made him look feral.

He laughed. "Where are you going?"

My voice came out weak and hoarse, "Please, let me go."

He grinned at me. His full lips turned up in a half-smile like he enjoyed me begging for my release. "Let you go? We're just getting started, pet."

Fucking pet? I wanted to be sick. I wanted to fight, but he didn't give me much of a chance for either. He grabbed me under my arms as if I weighed nothing. I tried to kick at him, but in a second, he had me flipped around and on my stomach. My legs were over the side of the bed, my ass out towards him. God, no. Not again.

"No! Please no!" I cried out just as he thrust his fingers inside of me.

"Shh, this will feel good, if you relax."

It was two fingers, then three. Nothing about this felt good. I cried and screamed, but the more I cried, the more of an assault he gave. I wished I could drift off and not endure this pain, but I was present and feeling every bit of it. I felt it when he slid in a fourth finger and then when he pulled them out and jammed his length into me, I felt that too. He was hard and brutal, smacking me in between thrusts. He played with me. Making me think he was almost done, only to laugh as I pleaded for him to stop.

"Got news for you, girl. Viagra and Cocaine. I'm going to fuck you all night, and just when you think your pussy can't take anymore, I'll take your ass. I'm going to fuck you in every hole and in every way, and then when I'm done fucking my new toy, I'll put you away until

107

I'm ready to play with you again. You're mine. My possession. I'm going to use you how I like, and there is no amount of pleading or begging that will make me stop. You're in my domain. No one here will save you."

I felt those vile words too. I felt them right down to my soul. I knew I was lost, so I closed my eyes and cried until I had no more tears. I screamed until my voice was gone. And sometime later, after he raped my ass and did things to me that I never imagined possible, I finally felt myself drift away.

When I woke up, I was no longer surrounded by black satin. The heavy scented cologne was gone. I was on a cot. A blanket covered my naked body and I no longer was tied. There was a toilet against a wall, as well as a shower. There was no curtain. There were no windows. I was in a cell. I realized I was, at least, by myself. I sat up wrapping the blanket around me and wincing in pain. I hurt everywhere.

I tried to remember how I got here. Everything was a blur. I was at the club dancing. I had gotten the picture of Gun. *Oh, God! Gun!* I hoped like crazy that he was safe with Mrs. Warner. I'd felt funny on stage. I think I saw Gunner. Was that even real? Did he kiss me? I'm not quite sure. Then, there was Enrico grabbing me, taking me. No one stopped him. Did I fight? I remembered asking him why and telling him people would look for me. "You're just another whore at a strip club. No one will search for you." I remembered him mentioning I was in my new home. *His* home, in Colombia. And then there was a sting in my neck and it was dark. Next thing I knew, I was being woken up by his dick choking me.

I rubbed my throat. It hurt so badly. I hated that man. Hated everything Enrico did to me. Hated every word he spoke to me. Looking down, I saw cum on my breasts. I decided I'd try to shower and wash his filth off of me. I attempted to stand and pain shot between my legs, bringing me to my knees. He probably tore something. I needed to wash him off. On my hands and knees, I crawled to the shower and reached up and turned it on. Ice cold shards pelted against my skin, but I didn't even care. I'd rather be numb from the cold, than feel what he did to me.

I'm not sure how long I sat under the spray, but at some point, the door opened making me curl up, afraid of another attack. A tray of food was slid inside along with a paper cup. I hadn't thought about food. I hadn't even thought about how much time had already passed, but seeing the tray, I realized I was starved. I shut the water off and crawled over to the food. My knees slipped on the cool cement as I moved. I knew I needed to eat, though. Enrico was a monster and I had no way of knowing how often I'd be fed. Fed like his fucking pet!

A peanut butter and jelly sandwich and applesauce sat on the blue plastic tray. It reminded me of a kids lunch at school. I ate it fast, too fast. I was thirsty and reached for the Styrofoam cup. Raspberry juice coated my sore, parched throat. I couldn't drink it fast enough, and before I knew it, my tray was empty. I crawled back to the cot, thinking about how broken I felt. Then, I climbed on, covered my naked body with the blanket, and felt my eyes grow heavy and fell asleep.

I woke up feeling groggy and unsure of where I was. Looking around, I realized I was in my cell. My thoughts moved to Gun. I wasn't sure how long I'd been here already. I hoped he wasn't afraid. I hoped he was safe. He must be so worried. I hated that for him. The waterworks began again. I needed to find a way out of this mess. I needed to figure out how to get away from Enrico. Maybe I could let him do whatever he wanted to me, and I could somehow escape?

I moved my legs and tried to see if I could bear weight on them. Pain still radiated, but when I tried to stand, I was able to hold myself upright. Well, that's progress. I moved to the toilet and relieved myself, and climbed back into bed. I needed rest and I needed my body to heal, even though I had no idea when he would decide to come back.

I pulled the blanket around me and stared at the cement wall. I wondered if Gunner ever thought about me? Staring at the wall, I replayed the time in my life when I felt loved.

You cuddle me close to your body. We're laying in the backyard of your house. It's late and I probably should've been home hours ago, but we both know no one really cares where I am.

"What are your dreams?" you ask me. It isn't the first time you've asked.

The stars are bright tonight, despite all the streetlights. I wrap my arm around your waist and squeeze as I answer.

"That it'll be us, one day."

"It's us, right now."

"Yeah, I know. But I guess I just don't want it to end. You're the only person I've ever really felt safe with, and you've always seen me."

"Trust me, Mouse. Too many people see you. You're beautiful."

I blush and attempt to pull away. I'm not good with compliments especially because you really believe them. "No, you don't do that.

You don't pull away. It's me and you, Mouse. The two of us against the world."

You kiss me. Your lips press against mine and you slowly kiss me again and again until my lips part. Your tongue eases inside, but it's nothing like the devouring kisses you usually give me. It's more. It's like you're making love to me with your mouth, and you're trying to get me to believe that I am beautiful.

After some time, you pull away from my mouth and you kiss me everywhere. You start at my forehead and move to my eyelids, then my cheeks and down my neck. You take your time, not leaving an ounce of exposed flesh without your kiss. Then, once you thoroughly kiss where you can see, you take off my shirt for the first time. The warm air hits my skin and you blow on my nipples making them instantly hard.

"So beautiful, Mouse," you say kissing my collarbone, the sides of my breasts, and skipping my nipples, you move to my stomach. It's one of the first times in my life that you make the need inside of me feel like it can explode. I had no idea I could want you so much, but I'm not ready and we both know that. Finally, after my torso is kissed completely, you move back to my breasts. With deliberation, you kiss my nipples. Slowly at first, alternating between the two until I am arching for more. You pull my nipples in between your full lips and suck them. Your tongue and teeth flick and pull making me moan.

"Jesus, you're sensitive. I could taste your skin all day, but you're making me so goddamned hard, it hurts," you pant. Your hazel eyes look up at me and they're wild. I wonder if your patience is slipping.

Unsure of myself and what to do, I reach down and rub my hand on your cock. You groan. I love the noise. "God, baby. This isn't supposed to be about me."

My breath hitches. You're so hard. I can feel you straining against your jeans. You reach down and undo a button and pull out your long, thick dick. I haven't seen it before, so I'm surprised by your size. My palm clumsily runs up your silky shaft. Your skin is so smooth, but my movements are inexperienced and jerky. "Relax," you whisper as you place your hand over mine, and set a steady rhythm. Once it seems like I have the hang of it, you let go of my hand and move your head back to my breasts sucking and making me want. Want what, I'm not really even sure. I just know I need more of the pleasure you're giving me.

"Can I touch you, Mouse?"

I look up at you and nod that I want that.

"Can I stick my fingers inside of you? Can I feel you squirm until you're cumming on my hand?"

God, I had no idea you could be so dirty. "Gunner," I whimper as your hand slips in my jeans and your finger begins to slowly swirl on my clit.

"Say it, Mouse."

"Yes."

You grin and then tell me, "Keep pumping."

I didn't realize I'd stopped, so I begin again, but my breath catches as you penetrate me. Your finger moves inside me. It's the first time I've ever felt anything in there. I would've thought it would hurt, but you push in gently and bring my moisture out and rub it around my clit. I have my first orgasm that night. It's exciting, but what is more exciting to me is that I give you yours. The look on your face was my precious gift. I'll always think about it.

The creaking of my door took me from my thoughts. I pulled my knees up to my chest waiting to find out what would happen next. Would it be Enrico? What would he do to me?

I steal a glance to see one of Enrico's men carrying a tray of food. "Please help me," I whispered.

The man blinked at me and then set the tray down.

"Why am I here? Why is he doing this to me? What did I do to deserve this?" I didn't think he'd answer, but I hoped. I needed something.

The man with nearly black eyes darted his eyes to the left and right making sure no one was listening. "Shut up, puta. You're a toy to him. This is what he does. He finds the girls with your look and he uses them for as long as he likes. You shut up and make your pussy useful, you live a while. You whine, maybe not so long you live. The last girl, live not so long," he shrugged like he was indifferent to it. Could that be the only reason I was taken?

The food tray clattered as it hit the cement floor and the man's boots echoed on the hard floor as he walked away like he hadn't just delivered another punch.

I was on borrowed time. I tried not to think about his words, but they sat in the back of my mind. What kind of psycho was I with that did this to women simply because he could? I had to survive this. I had to.

Eyeing the food, I wasn't as famished as I was the last time, so this time I kept the blanket wrapped around me as I grabbed the tray and brought it back to the cot. I took my time eating, then drank the cool juice. My throat felt better than yesterday. *Yesterday?* Could that have been a whole day ago? I had no way of telling how often they were bringing food or how long I slept. My thoughts moved back to Gun and I hoped he didn't think I abandoned him. I hoped he knew how much I loved him. What if Mrs. Warner calls DFS? What if they send him to a home that hurts him? No. No, I can't let my thoughts go there. I had to just pray that he was safe and if she did call DFS, he is placed with a loving home. My eyes begin to feel heavy and thoughts of a perfect life for Gun help me drift away.

Chapter Eleven

Charlie

I was being moved. Hands were under my armpits and my feet were dragging along the ground. I tried to blink, but my eyes were heavy. Too heavy. Blackness-- the heaviness felt like a blanket suffocating my senses.

Something was cool beneath my skin. I was laying down. My eyes still too heavy to see where I was. What was happening?

Pain, blinding pain, beyond anything I could imagine. I was screaming. My eyes flashed open just as they pulled away a large... Holy shit, was that a branding iron? The smell! Oh God, the smell. Was that my flesh? The pain was so intense. Bile hit my throat, and I couldn't help but throw up. The side of my face was pressed against a cold metal table, but I couldn't move my head. Vomit went off the side and hit the floor, the splash echoed in the room.

"So Carajo tenemos Alguen que vomita mucho." *"Oh, shit. We have a puker,"* a man said in Spanish. I took two years of accelerated Spanish classes, and would study more of the language at the library in my spare time. I couldn't let on that I understood them. I didn't even understand why, but my instincts said that I might need to use something I heard. Another man laughed, and I cringed as the pain on my back began radiating.

"It hurts. Make it stop. It hurts so bad," I cried out and heard yet another laugh. These men were all monsters.

"Ponga la perra de su miseria." *Put the bitch out of her misery.*

I felt a prick and then everything began to numb. A second later, my vision blurred and then... blackness.

I blinked. I was laying on my stomach back in my cell. Pain, so intense, made my back throb. I remembered the branding iron. Who the fuck brands someone? I needed to use the bathroom, but the moment I tried to move, nausea hit me and the room started to spin. I had to be drugged. As I l tried to lay still and not move, I realized you were here, sitting on the edge of the cot.

"You're here."

You cocked your head to the side and looked at me curiously. Your hazel eyes were soft and caring. The scruff on your face was days old.

"Why did you leave me? Why did you let him take me?" I wanted to touch you, but my hands were like jelly. I wondered if you were still the same.

You don't answer me.

I looked at your clothes, you were wearing a SAMCRO t-shirt, black jeans and boots. Your hands ran through your hair, the way they did when you were deep in thought.

"Do you know what he did to me? Do you know what they did to me? Do you know what I had to do?" I asked you question after question, but you did not answer. You continued watching me and then you

reached for me, but started to fade. You weren't there. "No, don't go," I pleaded. I needed you here. I began to cry. The pain in my back hurt. My head spun. I wanted out of this hell.

The door creaked open again and I couldn't be sure if it was really happening or not. A Hispanic man wearing all black entered. He had a glass in his hand with a straw sticking out of the top. I wanted to recoil, but I was too numb. He moved towards me, in what felt like a flash, and was in front of me. The straw was to my lips and he ordered, "Beber." I was to drink. I couldn't fight, so I succumbed to his order and I drank. The room swirled, he disappeared.

I see your face. You're back. Your hand hovers over my face, not quite touching me. I want you to touch me. I want your comfort, but then I'm light, like a feather floating away, until I am a cloud. Nothing was holding me down. I reach out trying to grab hold of something, anything. I'm falling, feeling like Alice tumbling through the rabbit hole. Everything begins to swirl again, and I close my eyes. Darkness.

I awoke to my head throbbing. My throat felt parched and I had to pee so bad it hurt. I sat up and felt the pain in my back. I remembered what happened, but thankfully, the pain wasn't as strong as it had been. My legs felt like jelly when I first tried to stand, but after a moment, I was able to move to the toilet. When I was finished, I decided I needed to shower as well. I turned on the water and stuck my face under it, drinking as much water as I could. When the water touched my back, it stung, so I avoided that as much as possible. I didn't even want to look at it. I wanted to pretend he didn't mark me, but the reality was, I was marked in so many ways.

I finished the shower and stared at the wall. At some point, the door opened and my tray was set inside. My stomach growled, and I realized I had no idea when the last time I ate was. I kept the blanket wrapped around myself, and grabbed the tray and ate. Peanut butter, again, coated my throat and I quickly drank the juice. My eyes began to get heavy and I wondered if they were drugging me? That was the final thought I had until I was out cold.

I woke up and actually had a bit of energy. I had no idea what day or time it was. My back still hurt, but it seemed to be healing, which made me think that I'd been sleeping a lot. I was used to working out and I wanted to try to keep up my strength so that if the opportunity presented itself to escape that I was still strong.

I dropped to the ground and began doing push-ups. I could immediately tell that I'd already lost some weight. I did three sets until my body screamed, then I moved on to squats and running in place. I broke a sweat and my body tired easily. Who was I kidding? I was no Sarah Connor. I wasn't going to get free and kick the bad guy's ass. I just had to survive.

The shower called to me, I didn't even mind the coldness of the water. Once finished, I laid on the cot with my blanket wrapped around me. I couldn't stop thinking about Gun. I was so worried about my little boy. It hurt badly, like a grip on my heart, when I thought of him, so I tried to stop. I tried to think of Gunner. I tried to think about the club. What I didn't think about was what I would do the next time the door opened and it was Enrico. I couldn't let my thoughts go there. He was vile and horrible, and the second I let my mind drift to what the monster might do was the second fear started to seize me.

Chapter Twelve

Gunner

"Dad! Heads up!" Gunner threw a football towards me. It was a neon-colored Nerf football. I quickly shot my hands up from my desk and grabbed it. He was getting along good with the guys at the shop and not much seemed to faze him, although the more days that passed without word about Charlie, the more I could see his light dimming.

"He's got a good arm on him," Shane said leaning against the doorjamb as I watched Gun run off towards the guys.

"Got any news?" I asked Shane the same question that was becoming all too redundant.

He shot me a look that said, "Not since that last time you asked me."

I sighed, "I'm sorry. It's just here with all of you guys, he's running around and having a good time, but when we get home it's different. It's..." I shook my head trying to come up with the right word, but before I could finish my thought, Gun came barreling towards us and he had something red in his hands.

"Ace said these were yours." He held up my gloves that I barely ever wore. I was more a hand to hand fighter.

"They're mine. Come on." I closed the laptop and led the way to the boxing ring. I glanced over my shoulder to make certain he was behind me. Once we got to the ring, I lifted him up and he climbed under the ropes and into the ring.

"These gloves won't fit you. Not yet at least. You want to learn to box, I'll buy you a pair that fit."

"Yeah?" he asked still unsure of what to make of me.

"Yeah."

"I'll give you your first lesson, right now."

He watched me with rapt attention, taking in everything I had to offer. I breathed in deep, not for the first time, trying to hold back my anger for the time I'd missed with him.

"What do you think is one of the most important parts to fighting? Your fist or your feet."

"That's easy." He held up his little fists and clenched them with his thumb tucked under his fingers.

"Guess again. Your fists are important, but to be a good fighter, you have to know how to move your feet." I opened his fist and moved his thumb to the outside, then I positioned his feet apart. I stood in front of him and showed him when I threw a punch, how I shuffled my feet.

"Move your feet back and forth."

The kid tried it, and he did okay. "We'll work on it. Try it again."

We did this repeatedly; him shuffling his feet, me teaching him how to move them. He was quick.

"Like this?" he asked, finally getting it exactly right.

"Yeah son, just like that."

We finished our lesson for the day and sat on the edge of the ring. Gun sat down next to me panting.

"Hey, Buzz! How about a couple of waters?" I called out to one of our prospects.

He brought them over and handed them to us.

I knew I needed to talk with Gun. I had to give it to him straight. "I don't have a good lock on your Mom yet. I'm looking. We're all looking. I'm trying, but I think while we're trying to find her that you should start school.

"Oh, man," he grumbled.

"I know it's not ideal, but she wouldn't want you missing school, would she?"

He looked up and away from me, "She wouldn't care," he lied.

"Oh, she wouldn't, huh? She'd let you miss school whenever? I took her as the type of mom who cared about her boy doing well." I had him there, I knew it. He did too. He looked at me and nodded, like he had no other choice.

"You'll start in a few days, after the weekend."

"Okay."

We spent the next few days hanging out at the clubhouse, and then Monday morning I enrolled him in school. Luckily, we had found his birth certificate amongst Charlie's things, so it wasn't hard for me to get his transcripts.

Dropping him off didn't go nearly as smoothly as I planned. He clung to me. I mean clung. It took everything in me to pry his fingers from around my neck. The school psychologist was right there with us, and she kept saying over and over again that if I gave in, then I would be setting myself up to make this even harder. I hated seeing tears in his eyes, but what could I do? Kids need to go to school, right?

I'd only been parenting for about a week and this shit was hard. I didn't know how Charlie did this for so long on her own. She must've been so scared. I tried to imagine how my quiet Mouse figured this shit out.

I was outside waiting for him when three-fifteen hit. He ran to me but instead of hugging me, he grabbed my hand like he was trying to hold on to being angry that I'd left him there. I shouldn't have been surprised. He was, after all, my son.

And so, this began our new routine. I would take him to school, and he wouldn't be happy about it. Some days, I'd be busy at the shop, and I'd have some of the guys grab him, and a few times, I'd ask for help from some of the legs that hung around.

Like today. I answered my phone as soon as it rang, desperate to hear how Gun was.

"How'd he do?"

"It was fine."

"Not what I asked Amber. I asked how he did?"

"He went in. No problem. I don't see what the big deal is."

Yeah, I guess she wouldn't. She was a woman who happened to hang around with the club. She had long legs and platinum blonde hair. She was hot. I let her blow me a few times after drinks, but that was it. She wasn't my taste, but now that I had Gun, I'd take any help I could get.

He was struggling and I couldn't blame him. He'd been with me for a few weeks. One day, after he got home from school, I decided that we should get him his own shit. I mean, we'd brought a lot from his place, but what kid didn't want to be spoiled? I had an extra room in my place that I had set up with a new bed waiting for him.

I was going to buy stuff, but I figured he'd want to help pick it out. So we went to the mall, and we decked it out. I let him pick out his favorite superhero blankets. I even got him his own TV and Xbox for his room. We picked out new clothes too. Half of the kid's stuff had holes in it, so we bought way too much. As much as I usually hated shopping, it was worth it seeing my kid's face light up. Plus, the kid got a kick out of how people reacted to me. Sure, I was big and my vest let them know exactly who I was, but the scowl on my face that said, "You better not fuck with me or my kid," was the topper. When we got home, we spent the better part of the night getting his room set up the way he wanted it.

I hated asking Amber for help, but I sometimes needed to. I asked her to help out and drop him off at school. I knew she wasn't Gun's favorite person, but I didn't have a whole lot of options. It wasn't like I could call my Mom up, and ask her to be a Grandma. I shook my head, she was whacked.

"Alright, Amber. Thanks." I was about to hang up when she stopped me. "Gunner, I can think of a real nice way you can pay me back," she purred. I knew what she was talking about, but I played dumb.

"I'll give you twenty bucks, the next time I see you," I disconnected and lifted my chin to

Ace as he walked into the machine shop.

"Brother," I said as he got closer, "You got any news?"

His eyes moved to the side connecting with Shane's, and Shane moved in like they had this planned.

"What do you got?" I asked impatiently. My temper had been wearing thin lately, a mixture of not knowing where my Mouse was, and not knowing what to tell my son. We'd confirmed with the strip club that one of the bouncers was beaten pretty badly. He watched out for Charlie. We also confirmed with one of the dancers that nothing was going on between Enrico and Charlie, and that he was basically stalking her. When I found out that tidbit of information, I had to hit the ring. My son needed me, so I couldn't afford to self-destruct, but damn if I wasn't waging an internal battle for not saving Charlie when I'd had the chance.

"It's not good," Shane said with a nod from Ace. "Our sources say he's been coming and going from Colombia pretty regularly. We can't get a lock on him, and I swear he owns half of Colombia."

"Fuck," I hissed.

"I'm reaching out to a contact. Trying to get eyes on his landing strip. I want to know if she is coming in the country with him or not. I'm working on getting us a way in the country without being detected, but it ain't easy," Ace added.

"There's more," Shane ran his hand through his hair. "There was heat between Hades Runners and the Mexicans. I can see Hades reaching out to Enrico. We have to be careful."

I rubbed my chin.

"What if we reach out to the Mexicans?"

"And risk Enrico thinking we double crossed him?" Ace asked.

This whole situation was so touchy, but if it meant getting Charlie back, fuck 'em.

"Any other players we can get involved? The Russians? Italians?" I asked.

"I'll put some feelers out," Shane pulled a smoke from his pack and lit it. The smoke made the air hazy.

"Fuck, it's already been almost a month. What if she isn't even alive anymore?" I gave my brothers my fears.

"You gotta have hope, and if this isn't a mission about getting her back, then it will be about getting revenge," Ace nodded agreeing with Shane.

"She was right there in front of me. I could've…"

"No, brother. No way you could've known. This isn't on you," Ace looked firm as he told me this and I wanted to believe him.

I sat with my head hung low for some time. I didn't know what I was doing. I was trying to make it okay for my kid, and I was trying to figure out how to save Charlie, but I felt like I was drowning.

"Kid, turn off the video game."

My son looked up at me, and that empty look in his eyes burned into my gut. He paused his game, his eyes silently questioned what I wanted.

I knew he was hurting, and I was hell bent on getting him through this. "Come on outside." He followed me through the house, and I grabbed a football on the way out.

"Let's play?" I asked.

He shrugged and I knew he was going to make me work for it, he'd been closing down more and more.

"My dad used to throw the ball around with me, when I was a kid." I tossed him the ball and let him get a feel for it in his hands. I couldn't imagine Mouse ever bringing him out to throw a ball around.

"We'd play two, maybe three times a week. Your mom lived across the street from me. Did she ever tell you that?"

He looked up at me, maybe eager to hear more about her, and then he tossed the ball to me. "Nope," was his one word answer.

"She was so quiet. She'd sneak around watching me. First time I saw her, thought she was the prettiest thing I ever saw." I shook my head at the memory and tossed the ball to Gun. He was a natural, and didn't even know it.

"What was she like?" he asked throwing the ball back to me. I smiled and took a step back giving him more room to throw.

"Like I said, she was quiet. It took her forever to talk to me, and then one day, I couldn't take it anymore, so I approached her." I threw the ball and continued, "I called her Mouse 'cause she was so sneaky and quiet."

"She's still kind of quiet." Ah, he was observant too. I caught the ball he threw to me.

"It took us a few years, but she talked to me. I never admitted it to her, but I think I loved her the first time she spoke. I was just waiting on her to get older. We were kids, but I was so taken by her."

"Well, then what happened? Why'd you leave us?" he asked walking over to the stairs of my front porch. He sat down, and spun the football. I grabbed the ball and his eyes met mine.

"First, I didn't know your mom was pregnant. No clue. At the time, I thought I had no choice, but the one I made. I messed up and was given a choice to join my mom's boyfriend's motorcycle club, or go to jail. I chose wrong. I should've gone to jail. Those guys…" I sucked in a breath, "they're nothing like my club. They wouldn't let me leave and when they finally did, I went to find Charlie, but she was gone. I searched. I looked for years. But I'm so sorry. I wish I could've found you sooner. I'm so sorry we missed out on all this time. I'm sorry I wasn't there. I'm sorry we don't have your mom back yet, but I promise you kid, I'm doing everything I can to get her back to us."

"I miss her," he said quietly.

"Will you tell me about what it was like for you two?"

He nodded, "When I was little," I grinned because he was still little, but kept quiet and let him continue, "we slept on this air mattress together and then eventually she got more and more things to fill our apartment. She was always hugging me and telling me she loved me. She'd work late and come and get me from the sitter's. Sometimes, she still snuggles with me."

I had to ask 'cause I was too fucking curious, "She ever have any boyfriends around?"

He shrugged, but gave me nothing more. I didn't push, even though I really wanted to. I wanted to put him in a lighter mood."You want me to teach you how to grip this better?" I showed him the laces on the ball and how to grip it, and then we spent the next twenty minutes throwing the ball back and forth.

I tucked him in that night. As I watched him struggle to keep his eyes open, I knew that no matter what, me and my boy would be okay. I'd figure this Dad thing out. I had too.

Later that night, I was sleeping in my bed when my cell phone woke me. I immediately answered it, and with a groggy voice answered, "Yeah."

"She was spotted," Ace responded. My heart hammered with confirmation that she was alive.

"Go, on."

"She was spotted with him. Report says she looked thin, didn't interact, but she was alive."

"Thank you, brother."

"Knew you'd want to know as soon as I did. Go back to bed. We'll meet after you take Junior to school."

"Night." I hit end and released a breath. She was alive and one way or another, I was going to get her back.

Chapter Thirteen

Charlie

I wished I could say my isolation lasted, but Enrico returned. I was staring at the wall imagining what my life could've been like if Gunner hadn't disappeared and he knew about our child. I'd spent endless hours going over what my life was like with him, and what it could've been.

I'd been pouring out the juice they'd bring me with lunch and drinking water from the shower, so I'd stayed awake more often than not, thus, my suspicions about the juice being drugged were confirmed. My food was brought a while ago, and I was certain that I should be sleeping, but I wasn't. The door opened and in walked Enrico.

My back was to the wall, but I immediately recognized the scent and curled as close to the wall as I could get.

"Ah, you're awake. I see you figured out about the drugs. Pity, really. Those are more for your benefit than mine. Most of my toys don't like to be conscious. It's easier that way. But trust me, I don't mind you being alert. It's more fun that way."

"Fuck you," I gritted out.

"No, dear. I plan to fuck you. Let me ask you? Did you miss me? Miss my cock in that tight little virgin ass?

"Why are you doing this to me?" I cried.

"Why does a man of my power and wealth do anything? Because I can. Plus, I got word that you're something to someone. Let's just say, I knew who you'd belong too, even if you didn't know it, and I wanted you for myself. I get to have the best toys."

The air whooshed out of my lungs. This was because of Gunner. I'd thought it, but I wasn't sure.

He sat down on the bed. I still hadn't turned my head to look at him. His fingers trailed along the branding on my back and I shuddered at his touch.

"My mark on you makes me hard."

"Don't touch me," I said with way more bravery than I really felt. The truth was, I was scared out of my mind, but I didn't want him to see that.

"You have a lot of fight. I like that."

I heard his belt buckle and I cringed at what would come next. Before I could even plan any type of defensive move, the leather was around my throat. The buckle bit into my skin and my breath was stolen from me.

"On your stomach," he demanded and then added, "You comply, you breathe."

I gasped for air as he loosened the belt. I did as he said and moved to my stomach. One hand palmed my ass as the other held onto the belt strap. "Where should I fuck you? Huh? Your asshole?" His fingers moved over my tight hole. I reflexively squeezed my ass cheeks together and was met with a tug on the belt, stealing my air.

"You want your pussy instead?" he asked shoving his fingers inside of me. I wanted to scream out at the violation. My air was given back to me, but only long enough for me to suck in a lungful. I heard him spit and then his fingers were inside of me again, pushing in his saliva. Then, his dick was at my entrance and he was forcing himself inside.

Tears slid down my cheeks as he slammed in and out over and over again.

He'd loosen my leash as he thrust in, and then tightened it as he pulled out. I wasn't sure how long the assault went on for. He definitely didn't last as long as he did with the Viagra. My vision had tunneled in and out. I was so focused on breathing that by the time he was finished, and had released the belt, I barely moved as the door latched on his way out.

Sometime later, the door opened. I braced. One of his men stood at the door. And thrust out a brush and two small bottles along with a pale pink nightgown.

"Boss wants your hair taken care of."

Once the door closed again, I didn't wait to shower. I didn't care it was what he wanted. I needed the shampoo. I needed to wash his filth from me. I reveled in the fresh scent that replaced his musky one. I rubbed my hand over my throat and could feel the burn from the leather's bite. I let the cold water numb it and stood under the spray until I could barely feel my body. When I was finished, I picked up the pink night gown. It was silk and skimpy, but I hadn't had clothes for a long time, so I didn't think about the implications of wearing it;

the low cut lace front, or what the lace slits might mean. I only thought about the fact that I was no longer naked.

I laid down on the bed and tried to push all images of what just happened out of my mind. It was the only way I could seem to calm my racing heart. I thought about Gun, and how clumsy he was when he first learned to walk. I thought about how, one day, I would get out of this hell and I'd see him again. It wasn't an option for me not too. I needed to hold onto that. He was my whole world and I was his. I wouldn't let him think I'd abandoned him. I know what that felt like and I loved him too much for that. I daydreamed about reuniting with my son. Eventually, I fell asleep.

When I woke again, the familiar tray with the familiar sandwich was by the door, but there was no juice. I ate, like I did every time, and used the water from the shower to wash down the peanut butter. I slipped into the routine I had been in, and after I ate, I dropped to the ground and did push-ups. My arms, despite the fact that I had little food, were strong. I'd put my energy into my workout and kept my mind off of the fact that Enrico would probably be back. Sometime into my third set of sit-ups, the silky material against my skin started to feel different. It was as if a thousand soft threads were brushing up against my legs.

My heart was fluttering and my mood seemed like it was changing. I didn't feel like I had, for however long I'd been here. Everything around me felt vibrant. As I continued to move, I realized that my nipples were now straining against the material of the nightgown. It was all I could do to get at them and tug. What was wrong with me? I felt hot and cold all at once. My skin prickled. The door opened, and I was sitting on the floor playing with my nipples. I didn't even stop because it felt so good. I paid no attention to whomever was. I finally felt something other than isolated agony, and my mind clung to the blissful sensation.

"I see Molly's working her charm."

Enrico stood in front of me. I knew I should be afraid, but for some reason, I couldn't grasp that emotion. He dropped a duffle bag on the cot and ordered me up. I didn't listen, so he grabbed me, making me stand, and then sat me down on the bed.

"Do you feel good?" he asked.

I nodded dreamily.

"Open your mouth. This will make you feel even better," he ordered and I complied. A small pill was placed in my mouth. I felt good and I wanted to feel better.

"Good girl. I want to feel you wet on my cock." He unzipped the bag and I watched in fascination as he pulled out a metal bar with thick leather cuffs on each side. He secured them to my ankles. I should've pulled back, but for some reason, I couldn't.

Next, he pulled something out of the bag that looked like an over-sized microphone. I watched Enrico, with his fancy suit and devilish eyes, smile like he couldn't wait for what he was about to do. He flicked a switch on and the black top started to hum. It was loud, the hum echoed around the room, sounding like a pulse. Then, it was being pressed to my core and my insides were coming to life. My pussy throbbed with sensation and it wasn't long before I was moaning into the pleasure.

"Oh, yes!" I cried out. But maybe it wasn't a cry, but a plea? I wanted more. More of this pleasure that felt too great to handle. I wanted more of whatever he gave me that made me enjoy this, and I wanted to come. Another moment later, his lips were at my throat. It was the first time I'd felt them on me. Against everything in my head that said it was wrong, my body opened up to him, giving in to what was happening.

His tongue lapped my skin, and the wet trail he left made me break out in tiny goosebumps. I could feel those, like I could feel the walls inside of me tighten as I let out a strangled scream. It was too much. Too good.

Before I knew what was happening, he had me flipped over the cot and he was driving inside of me. I could feel everything. The way the blanket roughly scratched against my face. The cool cement floor against my knees. His cologne filled the room and his white dress shirt pressed against my back. Each sensation was like a tickle to my senses.

His finger pressed at my asshole and my body betrayed me, rearing back into it. He slid his dick out and whispered. "Knew you'd be sweet, all wet for me."

And then he moved his finger away, pressed the large vibrator to my clit and slowly slid his dick into my ass. I was on fire. My knees trembled and sweat trickled into my eyes. Another orgasm tore through me and as my head was thrown back, the room spun. Traces of colors, followed my line of sight. The dull room was a prism of light and I was so caught up in it, I barely registered Enrico sliding out of me or the light trickle of wetness following after him as he left me behind. I didn't even really notice when my cuffs were undone and I was left on the cot. My eyes danced in delight at the pretty rainbows and I had no idea that when the fog cleared, I would hate Enrico even more for what he'd just done.

I awoke with one thought in mind, water. My throat was so parched all I wanted to do was drink. I moved to the shower, turned it on and stuck my head under the spray drinking as much as I could. My nightgown began to get wet. I suppose I had forgotten that I even had clothes on. And then, I remembered last night. Oh, God. I came. I didn't fight. I enjoyed it. Guilt coursed through my veins and I immediately bent forward and threw up all of the water I just drank.

I threw up over and over again. My body shook under the cold spray. How could I get off with him? That was the most vile thing to ever happen to me and I liked it. At that moment, I hated myself. I also hated Enrico even more. Feeding me drugs that made me enjoy sex with him was his own power play.

He took my orgasm and my ability to consent. I felt dirty and no amount of cold water could wash away my filth.

Chapter Fourteen

Charlie

"Eat," one of Enrico's men ordered. My peanut butter sandwich sat there from the day before. I ached from hunger pains, but I was so disgusted with myself that I couldn't stand to stomach anything. I stared at the wall and prayed the man would go away.

"I said, eat." I heard him shuffle behind me, then my hair was being yanked, and the sandwich was being shoved into my mouth. He stuffed the entire thing in gagging me. The thick, white bread mashed into a ball and blocked my throat. I tried to suck in air, but my airway was clogged. I coughed and gagged. The juice was poured over my mouth and I felt like I was drowning.

My hair was let go and I backed to the side coughing and choking. The man in a black military uniform laughed, then said, "Next time you eat, you filthy pig."

The door closed behind him. The sound of his boots echoed down the hall as he walked away. Tears stung my eyes and I coughed and coughed trying to clear the rest of the food from my throat. I moved to the shower and again ran the water over my face, swallowing as much as I could. My hand was braced against the wall, when I heard the door open again. I turned to glare at the goon who just left, but was met with Enrico's stare. It was the first time I'd seen him since he'd drugged me. My eyes immediately shot downward. I didn't want to look at him.

"Heard you like to choke on things." He prowled towards me. I wanted to strike out at him. I wanted to spit in his face and tell him how much I hated him. I didn't do that though. How could I? He'd already proven to me how much power he had over me.

"Look at me," he ordered and I did as he demanded. "If I send you food, you eat it." I gulped as the water continued to pour over me. Trickles of water moved into my eyes and I blinked staring at the monster. He took off his coat and set it on the cot ,then rolled up his sleeves. He prowled closer to me. I wanted to flinch, but I wasn't sure what the consequence would be. His hand shot out and turned off the water. I was all too aware of the wet nightgown clinging to my skin.

Enrico didn't miss it either as his eyes moved down my body. "Choke on this." He unzipped his black slacks and pulled out his hard dick. Oh, how I wanted to bite him, but I didn't. I did like he said and I dropped to my knees. My throat burned and all I thought about the entire time was that someday I would figure out a way out of this. I would close down and do as he said, but one day I would be free. I had to for Gun. So, as he finished, that was my thought. I held onto Gun.

* * *

As weeks passed, I knew all I was to him was a plaything. I'd been in the dungeon, as I referred to it, for God knew how long. Enrico was sometimes gone for days, and then he would return, and I would do as he said. I didn't fight him. If he said I needed to be on my knees, I was. If he wanted my ass, I gave it to him. I could be quiet and compliant. It wasn't just that it was easier than fighting him, but somehow I had convinced myself that if I went along with it, it would be easier. It wasn't. At night, I'd still cry, and each time after he left me, I felt less like a person and more like a receptacle. Sometimes, he would hurt me just to hurt me, but for the most part, he took what he wanted and left. I went back to wishing I was invisible and often, when the guards would come in, I thought I was. They didn't really look at me, and for that I was grateful. It was bad enough being raped by one man. At least the monster didn't share.

I lived in a constant state of anticipation and fear. Every time the door opened, I fought the urge to curl into myself. I hoped he would take me from the dungeon and I'd figure a way out of this hell. I was determined that I would get back to Gun. I was staring at the wall that I'd memorized every crack and crevice of, when the door opened.

"Come," one of Enrico's men ordered. I was afraid, not really sure what was going to happen to me. Maybe he was done using me, or maybe a new hell awaited me, what I didn't expect was for the goon to lead me to Enrico's room.

Enrico's room was opulent. I'd been in here once before when I'd first gotten here, but it was all a blur to me. The one thing I remembered was the black sheets on the bed. Images of Enrico raping my throat assaulted me, making me swallow back the bile.

"You have specific instructions. You're to shower. There is makeup and things for your hair. A dress is in the closet. You're to accompany Mr. Santos' to a dinner this evening. You'll not speak to anyone. You will keep your eyes down. If you don't follow these rules, he will not hesitate to kill you in front of his company. Do you understand, Senorita?"

"Yes," I whispered.

"Yes what, estupido puta."

"Yes, sir."

He looked smug as he closed me in the suite. I knew better than to look around. I didn't doubt that a camera would be on me. I'd already surmised that there was a camera in the dungeon. Besides the fact that Enrico made comments about getting off as he watched me, I'd spotted it in the ceiling. It was inconspicuous and blended in and if I hadn't been searching the ceiling for exactly that, I'd never known it was there.

Tonight, I would do as I was told. I would try to observe as much as I could, and I would do everything I could to stay safe. Well, as safe as one could be in the company of killers.

I showered. There was a fresh razor, I assumed was for me. As I shaved, I wondered if I'd be able to remove the razer-blade and use it as a weapon? I gave it a pull to see if it would come loose and nicked the skin on my finger. He'd notice any new cuts on me. I needed to be more careful. I finished showering and saw the brand new make-up that was left for me on the bathroom counter. It was all better quality than the drugstore brands I was used to purchasing. I used bobby pins to secure my hair into an up-do, then used the black charcoal liner to darken my eyes and finished off my look with a dark red lipstick.

Inside the closet, a black mini dress hung above a pair of red stilettos. They were all high fashion brands and I thought how funny it was that he didn't want to dress me like the whore I'd been turned into. After slipping into the dress and the securing the heels, the door opened and in walked Enrico. He walked around appraising me.

"You did well," his thick accent appraised me. Although to me, it felt more like sharp shards being thrown at me. I didn't want his assurances. I kept my face devoid of any emotion.

"Emanuel explained to you the rules for tonight?"

"Yes sir. He did."

"You don't talk to anyone. Do you understand? You do as I say. I'm not done playing with you yet, and if you fuck this up, I'll be forced to do something I'm not ready to do. Get it?"

"Yes."

"Dammit. Yes, what?"

Fuck, I'd screwed up. I waited for a blow as I quickly answered, "Yes sir." The blow didn't come. I watched as Enrico opened a safe and took out two large, silver guns. He wore a holster over his finely pressed white, linen shirt and then put a suit jacket on top of them. I know he did this as a show to me. I couldn't help but notice the stacks of cash inside of the safe. Maybe I could use that one day? Maybe I could escape?

I was dreaming about a way out of here when I'd heard, "Follow me, pet." Enrico motioned me out of his bedroom. I passed by a vase and I momentarily thought about grabbing it and smashing it over his head, but then what? I needed to be smart. I needed to come up with a plan.

A woman's voice caught me off guard. "Fine, you win. I'm sorry. Now, let me out!" She banged on a door as we passed. I couldn't lift my head as much as I wanted to, but something about the way she yelled at Enrico made me think that she wasn't in the same boat as me. Enrico ignored her. There wasn't even a pause in his step. I wondered if she was who normally escorted him. She was quickly forgotten by me, as he led me through the mansion. I followed Enrico, and although my head was down, I tried to keep track of how many guards I'd seen. I counted six, and I inwardly cringed--that was a lot of men.

We exited the mansion and a convoy of black SUV's awaited us in the hot Colombian sun. This was the first time I'd been outside, and I was surprised to see that we were surrounded by what looked to be a jungle. Thick trees and shrubs surrounded his nicely manicured lawn.

I was lead into an SUV. The air-conditioning was on full blast giving me a chill as I slid across the black leather interior. I kept my head turned towards the window, and noticed once we were past his property, the jungle thinned out and we were actually not far from an urban metropolis. There were people everywhere. Houses seemed to be stacked on top of one another and in every direction, there were herds and herds of people. I'd never been to New York, but I imagined that's what it was like, crowded.

Within ten minutes, we pulled up in front of a posh looking restaurant. As Enrico's car came to a stop, the SUVs in our convoy pulled up on each side of his vehicle. Guards surrounded us as they ushered us into the restaurant. Every worker inside seemed to scurry away as we passed by. A hostess lead us to a private room in the back of the restaurant where there were men surrounding the table with women at each side of them.

Before I sat, down Enrico grabbed my arm. "Be on your best behavior," he whispered into my ear. A quick glance at the table told me no one paid his dominance over me any mind.

"Armando, Luis," Enrico greeted the men who stood until Enrico sat.

I was to keep my eyes down, I knew this, but every once and awhile I would glance at the women. They had blank expressions similar to mine.

"Your new pet is beautiful." The man, I learned was Armando, spoke.

"That she is," Enrico responded taking a sip of a dark, amber liquid the server had poured as soon as we sat down.

The men began talking in Spanish. I kept my head down and did my best to remain unaffected. The other women seemed to do the same as I didn't hear a single sound from them.

Instead, I listened closely.

"You sold Lucia pretty quickly." The way he said it, I imagined Armando smirking. It made my skin crawl. I had to pretend I had no idea what he was talking about, even though my worst fears were being confirmed.

"I would've snapped her neck, if I didn't. She never shut up. Bitch would wail nonstop. I had her gagged and I could still hear her whimpering."

"Ah, that's how this one was, but a couple of lashings and a few goes with my men and it broke her pretty quickly," Luis snickered. He fucking snickered like they were talking about training dogs. I was reminded of every time Enrico called me pet. Perhaps in his mind, that's exactly what I was. I knew this, but somehow I was starting to think that maybe his obsession with me was more than that, like I was valued, but this conversation was telling me how expendable I was.

Most of the dinner was spent talking about production. I assumed it was drugs because every now and then, they would talk about fields. Before the men finished, the conversation had shifted once again.

"How did it go with Hades?" Luis asked.

"Good, they'll pay what I want. Those stupid Scars will pay up too. They'll be gone before they even know they were double crossed," Enrico started laughing and the other men joined in. The cackle was sinister and would be a sound that haunted me for nights to come.

We left the restaurant, but my mind was so preoccupied with what I'd heard Enrico talking about that I wasn't really on my game. They'd said Hades and Scars. I wondered if Scars was Gunner. I couldn't remember what Gunner's vest read, but my gut told me that part of the conversation had everything to do with him. I hated that he had anything to do with Enrico. It was another reminder that I had no idea what kind of man he'd become. Obviously, he had business dealings with Enrico and that didn't bode well for me. The thought had crossed my mind more than once, I wondered if that was one of the reasons why Enrico targeted me. I usually convinced myself that I was just a shiny toy that Enrico saw and wanted to add to his collection, but what if I wasn't? Those thoughts plagued my mind, so I didn't hear Enrico when he told me to take his cock out and suck.

"Now, Pet! When I say drop, you drop to your fucking knees. I just rewarded you with a meal, and this is how you repay me?" I was stunned when a smack landed across my face, splitting my lip. The bitter reality that I was in the back of Enrico's SUV stung as much as my face. I immediately did as he said and dropped to my knees. He was forceful and unkind, often cutting off my airway. I prayed it would end. When we got back to his home, everything changed, just not in a good way.

Chapter Fifteen

Charlie

Enrico grabbed me tightly by the arm, angry that blood from my split lip had gotten on his black dress pants. Once inside, he threw me to the ground. "You stupid bitch, maybe I'll sell you too."

"No, please don't!" I pleaded. As his eyes grew dark, I realized my mistake. He spoke to me in Spanish and I responded. It was careless. My mind was still on all that I had learned tonight and I wasn't being as careful as I should've been.

"You can understand me? You lying whore! All this time, you've been playing me." I was forcefully yanked by the hair.

"No, I'm sorry. I'll do anything. I'm sorry," I begged. I still had the idea that I needed to hang on for Gun. I couldn't let him kill me or sell me. I was so afraid that if he sold me, I'd end up somewhere even worse. What's the saying? Better the devil you know… Yeah well, at least I was learning what to expect from Enrico.

"You think I care about your pleas? You begging only makes me hard, you lying piece of shit."

"I'm sorry," I cried with tears streaming down my face. I don't know why I thought it could stop the devil. No. Not him.

I was met with a hit to the face, only this time it wasn't a smack. This time, his fist connected with my flesh. His gold ring he wore with a lion's head protruding from it came at me violently, breaking my skin. I tried to curl into myself the pain was so fierce.

He wouldn't let me. He delivered a kick to my ribs, and then with a fist in my hair, he began dragging me. I cried out. My legs barely worked as I tried to scramble to keep up with him, so that all of my dark hair wasn't ripped from my head.

I stumbled and fell as he led me down the basement steps to the dungeon. Every part of my body screamed in agony. He opened the door to a room I hadn't seen before. If I had thought my room was a dungeon, I was wrong. This was a dungeon. I was thrown to the ground. My hands dug into a cold damp floor. Small rocks and dirt surrounded me. One of my eyes had already begun to swell shut. I could vaguely make out a wall, and then I was being hauled upwards. Enrico was putting something on my wrists. Next thing I knew, my face pressed against a cold wall and my wrists were secured over head.

"I'll teach you to lie to me. You'll never do it again. This is it. Your only chance, and if I ever find you keeping something from me again, I'll destroy you. I will find your son and peel his skin from his body while you watch, but first I'll make him watch as I fuck your asshole 'til it bleeds. Then, I'll sell you to some friends of mine whose idea of play makes me look like a saint."

Tears poured down my face and I knew better than to open my mouth. I was silent. I'd learned to be a mouse in the past. I'd never make a sound again. A part of me hoped to die now before I did anything to jeopardize my son. He was my everything. I'd never comprehend how I ended up in the clutches of such a monster, but I'd do whatever I could to make sure this evil didn't touch him.

My dress was ripped from my body, the tearing sound and our deep breathing were the only sounds in the dark cell. I stayed silent as Enrico's belt lashed out and dug deep into my back. I stayed silent as he raped me. I was silent as he left me with my arms above my head.

Even then, I wouldn't make a sound. I wouldn't do it. My idea of escape had vanished. Now, my time here became about playing my part to keep my son safe. I prayed for death. I prayed over and over again. My prayers weren't answered.

Time seemed like it went on forever. My arms were long since numb. My body had ached so much, that consciousness was limited. I'd wake with nightmares of Enrico and his friend's laughing as my son was torn in two. I wanted nothing more than death, and as my body grew weaker and weaker, I knew it was coming for me. I closed my eyes, barely hanging on, and thought about Gunner and Gun. I thought about how he protected me from anyone who seemed to want to do me harm. I thought about all the ways I'd hoped Gun would be like him. I wanted Gun to have a good life one day. I wanted Gun to have his first girlfriend, his first kiss, his first motorcycle, and his own babies. I thought about how maybe one day, he'd reunite with his dad, and they could grow old being friends. These thoughts were the only peace I had while I hung from the wall, slowly bleeding out my life. These thoughts were the last ones I had before I drifted off for good.

Part Three

Chapter Sixteen

Gunner

"Kid, wake up." I didn't want to wake Gun in the middle of the night. I didn't want to say goodbye, but I had too.

"Dad?" His sleepy voice filled the bedroom. My chest ached in that way that only Gun calling me Dad could create.

"Yeah, Gun. Wake up."

He sat up, his Ninja Turtles pj's reminding me of how young he was. Sometimes, it was easy to forget because he'd already been through so much.

"What is it? Is it Mom? Did you find her?"

I couldn't tell him anything as much as I wanted to.

He blinked his eyes at me. The light from the hallway filtered into his bedroom. "Why are you dressed? Are you leaving me?" I hated that. My boy was so insecure about not having anyone, and I knew this conversation was not going to be easy for me.

"I need you to listen to me, and do your best to be as brave as you can. You hear me?"

Gun sat up even taller and nodded his head.

"I do have to leave. Reggie's going to stay with you. He's going to keep you home from school for the next few days and play video games and shit with you. Whatever you want, 'kay?" Reggie had really taken to Gun, so I hoped that he wouldn't be too disappointed.

He looked dejected. I had to give it to him straight. I owed him that, and if I didn't come back, I didn't want him to think it had anything to do with him.

"I got a lock on your Mom. A bad guy has her. I'm going after her, and I'm going to do everything I can to bring her back to you. Love you, kid."

"What if the bad guys win?" his chin wobbled as he asked.

"None of that. You hear me? Bad guys don't win. You be brave and do as Reggie tells you and hopefully, all this will be over before you know it."

"Is she okay?"

My eyes turned down because I really didn't know and I didn't want to lie to him. "I really hope so. I really do." I hugged my son for a few minutes, and soon his tired body started to grow lax in my arms. I started to leave his room when I heard him call out, "Dad, love you too."

It was the first time he'd ever said that to me and I needed to hear it. I needed that extra something to get me through this because, in all honesty, I wasn't sure how the fuck I was going to save her, but I was going to try. If I failed, my club would raise Gun.

• • •

I had parked my bike and was walking up to the private airstrip I'd arranged to use, when Ace and Shane came into view.

"Fuck, I thought we talked about this? I thought we decided I'd go it alone, and you guys would take care of the club? They need you."

"No, fuckwit. You decided you'd go it alone. We didn't decide that shit." Shane slapped me on the back, and I flashed him a look of irritation.

"It's decided. Club voted tonight. We're with you. One way or another, either you're coming home with us, or none of us are. We don't do it alone. Didn't you learn that lesson?" Ace shot me a glare. That was one of the longest sentences my brother had ever said to me. I knew I couldn't argue if my club had voted on it.

"You fucks voted without me?"

"Yep," Shane answered.

"Plane's loaded," Ace lifted his vest showing me all the guns strapped to his chest.

The first twenty minutes in the air was spent getting ready for war and the remaining part of the flight, we went over every detail of our plan. Which wasn't a solid plan, but it was all we had. The danger was great, but they were willing to risk it for me. They were willing to risk everything. I couldn't be pissed, even though I wanted to be. Truth was, I needed the help.

We landed in a makeshift airfield in the middle of a fucking field of cocoa plants. The heat from the early Colombian sun made my brow sweat almost immediately. Men with guns walked around in the field and a group of young boys harvested plants. They didn't look up at us, and the pilot acted like it was business as usual as he paid the armed guards a small fortune to keep their mouths shut.

"You need to be here by midnight tonight, otherwise I leave and you never see me again," the pilot said as we got into the SUV that was waiting for us.

"We understand. See you soon," Shane said before we pulled away.

Our intel finally came in, and we paid a mint for it. We were confident that we could get in and out. It was a decent plan; it wasn't perfect. When we were in the air going over everything, I couldn't have been more glad that Ace and Shane were with me. Ace knew his shit, way more than I ever gave him credit for. He came strapped like motherfucking Rambo. Of course, it didn't hurt that one of Enrico's guys sang like a fucking canary when offered the right amount of money. There was no loyalty among these men. His employees worked for him out of fear or money, not because they were brothers. That meant they could be bought. And our inside guy told us exactly who we could buy.

There was a change in guards every six hours. We had a by-the-minute time table of how we could get in without getting caught. For three hours, we sat in the brush waiting for our signal. When it came, we were ready and did exactly like we were instructed.

We moved through the path in the thick jungle surrounding Enrico's property and came out of it at the rear of the house. Once at the back of the house, Ace kept an eye on his watch until it was time for us to move again. Another minute passed, and we were going to the sliding door. It opened just like we were assured it would. We moved down a hall, and came to his office door. I threw open the door and there he sat at his desk, dressed in a tailored suit. His hair was slicked back. I caught a flash of concern cross his features as his eyes crinkled in the corners, the only real sign that he was much older than me, before he quickly put on his steely reserve. The room wasn't overly large. There was an opulent desk with a briefcase opened on it and a laptop next to that. Besides that, it was meticulously clean. Even the pen that sat on the desk looked like it had been set in that exact location on purpose. There were several large bookshelves lining the back wall and across from that were two large, high back chairs with ornately carved wooden arms.

There was another man in the room who quickly moved into action. He lifted his gun to aim it. Ace didn't hesitate. He shot him before the man's finger was even on the trigger. The man fell to the ground with a bullet hole in his head. A red pool started to form around him.

Enrico Santos sat calmly. "Tsk, tsk. Juan was one of my best men, you really didn't need to do that. Now, you're here for a reason, si? What is it? We had a deal on the guns. Or is it money? Drugs? Why have you come into my home disrespecting me, when I've shown you nothing but respect?" His accent was thick as he coolly demanded answers.

Shane stealthily moved behind Enrico with his gun aimed at his head while Ace covered the door. I stood in front of Enrico with my gun aimed ready to blow his brains out, but knowing I couldn't do it, not yet.

"Respect me? That's why you were meaning to undermine us with Hades?"

His eyes flared for another brief second. I saw it. He was surprised we knew.

"Respect?" I scoffed again, "That's why you have the mother of my child? You have my woman, and you want to talk about respect?" My nose flared and I was so close to pulling the trigger.

"Gunner," Shane said my name trying to calm me. I couldn't kill this piece of shit until I had Charlie.

"Where is she?" I asked through clenched teeth.

He laughed, actually threw his head back and laughed. "That puta? That's what's got your panties in a bunch?"

Shane aimed his gun down and shot him in the leg. His pant leg darkened.

"Fuck! You'll pay for that," Enrico said through gritted teeth.

"Flesh wound. Next one will be worse. You think we don't know how to make a man bleed? Get up!" Shane ordered.

Noise from the hall alerted Ace to the fact that some of Enrico's men had begun making their way toward the room. Ace shouted, "Tell them to fall back, or I take your knees." The men in the hall must've heard this, because the noise from their loud clumsy asses quieted.

"Pare, no vienen más cerca!" Enrico yelled in Spanish. I didn't speak Spanish, but I imagined he was telling them to stop.

I kept my gun trained on Enrico. My brothers' covered me as we forced a limping Enrico to his feet. "Lead us to her."

As we moved into the hall, his men fell back sensing the danger their boss was in. We were led down a set of stairs, through a few doors, and then down another three stairs. It seemed to get colder and darker, the further down we traveled. The air smelled dank. At the end of what seemed to be a tunnel, we came to a wooden door. My blood boiled at the thought that she was being kept here. I gripped the back of his neck, doing everything in my power to not kill him yet. I needed to make sure she was here. Enrico moved his hand to his pocket. "Easy," I said reaching in and fishing out a large set of keys. There was no way I would know which one unlocked the door. I handed them to him, "Open it," I ordered. He grabbed them and took his time, infuriating me even more. Finally, he put the key in the lock and turned it. What I saw when he opened the door took my breath away.

A woman, I wasn't even sure yet was Charlie, with bound wrists hung from a hook. She was naked. Her back was to us, dried blood and deep, large, red welts covered her gaunt body. Her head lulled to the side and I had no idea if she was even alive. "Son of a bitch," I hissed. "Release her."

Enrico sifted through keys on the ring and unlocked her wrists, but not before his hand ran down her back. I shoved him aside and grabbed the woman. I gasped when I saw her face.

It was her.

My. Fucking. World.

And she was destroyed.

Ace, with his military background, grabbed her wrist, "She's got a pulse, but barely."

"Let's move," Shane said, as I scooped Charlie into my arms. He held a gun on Enrico as we began moving out of the dungeon and back the way we came.

"Baby, hang on. I'm here. Hang on," I whispered and kissed her forehead, praying to God that I wasn't too late.

We had just made it to the kitchen, when a flash of silver caught my eye and a bullet grazed past me. Ace fired back and before we knew it, we were in a shootout.

The kitchen was open layout with the fridge and range against the wall and the rest of the deep mahogany cabinets were an island in the middle if the room. Across from one side of the kitchen were windows and patio doors. On the other side, there was a formal dining room and a hallway. The hallway was where the bullets began flying from. We ducked behind the cabinets. Shane still held a gun to Enrico, but we needed Shane's help, so with Charlie in my arms, I aimed at him. There was an all out war around us. If Enrico didn't make it, I needed to know why. So with my gun trained on him, in the midst of chaos, I asked, "Why did you take her? Why her? Why me?"

The sick fucker smiled at me. "Why don't you ask your mother about how I like pretty things?"

What the fuck?

Enrico, thinking he took me off guard, went for a knife from the butcher block. I pulled the trigger of my gun and shot him in his other leg, and this time it wasn't a flesh wound. Enrico hissed in pain, not wanting to show how much that must've hurt.

"Tell them to stand down. The only reason you're still alive is to ensure we get the fuck out of here. If they don't back down, you're dead," Shane said through the rapid gunfire.

A bullet grazed Ace's shoulder and he shouted, "Fuck this!" He took out a fucking grenade and threw it. The room seemed to explode, dust was everywhere. Men were screaming.

"Fuck," Shane shouted. Somehow during the explosion, even with his wounded leg, Enrico managed to get away.

I looked down at Charlie. I wanted to go after Enrico. I wanted to make him pay. Shane, seeing my torment, shook his head. "Not now."

"We don't have time! Let's go!" Ace shouted.

I wanted to kill Enrico, but my focus needed to be on Charlie. Above everything else, I needed to keep her safe. We moved through the hole in the wall to the outside. As we did, Ace pulled out another grenade and threw it into the house. I just prayed that this explosion killed that sick fucker. Flames were everywhere. Smoke filled our lungs, but we moved quickly.

Once outside, there were far fewer men, so Shane and Ace flanked my sides taking men out as we left the burning building behind. We could hear screaming and shouting, a mixture of pain and revenge. Those men wanted us dead.

We moved through the jungle and before we knew it, we'd made it to the SUV. I climbed in the back still holding Charlie close to me. Shane and Ace got in the front, and we sped off. We zoomed through the Colombian streets, and in what felt like seconds, but was surely longer, we were at the airfield. Shane had called ahead to the pilot and within minutes of arriving, we were in the air. I wrapped Charlie in a blanket, and continued whispering that she would be okay, even though I wasn't really sure if that was the truth. She wasn't conscious and from the way her breath labored, I wondered how long we had.

"We need to get her to a hospital. I don't know if she'll make it to the States."

Shane went to the cockpit and spoke to the pilot. "We'll land in Costa Rica. He knows someone. They'll meet us as soon as we land." I looked up to the heavens and said a silent prayer.

"ETA?" Ace asked.

"Fifty minutes," Shane met my eyes. The look he gave me made me feel like he thought I was fighting a losing battle.

"She's not gonna die," I gave him a hard look, daring him to challenge me.

"I know, brother."

"No, she's not going to die. Are you, Charlie? You're going to hang on." My voice cracked and I realized I was fucking crying. "I have Gun. He's such a good kid. You did so good with him. I promised him I'd bring you home, so don't you make me a liar to him. You hang on. You hear me? Hang on." I was rocking her back and forth praying that I wouldn't lose her.

We landed at another airstrip in the middle of nowhere. A woman with a medical bag boarded the plane a few minutes later.

"She's going to do what she can from here. Enrico still has reach here, and if he made it out of there and finds out we landed here, we'll have more problems than we can deal with." I nodded to Shane understanding.

I couldn't miss the way the woman sucked in a breath when she saw Charlie. "This woman needs a hospital. What happened to her?"

"A monster," Ace answered for me. The lump in my throat was making it hard for me to talk.

She took a stethoscope from her bag and listened to Charlie's heart, and then she felt her gaunt stomach. "Pulse is faint. Can you lift her, so I can hear her lungs?"

I cradled her front to me and moved the blanket revealing her back. A loud gasp escaped the doctor's lips. "Lord have mercy," she whispered. As I moved Charlie, she was completely limp in my arms. Her body felt lifeless. I couldn't let her die. It couldn't be too late.

"This woman is barely hanging on. In fact, I'm surprised she's still breathing. Without a CT scan to make sure there's no internal bleeding, I'm limited in what I can do. I'll start an IV. She obviously needs fluids. I'll give her antibiotics and hopefully, that will tie her over until you can get her to the States. You'll have to change the bag, when this one is empty."

I found my voice, "Will she make it, Doc?"

She looked at me with a small amount of pity. I hated being pitied. "If I were you, I'd pray."

Ace led her off of the plane and ten minutes later, we were back in the air. I held Charlie close to me, rocking her back and forth. Ace and Shane remained quiet the rest of the flight. By the time we landed, Charlie's skin looked a little better. She wasn't as pale. She was still unconscious, but the small amount of pink in her cheeks gave me a little hope.

"We can't bring her to the hospital," Ace said as we exited the plane. I had been thinking the same thought, so I nodded.

Shane handed the pilot a large envelope. I had no doubt that everything the pilot did for us today would cost a pretty penny.

"We just pissed off a whole lotta bad guys. We bring her in, we'll be a target." Ace wasn't saying anything I hadn't already suspected.

"I think we all need to head to the mountains. Safe-house should be ready to go. I'll make the calls and get Doc to meet us there." Shane pulled his phone from his pocket and started calling the brothers.

He powered off his phone. "Reggie said your kid's doing fine. He'll pack up some things for him, and they'll be on their way."

My brothers helped me place Charlie in the truck that I'd left parked at the airfield. I hated to even move her from my arms, but their bikes were here and we needed to get to cover. We had just started a war and we had to be prepared.

Chapter Seventeen

Gunner

"Her vitals look good. I'll keep her on the drip for at least the next twenty-four hours, and then we'll go from there."

"Thanks, Doc. When do you think she'll wake up?"

"There's no telling, right now, exactly how much trauma she's been through. She needs to heal right now, and the best way her body knows to do that is for her to remain asleep. Plus, her mind could be shielding her." He rubbed his white beard while the wrinkles around his eyes softened, "If I were you, I'd talk to her as much as possible."

I nodded and felt a little of the heaviness weighing on my chest lighten. Doc gave me hope that she was going to make it, and that's more than I had a few hours ago. A knock on the door interrupted us, "Reggie's here," Austin, one of my brothers, poked his head in.

"Will you stay with her for a few minutes? I have to figure out what I'm going to tell my boy," I asked Doc.

"You want some advice?"

Considering the whole parenting thing was brand new to me, I'd take any advice I could get, so I conveyed that to him with my eyes.

"I know she looks bad, but if I were you, I would let him see her. He's been without her for some time now, so he's probably already imagined the worst."

He'd answered the question that I'd been going back and forth on. Truth was, a part of me was afraid to damage him even more, but I knew Doc was right.

"Thanks, Doc."

I hated leaving Charlie, but my son needed me. Reggie was just grabbing a suitcase from the trunk when I approached. I didn't see Gun at first, and then I noticed him kicking dirt on the other side of the black sedan. "A Camry? Really?" I said to Reggie as I passed him.

"It's my mom's. I didn't really have much time to figure out how I'd get him here. I haven't owned a cage in years."

"Dad!" Gun rushed forward and threw his small arms around me. "You're okay!"

I ruffled his sandy, blonde hair, "Told you I'd be back."

"Where are we?" he asked.

"He was asleep most of the car ride. That kid of yours could sleep through anything. I even cranked up some metal."

"Reg," I gave him a 'what the fuck' look.

"We're in the Allegheny Mountains in Pennsylvania. It's a few hours east of home. These are safe houses no one knows about." I moved my head toward the five small cabins behind me. This place was once rented out to campers, but the owners went belly up and we bought it through a shell corporation a few years ago.

"Safe houses? Why are we in danger? Is it Mom? Is she okay?"

Fuck, why did I use "safe houses"? Sometimes it was easy to forget how smart this kid was.

"We're safe here. Follow me." I motioned my head towards the small front steps of the cabin and sat down. Gun sat down next to me and peered up at me through his long lashes.

"A real bad guy had your momma. Me and the boys got her back."

"She's okay? She's here? I need to see her."

I put my hand on his shoulder to calm him, "Kid, she's hurt. She's inside and the doctors have seen her. They think she's going to be okay, but she's sleeping and might be asleep for a long time."

"I need to go to her." This kid. He was already so brave.

Doc grabbed his bag, "I'll be in cabin four, if you need me."

He stood up and I followed, "I want you to be prepared. It's not good."

He raced inside and I stepped in front of him placing my hand on top of his before he was able to turn the door handle. "Son, I'm right here. She's going to get better, alright." His lip trembled and I could tell he was trying to hold back tears. I opened the door and Doc had put Charlie under the blankets. The IV drip was next to the bed.

Gun spoke up, startling me, "Is she… Can I touch her?" With a shift of my head, I silently told Doc that I had this, and he left, closing the door behind him.

I grabbed Gun's hand and sat us both on the side of the bed. He watched as I held her hand. "Mouse, Gun's here. Want you to work on getting better and coming back to us." I lifted her hand to my mouth and brushed my lips across her knuckles. He eyed us, and then he climbed closer to her, laid down next to her and wrapped his small arm around her waist.

He didn't say anything, at least not for a while. He held her, and I stared at the two of them, suddenly slammed with more possessiveness than I'd felt my entire life. These two were my everything. Charlie might be broken, but I'd move heaven and hell to put her back together.

I leaned over the bed, kissed my son on his forehead and then dipped a knee into the mattress so I could kiss Charlie's forehead.

"Don't knock the IV, yeah? If she stirs, even a little, you come get me."

"Where are you..."

I cut him off. "I'm not going far, just need to make sure that the bad guys don't get away with this."

"Dad?" That word alone coming from my son's mouth made my chest tighten every time. His chin wobbled and he barely got out, "Hurry back."

Ace and Shane were in the living room/kitchen area of the cabin when I walked out. It was like they knew I'd need to meet with them.

"Are the last of the guys here?"

Ace gave me a head nod.

"Call church then. Need to see where everyone's heads are. If I don't have everyone's support, I'll..."

Shane cut me off, "You'll nothing. We were there--saw what he's capable of. There's none of that going it alone bullshit. When will you get it through your thick skull?" He smacked me upside the back of the head. I supposed I needed it, but I glared at him anyway, to which he returned a toothy grin.

Fifteen minutes later, myself and roughly thirty other members were situated around a campfire, while huge tents wove between the cabins which were saved for families. There weren't a ton of families, but enough that we wouldn't leave them out in the open for anything to happen to them.

"Listen up," Shane bellowed, "Most of you have heard what went down. It went, for the most part, as planned. We got Gunner's woman back, but not sure if we got the sick fuck."

"Threw a few grenades at his ass," Ace sat and sharpened a large M-9 Bayonet, the metal made a loud, scraping noise as it moved fluidly against the sharpening stone.

Shane continued, "We're not sure if he made it out or not. I've already put out some calls and am waiting for confirmation from our contacts. That's why you're all here. I don't want to take any chances. Until we know for sure, you're all to remain here."

"Let's just assume he's alive, and start planning on what we're going to do next," I suggested knowing that I'd rather be prepared.

"Going to Colombia just depleted a huge chunk of our funds," Ace added barely looking up from that damn blade.

"So, we have to be smart. He doesn't know where we are so, that'll be in our favor." Shane and Ace looked at me nodding their heads, agreeing as I spoke.

"Anyone hear anything about Hades lately? They've been awfully quiet," Razor, one of the brothers, asked.

"Good point," I added.

"We need to make calls, make sure every Bleeding Scar knows what's going on. I want all eyes on this. Every contact we have needs to be looking out for signs of Enrico, and I need an ear to the ground on the Hades Runners," Shane began barking orders.

Ace stood looking like the Marine he once was, "Need you men to think like soldiers on this one. We need to learn every in and out of these grounds. There's no one around for miles and leading the enemy here might just work to our advantage, if we play this right."

"All due respect, Ace, my wife and kids are here," Porter flicked his cigarette into the fire.

"Mine too," another brother added, "And I got a newborn."

I put my hand up to stop them, I'm sure Ace had a plan. "My whole world is right there," I pointed, "How do we protect them?"

"Rocket launchers are a start," Ace laughed, but I knew he wasn't fucking kidding. I saw them. "We scout, for now. Get the lay of the land. And then, when the time is right, we take the women and kids out of here and end those motherfuckers once and for all," Ace finished his go get 'em speech adding more inspiring lines about loyalty and family.

By the end, the men all agreed. That was followed by the usual campfire shit, not the kumbaya shit, but the haze and blaze shit. Weed was plentiful and the booze ran freely. I didn't partake, though. No, I went inside the cabin and found my son curled up next to his mom asleep. I made sure loaded guns were within grabbing distance and then laid down on the other side of Charlie.

I was careful not to move her IV as I shifted Charlie so that my arm was around her. Her neck laid against my bicep and my other arm was around her waist. It laid on top of my son's. He blinked up at me and momentarily stirred.

"She didn't open her eyes," he whispered.

I didn't imagine she would. "She's not ready yet. It'll happen. In the meantime, get some rest. Yeah?"

He shifted so he was under the blankets, "You won't leave, will you?"

"I'll be right here," I squeezed his hand which had found mine again and listened as his breathing evened out. Once he was good and asleep, I talked to Charlie. I'm not even sure what I said, quite honestly. I babbled until I could no longer keep my eyes open. The last thing I remembered was reassuring her that she was safe, and begging her to come back to me.

When I woke up, the room was just beginning to glow from the early morning sun. I gripped the sheet around Charlie and held her closer to me. I closed my eyes, not wanting to face the horrors of what had happened to her, and thought about the two of us laying underneath the stars. I thought of how quiet she'd been with everyone else, but how she seemed to speak to me with no hesitation. I thought about how pretty I always thought she was, even when I was only a boy. I thought about how she thought that I didn't notice her, even when I did. She was always so strong. "Be strong for me, Mouse," I said in a hushed whisper as I opened my eyes to face another day.

I noticed the empty IV bag and hurriedly sat up to change it. That's when I saw the door was slightly cracked and that Gun wasn't here. I jumped up, angry at myself for sleeping so soundly. I moved out of the bedroom and rushed to the common area about to call his name. There he sat at a small table with a box of Lucky Charms in front of him. Reggie sat across from him and he lifted his blue plastic bowl towards me, "Want some?"

I let out a breath, I was so nervous. "Nah, gonna hit the head," I said and moved to the bathroom to relieve myself.

When I came out, Doc was there pouring himself a cup of coffee. "I was about to change her drip," I told him.

"I can do it. I need to change her dressings anyways." He took a sip of the steaming hot liquid and picked up his black medicine bag.

"I'll help. Reggie, you good keeping an eye on Gun?"

"No problem. I was just telling Gun, that I'd beat him at Grand Turbo Three."

"What! You haven't beat me yet. You're on!"

I couldn't help but smirk, but then Doc placed his hand on top of mine. "You might want to sit this out. You weren't here when I dressed them. It ain't good, Brother."

I looked at him pointedly, "That woman in there, she went through that. She felt that. I won't shy away because it'll hurt. What kind of man do you take me for? Now, you going to stare at me all day, or can we take care of Charlie?

He nodded his head, resigned to the fact that nothing he could say would stop me. She was still out of it as Doc took her vitals, "She's a fighter, alright. Heartbeat is stronger today." He rolled her onto her side so that her back was to us and moved the blanket exposing her. I hadn't realized last night that she was basically wrapped in sheets. There was a sheet around her front, even covering her shoulders and then there was another on her back. He moved the sheet on her back, and ordered, "Well if you're here, you might as well be useful. Get me some clean water and a trash can."

A minute later, I returned and when I walked into the room, my breath caught. I'd seen Charlie when she was hooked and hanging, but I was fueled with adrenaline. Now, her back was bare to me and the damage to her flesh was a lot more visible. She was cut wide open in thick gashes.

"Some of the tissue has already started to heal, so I can't stitch it. I need to keep an eye out for infection. We're going to clean it, put ointment on it, and then re-bandage it."

"What's that?" I pointed to her lower back. I moved my face in closer. There was an angry gash through it, but I made it out. Branded into her skin, were the letters ES. "Motherfucker," I roared.

"Need a minute, Doc."

"I can do this alone, you don't..."

"I said a minute," I said through gritted teeth. I walked out of the room, saw Gun in the living room playing video games, and knew I couldn't lose my shit in front of him. I cut Reggie a look and knew my brother would shield my son, then I walked outside.

"Fuuuck!" I bellowed as I dropped to my knees in the dirt. I breathed in and out, inhaling the moist air. I wanted to hit something-- someone. I wanted to scream to the universe that my Mouse didn't deserve this. She didn't deserve a thing that had happened to her. She didn't deserve to be in pain.

When I'd seen her on that stage after not seeing her for so long, I thought she was doing okay. She was high, so not great, but I thought she was okay. I was so angry at myself. If I'd only seen past my own bullheadedness, none of this would've happened.

171

I did this.

Me.

I might not have branded her, but if I'd only found her sooner… If I'd only seen past the glassy eyes… If I'd only saved her before…

I couldn't even finish my self-deprecating thoughts, too many 'if only's' passed through my mind. My shoulders rose and fell rapidly. I was a man on the brink. I'd lose it or channel my anger. I felt a hand on my shoulder and heard Ace's deep voice, "Reign it in. That shit you got going through your head, It ain't on you."

I don't know how he knew what was going through my mind, but I shouldn't have been surprised. It was, after all, the ever observant Ace.

I took a few more deep breaths and heard, "Reign it in," again.

After another minute of trying to get myself under control, I stood. I didn't glance at Ace. I needed to get back into Charlie.

"You good?" Doc asked as I walked back in.

"Not even a little, but let's do this."

Doc eyed me, feeling out my temperament, and then began to show me how much ointment to apply and how to bandage her wounds. "I'm only going to do this for another few days, and then I want the air to hit it. It might start to scab better, so be prepared to find something for your kid to do, so he won't have to see it."

I agreed with the plan and once we were finished changing her, I got a hair brush and a fresh bowl of water. I cleaned her skin with care and then brushed her hair. I don't even know how long I focused on each strand, but it was nearing lunch when Reggie knocked. "Going to make some burgers, you want one?" I couldn't think about eating at a time like this. I just wanted her to wake up, flinch, something. The rise and fall of her chest, the subtle pulse at her throat, were the only signs that she held life. I needed more. I wouldn't leave her.

"I'm good. Take care of Gun, would you?"

"I'm on it, but Gunner, he's going to need you to look strong, even if you're not. He'll need that from you. You got it in you to give it to him? You don't, then I'll do my best, but he needs that from you."

"Hear you, Brother."

Reggie turned to leave. "How's he seem?" I asked, knowing Gun needed me too.

"He's a great kid. We're keeping him busy. I think Shane is going to bring him to the lake to fish in a little bit, but he's got that look in his eyes." I knew what look, it closely resembled my own. I couldn't let him get lost.

"Stay with her for a few, would you? She as much as flinches, and you call me."

"Got it."

I found Gun sitting at the same table as earlier playing something I couldn't make out on someone's phone.

As soon as he saw me he stopped, "Is she awake?"

"Not yet, but she will wake up. As soon as her body has had enough rest. It's going to be okay."

He looked down not believing me.

"I know this is hard. It's hard on me too. She's the strongest woman I've even met, and she loves you too darn much to do anything other than wake up. Doc says she continues to get stronger."

173

To that his eyes met mine, "Shane said he's going to take me fishing after we eat lunch. What if she wakes up, and I'm not here?"

"Kid, I'll send someone for you. Don't you worry. I'll be with her. If anyone loves her as much as you, if not more, it's me."

He had doubt in his eyes still, "I'm the one who's been with her."

"Told you, kid. I'd have been there, if I'd been able to find her."

"You found her now. How come you couldn't find her then?"

"I tried, I failed, son. I won't fail you again. Now, stop worrying over everything. It'll be fine. You ever hook a worm before?"

"Never."

"It's fun. I'll fish with you too, as soon as she's moving around." I wanted to be the first man to do this with him, but I knew he needed the distraction.

"Promise?"

"Have I broken a promise to you yet?"

He smiled, and I hoped he got it. I was going to do everything I could to be there for my family.

Chapter Eighteen

Charlie

The leather cut into my flesh again, burning and peeling. And then the monster pushed inside, taking and taking. I'd cry out, but I was so used to his violation that I couldn't give in. I'd never give him that from me again. Hands gripped around my throat and I struggled to breathe. My legs involuntarily kicked and thrashed about.

"Shh, you're okay. I got you. Get Doc!" The voice sounded mumbled and I wanted to hang onto it, but no sooner did it bring me from the horrible things that were happening to me, then I'd slip back into another state.

You watch me as I hang. You look over me up, down, side to side. I want to talk to you, but I can't speak, my mouth sewn shut. I want to scream, but it's impossible. Your head moves to the side in an unnatural way. I don't understand why you don't speak to me, even though your familiar hazel eyes bore into mine. My flesh begins to melt, and panic flashes wildly in my eyes before I dissolve into nothing.

I am laying in a bed. Alone. The room is dark with a small amount of light. You walk through a door, but don't see me. You're followed by Marjorie, who takes a seat across from you at the small table. Her long red hair hangs over one shoulder and her exposed leg runs along your jean-clad legs. She rubs your arm, flirting with you, but all I can do is watch. She is beautiful. I am... Well, I am gone. I disappeared into sheets from so much damage, and now, I'm nothing. I'm invisible.

You stand in front of me. You're shirtless. I smile at you and you grab my hand, "What is it, Mouse?"

"Whatever do you mean?" I laugh and smack your shoulder. You're getting so strong so quickly. I run the pad my thumb over the tiny stretch mark that only I'd ever notice. I like it because I see it. I see your small imperfections because they're beautiful. They tell your story-- that you're becoming a man.

"You know you can't stay here forever, right? You need to wake up, Mouse?"

"I don't want to wake up. It's bad out there. I'm safe here with you."

"Always safe with me, Babe. Wake up."

I blinked and then squinted. The room's light hurt my eyes.

"Charlie! Thank God, Charlie. Stay with me. Don't leave me. Hang on."

I recognized that voice. It felt so real. No, it couldn't be. I squinted again and through my hazy vision, I could make out Gunner Reed.

Those beautiful flecks of brown and green stared at me as if I'd hung the moon.

"Here's some water. Take a sip. The Doc is on his way," he spoke softly. I tried not to blink, fearful that this wasn't real. A straw was placed against my lips and I did as he instructed. He pulled it away, "Easy doll, not too fast."

The room was beginning to fade again. I heard another man, "Charlie, I'm Doc. You're with family. I'm going to take your vitals."

I briefly felt a something cold against my chest, and then it was all blackness again.

I opened my eyes. The room was shrouded in darkness. I felt a weight settle over my stomach and I looked down to see what it was. My breath caught and my chest ached. I couldn't believe it. My boy, my sweet precious Gun, was curled tight around me sleeping. How could this be? I must be dreaming. I moved my fingertips, they worked. I wiggled my toes; yep, still there. I took a chance on reality, and moved my arm to run my fingertips through his dark blonde hair. It was soft and gave me hope that this was real.

"Mom?" I heard his small voice that held so much uncertainty. I continued moving my fingers in his hair until they felt weighted. Before I knew it, I was drifting into darkness again.

The next time I woke, it was daylight and my boy was no longer curled around me. I wondered if it was a dream, but there was something familiar about the room, like I'd woken and seen it.

"He's fishing with the boys," I heard from across the room. I tried to sit up, but the slightest shift in movement, made my body scream in agony. The bed dipped next to me, and there he was, Gunner Reed. His dirty blonde hair fell slightly around those beautiful hazel eyes. Tattoos covered his arms, then a white t-shirt covered by a black motorcycle vest.

His presence confused me and I squinted my eyes and furrowed my brow. Gunner must have read my confusion. He began to explain, "The day after I saw you in the club, I regretted the way I treated you. I was angry. I can never explain to you how sorry I am. I should've seen past how high you were. I got your address and went by your place. That's where I found Gun. Knew right away he was mine. He's been with me ever since, well, I mean, I had him stay with Reggie, one of the guys, when me and the boys came and got you."

I wanted to ask him how they rescued me. I wanted to ask him if Enrico was dead. I hoped like hell he was dead, but when I opened my mouth to talk, nothing came out. "You've been out for a few days. You woke up a few times, but it didn't last. This is the most alert you've seemed. Here take a sip," Gunner pressed a straw to my lips and I took a small sip of the cool water.

"You have a lot of gashes on your back. I was getting ready to turn you over on your side and change your bandages. I didn't want Gun to see, so while he's out, I was hoping we could let the air hit it."

My eyes said okay as my voice remained silent. He leaned in, I presumed it was to move me, but then his facial hair scratched against my face and his soft lips pressed against my forehead. "I'm so damn thankful to see your eyes open. Missed you, Mouse. Missed you so damn much." He was pulling away and gently rolled me on my side. He began the painstaking process of removing the bandages. I could tell he was hurrying as the bandages were sticking to my wounds. I didn't have to see my back to understand how it looked. I knew what had happened to me. I was there. Well, at least, until I wasn't.

While he did his thing behind me, I tried to process everything I learned. Gun was safe and had been with his dad. Gunner saved me. Gunner was here. This was real. He rescued me from what I'd thought was the impossible. Hanging from that wall, I'd lost hope, yet here it was; real.

I must've dozed off again, but not for very long. I was laying on my stomach and Gunner was sitting next to me, stroking my hair. I wanted to cry at the sensation. I'd thought I'd never see him again, yet here he was, taking care of me.

"You've been asleep for a few hours. I have some broth, I want you to drink some. Do you think you can do that? I nodded and then he continued, "You'll have to sit up, but I want to keep your back uncovered, so I'm going to keep a sheet tucked around your breasts. You had an IV in your arm but Doc removed it yesterday when you woke up. You were thrashing around and he didn't want you to hurt yourself, so your arm might be sore too." I sat up, pulling the sheet with me. Gunner gave me a look that said, he wanted to help me, but I need to see how I could move. My body was sore, but it wasn't as bad as I'd thought. My limbs felt stiff, but I had some strength. My hair hung over the white sheet and I was surprised to see how nice it looked. Without him saying it, I knew that was Gunner's doing. He lifted a spoon to my mouth and I sipped broth over and over again, and then when I'd drunk about all I could, he set the bowl down, knowing I'd had enough.

A deep pain low in my groin made me squirm. I had to use the bathroom and badly. I grabbed Gunner's arm and squeezed my legs together. At first, he looked confused and then as if a light bulb went off he said, "Shit, I should've thought of that. There's not a bathroom in here. It's down the hall." Before I knew what was happening, Gunner had me up and was cradling me in his arms. We were moving down a hallway, I briefly saw a few guys sitting at a table and then I was in a bathroom, being deposited on my feet. My legs felt wobbly, "Hold on to me," he said and then moved my sheet and held it in front of me trying to give me some type of privacy as my ass hit the toilet seat. I couldn't care about privacy, the stream of pee began almost immediately. I wiped and Gunner helped me up, wrapping the sheet around me so that my front and bottom were covered but also so that my back wasn't touching anything. "Put your arms around my shoulders."

I did like he asked and we were up. I caught a glimpse of myself in the mirror, what I saw was haunting. My face looked hollow and my eyes were vacant. My hair was thinner and I knew immediately it was because Enrico had ripped so much from the scalp. I hated my reflection, but no quicker did I see it, than we were moving again. As we passed down the hall again, Gunner stopped and spoke to one of the men in the kitchen. The man looked at me with sympathy. "Text Shane for me, and let Gun know she's up. Then, call Doc, would you?" The man nodded and then in a deep scratchy voice said, "Glad to see you up, doll."

We moved back to the room and Gunner started to lay me back down, but I felt safe in his arms and I didn't want to lose that, so I clung my arms tighter. "Alright, Mouse. I got you." He laid against the headboard and I held on tight. His arms circled around me and I heard him whisper, "I got you," before I fell asleep again.

I felt warmth wrapped around me and I still felt the heat from Gunner's body. "Doc, she hasn't said a word. Is that…"

"The mind is a funny thing. It could be the way her brain is coping with the trauma she's been through. She could open her mouth and talk today, or it may take a while and by a while, I mean years, if ever. You can't rush these things. As soon as this shit is over, you'll need to get her into counseling."

I blinked and opened my mouth to speak, a squeak of a sound came out, but then I felt hands gripping around my throat. I was right back in the dungeon. Enrico was inside of me. I began to thrash and vaguely heard Gunner's voice. "Doc?"

"Panic attack," was the garbled mess I heard the doc murmur, and then I felt a prick and was slipping under into the darkness; again.

It had been three days since I'd woken up. Gun had been in and out with me since he'd learned I'd woken up, however, Gunner explained to me that he was trying to shield him from my back. I didn't communicate this, but I was grateful for the fact. I was also beyond grateful that Gunner had Gun. I was so happy to watch the two bond, even if it was only over solitaire at my bedside.

Gunner would use the silence to tell me about his life. He started where we left off. "Babe, worst mistake I ever made was thinking I could trust those Hades Runners. I thought because it was my Mom, I'd be okay. I was wrong. They wouldn't let me leave while I prospected. I should've fought harder. I mean, I did fight them and got my ass handed to me once, but then I'd accepted my fate. I wished like hell I kept trying. When I finally could leave and went back, I saw the house burned." I grabbed his hand to stop him and looked at him confused. "Oh, you don't know. How could you? Well, after you left there was a fire. Your foster parents were killed. I had the club search for you, but no one really cared. It wasn't a brotherhood. They're savages. Nothing like us."

I didn't know how I should feel about Claire and Mitchell, but I supposed I felt much like what they felt for me, nothing.

"I would've thought some caseworker would've told you. But then, I couldn't find where you went... God, I wish you could tell me." He let out a large breath and continued, "It was like you vanished. I must've searched every group home and foster home in all of Ohio. I searched for years. I was in a bad way. I hated that I'd lost you. I can only imagine what you thought."

He'd searched for me? For years? I'd left Ohio. What if I'd stayed? Oh, I probably would've been arrested, but I couldn't believe he looked. I'd convinced myself over the years that I was just another notch in the never-ending bedpost of Gunner Reed's. This story went against so many things I'd believed. By the time he finished telling me of how he walked away, my emotions were in overdrive.

I placed my hand on his arm to stop him from continuing. He could tell I needed a moment. I grabbed the robe that was near, cinched it tight letting the sheet that was covering me fall away, and swung my legs over the side of the bed. I gave a head nod towards the restroom.

He began to lift me and I stopped him with a shake of my head. I could walk.

I saw in his eyes that he didn't like this, but I needed to get stronger. I needed to stand on my own two feet.

He followed closely behind me.

"Mom!" Gun shouted setting down a controller to the game that he was very obviously kicking Reggie's butt at. He rushed towards me, threw his arms around my waist, and declared, "You're up!"

I squeezed my arms around him and held him for a moment.

"Mom's gotta use the bathroom, Gun," Gunner said softly.

Gun dropped his arms, gave me a grin and said, "This game rocks!"

I did my best to grin back, even though it was forced, and made my way to the bathroom. Gunner attempted to follow me in, I put up a hand to stop him. I didn't want him to go in with me. I could do this on my own.

"Mouse," he ground out, but I ignored him and closed the door. I did my business and then looked in the mirror. The bruising on my face was yellowing, but it wasn't as bad as it was. My cheeks looked hollowed out, and my eyes had a look that would haunt me for a long time to come.

Suddenly, I wanted nothing more than to bathe. I couldn't shower. I didn't want to think about my showers in the dungeon, so I turned on the water for a bath and pushed the stopper. I dropped my robe to the floor and looked at my body in the mirror hanging on the back of the door. My ribs protruded a little and were covered in shades of yellow and blue. I moved to the side and saw my back, finally able to see the extent of the damage. A loud gasp escaped my throat.

"Charlie?" Gunner wanted to know if everything was okay. I needed to face this on my own. I turned the lock on the handle a moment before Gunner tried to come in. The gashes were healing. They were just more scars. I was already cut wide open on the inside, these just clued Gunner in on a little of the pain on the outside. What made me truly gasp was his initials--the ES, branded on my skin.

I wanted it off. I knew there was something there, but seeing those letters etched in my skin made me feel vile, like somehow, even in this bathroom, he still had a part of me. I sat in the warm water and grabbed a washcloth that was left hanging from the last person who used it. I didn't care. The water stung on my back. I didn't care about that either. I began to scrub. The harder I scrubbed, the more the water stung. Didn't care. I sobbed out loud. I wanted it gone.

I barely noticed the door shaking and the yelling from the other side. I needed to be clean. Sound was coming from me, I couldn't even register what I was saying, all I knew was that I needed him gone. I needed it gone. There was a loud crash and then the shower curtain was thrown open.

Gunner grabbed my shoulders and shook me once, then twice. I realized then that I was screaming, "Get him off of me! Get him off of me!" I scrubbed at my back as I rocked back and forth.

Next thing I knew, Gunner, still in his jeans, was in the tub crouched down in front of me. "Shh, Mouse. Shh. It's okay." He grabbed my wrists and pulled them in front of us. "As soon as it's healed completely, I'll either have a plastic surgeon take a look at it, or we'll get it tattooed. It won't be much longer, but you're destroying the good skin. You have to stop. Have to let it heal." His voice calmed me in the way that only Gunner's could.

I realized I was quiet again, and I was no longer screaming. I was staring into his hazel eyes, and could almost see the boy I once knew. He was different too. There was so much behind his eyes. There was the look he always gave me, that felt reserved for me, but there was pain there too.

Chapter Nineteen

Gunner

She spoke. It was pain-filled and broken, but it was her.

"Mouse, you're safe. He'll never come near you again. He'll never hurt you again. We'll get it taken care of," I tried to reassure her.

She shivered, and I let her wrist go to turn up the temperature of the water. "Let's get you washed since you're in here, yeah?" I grabbed the wash cup I left in here when I helped Gun with his hair. Teaching that boy to shower on his own was definitely on my priority list when this shit settled. I poured some water over her hair and grabbed the green shampoo bottle from the side of the tub. I took care with her scalp as I lathered, and then I pushed her hair over her shoulder so that when I rinsed not as much fell on her back.

Her beautiful nipples that were a shade between pink and brown peeked out from behind her knees that were drawn to her chest. My body, reflexively, began to react. Now was not the time, but even in her broken state, she was still the most beautiful woman I'd ever seen. I looked away and closed my eyes as my nostrils flared. I inhaled trying to will away my hard on. I opened them and accidentally caught a glimpse of her pink soft flesh between her legs, only there was dark bruising right alongside it. It was nearly black, and judging by how her other bruises already began to fade, these were the worst. My dick was instantly soft and I unconsciously gripped Charlie's arm. It was to steady myself, but then her worried eyes caught me by surprise. I loosened my grip and murmured, "Sorry." She caught the look in my eyes and I felt so much rage and then shame that she saw it. She didn't need my shit on top of what she was already dealing with, but it pained me to see it. I knew if I didn't let out this rage that was burrowing deep within me soon, something bad would happen.

I hurriedly finished her hair and got out. My jeans pooled water on the floor as I stripped them off and slung them over the shower curtain rod. My shirt was soaked through too, so I stripped that off leaving me standing in my boxer briefs. Charlie looked at me from the tub where she still sat, but she was no longer rocking, just staring. I'd given anything to know what she was thinking.

I grabbed a towel from the small closet and wrapped it around her, then threw her robe over her shoulders and scooped her up into my arms. Without being prodded, she brought her arms around my neck to hold on.

In the hallway, I saw Shane and he nodded to the empty spot where Gun had been sitting "Reggie brought him outside as soon as he heard you." I gave him a chin lift, and hurried Charlie into our room.

I laid her down on the bed, and pulled the blanket over both of us. Under the covers, I kicked off my briefs. I didn't care that I was naked next to her. It came naturally. I didn't even think. I just stripped myself bare, so I wouldn't soak her and then held her. Terrycloth separated our bodies. She relaxed into me, while my body was strung tight. I knew when I'd found her hanging from the wall that hell had been unleashed on her, but it wasn't until seeing those dark bruises that I really grasped it. The not-so-funny-thing was that I'd seen her naked already, but maybe my mind wasn't ready to admit what I was looking at. She fell asleep and not long after began to thrash. I hooked my leg over hers and squeezed her tight, only her thrashing jostled her towel loose and then my naked body was pressed against hers. I froze, not wanting to scare her. What if she woke and my dick was pressed against her thigh? I didn't really get much of a choice because she calmed almost immediately and then after another few minutes of her sleeping soundly she hooked a leg on top of mine. We became a tangled mess of limbs. I wanted to sleep and savor the feeling of finally having her in my arms. I wanted to put my mouth on her skin and wake her during the night like I'd dreamed of so many times doing. I wanted a lot of things, but life was a cruel bitch, dealing me a hand I didn't know how to play. I wasn't piecing her back together. I didn't know what I was doing, but it wasn't that. I was the dumb motherfucker who caused this, from one bad decision to the next. I wanted to stay with her all night like that, but I waited until she was in an even deeper sleep, then I unhooked my legs and slid away from her, careful not to wake her.

I got dressed and watched over her for a few more minutes before leaving her. Inside the kitchen, I saw a bottle of Crown. I didn't bother with a glass, but untwisted the cap and gulped it back. My son was on the couch asleep, and Ace stared at me from the darkened room.

"Not going to fix shit with that, and you know it."

I ignored him and took another gulp, "Need to do something."

"Not that," he nodded towards the bottle knowing that this was a slippery slope for me, and one I wanted to slide down. I wanted to fall away and not have any of this shit that I had going on to be real. I wanted to escape it.

"Fine. Need you to look after them for me, then." I grabbed my vest and took off. Outside, I opened my phone. I knew the lay of the land, knew the closest place to find a fight. There was one not but twenty minutes from here. I dialed Dimitri. "I'm in tonight. You get me a big ass motherfucker that won't fall easily."

Dimitri, the ever happy to do business with me Russian motherfucker, smiled into the phone. I could actual feel his fucking smile. I'd just made him a lot of money tonight. I'd thrown a leg over my bike when Shane caught up with me. I shot him a look that said leave me the fuck be.

"Where the fuck do you think you're going?"

"I need a few fucking hours," I snapped.

"So, what? You're going to get plastered while your woman and kid are going through hell?"

"Nope, I'm going to do that other thing I'm really fucking good at. I'm going nuts in there and if I don't let it out…"

"I get it. I'll come."

189

"No, need you here. No offense, but I need to do this alone."

He eyed me, "Don't think you going in alone when we're dealing with this shit, Brother."

"Fine, then send Donny and Knuckles with me. They'll have my back, and the two people I trust more than anything will be here to watch over my family.

He didn't want to give in, but I didn't really give a fuck. I saw it on his face when he decided to let me be "Fine, I'll get them."

A short while later, Knuckles, Donny and I were pulling into a warehouse in a podunk hillbilly town in PA. I knocked on the back door, that didn't look like an entrance, but was the only entrance that actually worked in this place. In my fighting days, I was here often enough, and even though it had been some time since I'd been on the circuit, I needed it tonight.

The crowd was thick, men huddled around in the dimly lit warehouse. In the middle of the cavernous room, a circle was spray painted on the ground, giving the men in the makeshift ring their barriers as they danced around each other waiting for the next hit to come. The fighters were lightweights, at best. Both men looked scrappy, but in their own way, were tough.

A minute of watching them had me placing a bet on the smaller one, McGuinness. He wore typical Irish flag shorts. He was getting knocked around by the faster fighter, Thompson. Odds were favoring Thompson, but I had an eye. I didn't even plan on placing any bets, but McGuiness had that look in his eyes that said he was hungry. It said he needed this win. It said he had something to lose. Whoever said a man with nothing to lose was dangerous was a dumb ass. The real danger was a man who had everything to lose. He would fight to hell and back. He would do anything to make sure that what he had was protected. He was the dangerous opponent. Yeah, my money was on him.

Thompson threw a hard right connecting with my guy's jaw. It was the moment I was waiting for. Every fighter has a limit, that is, if they're good. This was his. His stance changed, and then it was a new fight. A fight where the scrawny underdog showed the room what he was made of. Showed me what he was made of considering I dropped ten Gs on him.

A minute later, the room was shocked. Men were cursing. A few were shouting. McGuiness won by knockout.

Dimitri smacked me on the back and in a thick accent said, "You always did have a good eye. Whole room bet against him. You just made a fortune."

I pulled my shirt overhead and handed it to Knuckles. "You taping up?" he asked taking a pull on his Budweiser.

"Not tonight."

Dimitri laughed. His laugh was more like a cackle that men stopped to see what would follow. "Gentleman, bloodhounds, scoundrels alike. Tonight, I have a fighter for you that hasn't been in this ring for a very long time, but I can promise you, he's every bit as lethal as the last time he was here. Who will fight him?" He paused and looked around the room, "You?" he asked stopping at a man who fought often, a man I'd fought in the past.

"Not tonight," the man shook his head.

"I'll take a piece of him," A large man that had to be at least six-five said, stepping out of the shadows. This was all choreographed.

Dimitri knew exactly who I was fighting. He did it for the crowd. "Bull, so nice of you to step up." Dimitri's man started taking bets as I eyed Bull. We stood in the circle on the floor. The last fighters, long gone.

One of Dimitri's men took bets. I was smaller than Bull. The crowd was familiar with him, not me. He was clearly favorited. Bring it on.

This wasn't a professional match where a ref would stop us after so many minutes. Nope, this was the type of fight that you didn't walk away from easily. Rules were for pansies. We didn't kill each other, at least not intentionally, other than that, everything goes.

Bull was tall, broad shoulders, with a scar ran down his chest like he'd been split open before. His stance wasn't necessarily of a fighter and the way he circled me, I realized he most likely won based on size and force. He took up more space in the ring than me, but not by much. He was only a few inches taller than me. His arms were bigger, but that didn't mean much. He was the first to strike. It was intentional on my part. I liked to know right upfront what my opponent brought. When his right hook connected, it was a fucking force. He hit like a truck.

I let him get two more hits in. Truth was, I wanted the pain. I felt like I deserved it. Every time he struck me, the crowd went wilder. They thought he was going to be their big payoff. They thought fucking wrong.

Bull moved to hit me in the ribs. I ducked, swept my leg out, and a split second later, I took the legs out from under their mighty Bull. The room took on a murmur instead of a roar. I could've jumped on Bull and ended the fight. I didn't. I let him get up so that I could knock him down again. The second time he was a bit more prepared for it, so I changed tactics and hit him with a quick throat punch before knocking him down again. I could see he was beginning to get pissed.

While down, he lunged for my legs. I kicked and he grabbed my ankle. Using my other leg, I kneed the big fucker in his face. His head lulled to the side, and then all too soon, I let my rage out. I beat the motherfucker until they were pulling me off and raising my arms. I was declared the victor as more grumbles from the crowd ignited, because between me and McGuiness, tonight they were losing their wallets.

Dimitri clapped me on the back with a smile. "Thank you, I knew you'd win that one," he said to me, then raised my arm, "Ladies and gentleman, one of the best fighter's you will ever see, Gunner the hitman!" I gave a quick shake of my head because that name was stupid.

Fifteen minutes later, I was tilting back a beer , letting that ice cold Budweiser hit the back of my throat. Knuckles laughed beside me, "Never saw you quite like that."

Donnie shook his head, "You got it all out?"

I looked at my already bruising fist. "Don't know if I'll ever get it all out."

Knuckles sobered and sat up straighter.

Dimitri walked up with a small scowl on his face. "Thirty-five G's on the first fight, and your fight? Holy shit, man. What the fuck?" Alright, so we bet pretty fucking heavy.

I eyed him up and down, deciding an ally wouldn't be a bad thing. "I'll tell you what. You pay me my payout for the kid, and I'll let my fight go provided I get a marker."

Dimitri rubbed his chin and thought on this for a moment, then smiled, reached out his hand to shake mine, and said, "Deal."

Knuckles and Donnie followed me out. We threw our legs over our bikes and started the ride back. Thoughts of my Charlie before she was broken, plagued me. No, that wasn't quite right. She had always been kind of broken. I looked past how broken she used to be and saw it as her unique perfection. She was able to take her shit life, and still come out shining. I didn't want to see all of the pain she'd endured, when she was so young. It hurt to see something so beautiful, so damaged. So now, when she was really truly fucked, well now, it broke me too. I was used to being broken, I'd been in fucking pieces for so long. I just needed to keep a lid on my shit at least enough that I could carry Charlie's weight. Coming here to fight might have helped with my rage, but the more I thought about leaving my family, the more fucked up I knew I was. That ring wasn't where I belonged, and my brothers knew it. I was just so caught up in my rage that I had to get it out the only way I knew how. I needed to trust in what they had to say to me, because it wasn't just me anymore.

Chapter Twenty

Charlie

I blinked. The room was dark and I was cold. I didn't have the same heat at my back that I was becoming accustomed too. I was alone, but something had woken me, and then I heard it.

"Mom, don't go. Momma, stay."

"Shh, boy. It's just a dream."

His sobs followed and I couldn't lay here while my son fell apart. I shot out of bed, quickly tied the robe around me, and then left the room to find my son being consoled by one of Gunner's friends. Gunner wasn't here and my sweet boy was being comforted by someone I didn't know.

I'd been beaten down before.

I'd been broken.

But it wasn't about me. My son needed me.

Acting on pure adrenaline, I took him from the tattooed biker and scooped him up in my arms. He was heavier, or I was weaker than I realized either way, I didn't care. I held him to me. I attempted to walk back to the room but my tattered body wouldn't let me. I plopped us down into the nearest recliner desperate to not drop him.

"Shh," I purred. It was that simple sound that had my son look up at me and quiet his tumultuous mind. I couldn't think about anything, but Gun. I couldn't think about my trauma, or my body. I couldn't think about what I'd been through. I needed to get my shit together, because it wasn't just me. Gun needed me. He is what I held on to while I was in that hell. He is who I'd prayed to have in my arms again, and he is who needed me right now.

"Mom," he sucked in sharp breaths as he cried, "Don't leave me."

"I'm here," I whispered and then I began to hum to him. It was soft and quiet. I hummed "Amazing Grace." It was something I'd done plenty of times for him. I was lost in the moment and didn't hear the door. I was focused on my son, rocking him and holding him like he was much younger than his seven-year-old self. He needed so much. I hated what that sick fuck did to me, but I hated him even more for what he did to my son. No boy should have to lose his mother. I knew what it was like to lose the only person in your world. He must've been so afraid.

A hand on my shoulder had me looking up in surprise. Gunner was standing there. He bent low, leaning over us. He smelled of alcohol and cigarettes. Sweat and gasoline. The room was dim and my boy still rocked in my arms while I continued humming. Gunner pressed his head to mine. The feel of his forehead against my own was a comfort I had long forgotten. My son didn't flinch, or move when he felt Gunner at his back. It was like my son accepted his comfort on a subconscious level.

I finished the verse and Gunner lifted Gun from my arms. I looked up at him stunned by the ease with which Gun went to him. He held out his hand for me, which even in the dark I could tell was bruised and swollen. "He been up for a while?"

I shook my head not using my voice and clasped my hand in his. We walked quietly to the bedroom and I noticed his friend trying to give us privacy by not looking our way as he hung back in the kitchen.

The room was the same room I awoke in not ten minutes before, but somehow, now it seemed different. Everything that felt muted before now seemed more alive Moonlight filtered through the lone window. The wooden beams of the log cabin were a stark contrast to the black headboard that seemed to take up an entire wall. It was a masculine space, but somehow with the small nightstand and intricate woodwork, it felt almost homey. Gunner laid Gun down in the middle of the bed, and only once he laid him down did he notice the tears still streaming from Gun's eyes.

I couldn't hide in myself any longer. Gun needed so much. He needed his parents, both of us. "He had a bad dream," I admitted out loud, speaking to Gunner for the first time. His eyes were the only thing that gave away his surprise.

"That true, kid? Something shake you?"

I sat down on the edge of the bed as Gunner stood above us. Gun eyed me, and then moved in close, and put his arm around my waist.

"Baby, it's okay. I'm not going anywhere."

"Kid," Gunner spoke as he sat down on the other side of Gun. "Told you I'd bring her back to you, yeah?"

When Gun didn't answer him, he prompted again, "Didn't I?"

Gun lifted his head from my lap, "Yeah, Dad."

My heart clenched at hearing Gun say dad.

"I promised you, right?"

"You did."

"Well, I'll make another promise to you, and I always keep my promises. Nothing is going to happen to your mom. I won't let it. I promise."

He nodded his head accepting Gunner's promise, then placed his head back in my lap. I stroked the side of his head and it wasn't long before he drifted off.

Once asleep, Gunner placed Gun under the blankets and then grabbed my hand, walked me to the other side of the bed, climbed in next to Gun, and laid down saying, "Climb in with me. Need you near, but I don't want to leave him."

I did as he said and laid down beside him facing him. "God, let me hear your voice, Mouse."

I swiped my thumb along his bruised cheek, "You're hurt."

He sighed like it was the best sound he'd ever hear. "I'm fine."

"Where'd you go?" I asked and was met with the same question from Gunner, "Where'd you go?"

What a loaded question. Which time. Where did I go when my momma was getting high, and left me as her life drained? Where did I go when he left me young and pregnant? Where, after the foster home from hell? Where, after Enrico raped me? Where, after I was almost killed?"

I blinked unsure of the answer he wanted me to give. Noticing my internal dialogue, Gunner answered my question. "I fight. Used to do it all the time. Now, I do it when I need a release. Seeing you like that. Jesus. I wanted to break something. That's not even the right way to describe it. I want to kill someone. I want to find that sick fucker and not only kill him, but I want to destroy anything he ever gave two shits about. Can't do that and keep you safe, so, I found a fight and I fought." He shrugged his shoulders like no big deal. The heat from his skin radiated like a warm blanket. One would think after everything I'd been through that I wouldn't want a man to be near me, but this wasn't just a man. He was the only man. I'd never felt safe or loved except for Gunner, and then Gun. He was a part of me.

"Did you win?" I looked down feeling shy.

Gunner's slightly swollen knuckles lifted my chin, "What do you think?" His voice almost had a rasp to it, and part of me wanted to press my lips to his, but then the shame of everything my body had been through washed over me.

"I think if I remember your temper correctly, then he never had a chance."

He smirked, "It's nice to hear your voice." And then Gunner leaned forward and pressed his lips to my head, "Get some sleep. Yeah?"

I moved my arm around his waist and burrowed deep into his chest. Today was a hard day. Tomorrow would be better. I'd be better.

Chapter Twenty-One

Gunner

My God! Her voice! What a sweet sound. I laid awake with her in my arms, feeling like I could finally breathe. Even though she was frail, and her body was broken, there was something about her that gave me the peace that no amount of fighting, drinking, or sex could've ever given me.

I woke up when I heard Gun stir. Charlie was still sleeping. I peeled myself from her arms and sat up. I put my finger over my lips to shush Gun. I didn't want to wake her. She looked peaceful.

Gun followed me into the kitchen where Shane and Reggie sat drinking coffee. "You want some cereal?" I looked at Gun wondering how he was today.

"Any more Lucky Charms?" he asked telling me he wasn't letting last night get him down.

"Saved you a bowl," Shane said sliding the box down the counter, "This dipshit would've eaten it all." Shane shot Reggie a look that said, told you we needed to save some.

I poured him a bowl, then poured two cups of coffee. I liked mine black, but had no idea how she would take hers. I guessed she at least liked milk, but I had no idea, seeing as she was sixteen the last time I'd spent any real time with her. That thought made me angry. There was so much about her that I didn't know. Like the way she took her fucking coffee.

"I wish Lucky Charms was reversed," Gun said between bites, quickly snapping me out of my anger.

"What do you mean?"

"I mean, I wish it was like mostly marshmallows and just a little bit of the crispy cereal."

"Right on," Reggie laughed fist bumping my kid. I shook my head. When did he teach him to fist bump?

Shane got my attention, "How's she doing?"

"She talked last night, so we're making progress."

"And last night? Heard you didn't go easy."

I shrugged, "Do I ever?"

"I guess not. The guys were happy, walked out with a shit ton of money."

"There was a fighter last night, name's McGuiness. When this shit blows over, we should talk to him. Don't know if he rides or not, but he's got that look."

Shane knew exactly what type of look I was talking about considering we had seen it so many times in prospects eyes. He nodded his head in understanding.

"Going to bring this to your momma. You good?" I asked Gun.

He moved his spoon around his bowl searching for marshmallows and said, "Sure," in a peppy voice.

I walked down the hall and was surprised to see Charlie sitting up with my t-shirt pulled over her head.

She saw me and smiled. Actually, fucking smiled. I would've done anything for that smile and here it was so freely given.

"Where's Gun?" she asked like it was the most natural thing in the world for her to speak.

"Eating cereal with Shane and Reggie. He's in good hands. I brought you coffee. Didn't know how you liked it. So, there's some cream. I can get you sugar, if you want?" I rambled nervously. Why the hell was I nervous? It was just coffee.

"Coffee's good." She reached her hand out to take the mug from me and I took full advantage brushing my fingers over hers capturing her eyes, not daring to look away.

"He looks like you, doesn't he?" she broke the spell.

"I didn't even have to find out his name to know he was mine, spitting fucking image. I got to know Charlie, what happened after I left. I searched for you for years, I couldn't find you. Hell, I got connections and no one could find you. You turned into a fucking ghost."

She sighed, "I need to get out of this room. Do you think you can get me some pants, and maybe we can walk?" As much as I didn't want her walking around, I got how she could be stir crazy.

"One of the old ladies dropped off some clothes."

"Old ladies? How many people are here?"

"There's four cabins and a bunch of families are bunked up in those. Most of the single brothers are in the tents. There's about forty people here, in all."

"Wow," she breathed in amazement that there were so many people here.

"There's another bedroom off the living room. Shane and Ace are bunking up in there, and Reggie who's taken a liking to Gun, stays on the couch."

"Where are we?"

"We picked this property up a few years ago. Bought it through a shell company, so it can't be traced back to us. No one knows we're here."

"Oh, okay," she answered like it was too much too soon.

"I'll get you some pants." I left the room and saw Gun curled up on the couch with Reggie on the other side. On the television, cartoons played and I watched Gun chuckle, his little body shaking. In a bag next to the door, there was a stack of clothes that Roxanne, one of the old ladies, had dropped off. I brought them into Charlie, and didn't look away or give her privacy as she pulled up the jeans that were sizes too big. Maybe that made me a dick after everything she'd been through, but I didn't care. I always thought of her as mine and giving her privacy would've felt like I was admitting she wasn't. She slipped her feet into a pair of Uggs that she'd pulled from the bag and I asked again, "You sure you're up to walking?"

"Yeah."

"Well, it's kind of chilly. Wear this." I handed her my sweatshirt that was almost like a dress on her. Our Bleeding Scars logo spread across the back.

We walked out of the bedroom, but her slight painful stance made me hesitate going outside, but I knew she needed this.

I ruffled Gun's head as we passed. He looked up and his eyes got big when he saw Charlie dressed and walking around.

"Mom! You're up."

"Gunner and I are going to go for a walk. When I get back, how about you tell me what you've been up to since I've been gone?"

He anxiously nodded his head, and I put my hand on the small of Charlie's back guiding her outside.

The air outside was cool. Even cooler evenings left the trees all shades of reds, yellows, and oranges. Fires that had been constantly stoked still burned big. Various camping chairs with brothers, and some of their family members surrounded them. It was early, but to many of these guys, this was like a huge camping trip with their loved ones.

The cabin we stayed in was the largest of the four and was slightly more secluded than the rest. The other cabins were clustered together closer to a small lake. In the distance, I could see two teenage boys casting out a fishing line. Tents were crammed together, and as we silently walked past, snoring cut through the air. Walking past the final tent in the cluster, moaning and skin slapping against skin drowned out the snores. I checked to see Charlie's reaction. There wasn't one. She ignored it. Looking at her as she walked beside me, she was the same closed off Mouse that I'd met when we were so young.

I grabbed her hand and led us to a small path that ran along the lake. "Can you tell me what happened after you left the neighborhood?" I had to break the silence. I needed to know.

She walked a few more steps, then paused and stared out at the water. "I went to another foster home." She bent low, picked up a rock and threw it into the water. I didn't like how she seemed to be holding back.

"After that, I stayed in some shelters. I eventually got a place."

"Hold up," I interrupted her account because it was riddled with holes.

"What happened at the foster home?"

"They were religious freaks. I couldn't stick around."

"Charlie," I said her name, cutting her off. She was leaving out something huge. I could tell. "Don't sugar coat shit for me."

"Fine," she said with more fierceness than I'd heard from her. "You want to know? You sure about that? 'Cause once I tell you, I can't take that back. You'll know."

"Charlie," I was agitated. I needed to know.

"Your baby was in me and these bible thumpers, who thought their twin sons were holier than thou, let it happen. It happened once."

"What happened?" I struggled to hold onto my temper. I had the sick feeling I knew what she was going to say.

Chapter Twenty-Two

Charlie

"They raped me! Is that what you want to hear? They held me down and raped me. But you know what? The second time they tried, I was ready. I stole a gun and waited for them to try something. They weren't expecting me to defend myself. I shot the brothers, took their parent's car and money, then got the fuck out of there. I ditched the car. Hitched a ride with a trucker and stayed in shelters for a while until I stole someone's ID, and used that to get into the system. I didn't have much, but I eventually got into the system. You couldn't find me because I was hiding.

"I worked at clubs under the table and had been working at The Select Club for a while. I did all right. Not to say that Gun and I had it easy, but I got us by. I wasn't going to do it forever. We had a life, maybe not an awesome one, but it was okay," I finished. I hadn't even looked at Gunner to gage his response. I didn't know if he'd look at me differently for shooting those boys. I didn't know if he would pity me. I bent low and grabbed a pretty leaf that had fallen and I twirled it by the stem in my fingers. It calmed me and I needed that. My beating heart felt like it might explode in my chest. I wasn't even talking yesterday, and today I divulged things that I'd never admitted to anyone before.

I heard a flick of a lighter and then lifted my eyes to see Gunner pulling smoke into his lungs as his cherry glowed red hot. He was breathing in deep breaths. Like he needed to control himself too.

"I met them. I fucking met those people. I questioned them myself. Their sons were at football practice, but the mom and dad, they answered every question I asked about you. They told me you were only there a week, and then you were moved to another foster home. Fuck!" He gritted his teeth and took another long drag from his smoke. "I can't believe those Jesus freaks got one over on me. They're dead. All of them."

I wanted to argue with him and tell him that he didn't need to do that for me, but there were much bigger monsters for us to be concerned with.

He stomped out his smoke, his black boot grinding into the dirt. And then he did something I wasn't expecting. He grabbed me, pulled me into his arms and hugged me. His body was so large against mine that I felt cocooned as his broad arms enveloped me. We stood that way for an infinite amount of time. At least it felt that way. After a while, Gunner pulled away, "We should get back. You've been standing for a while. You need to heal."

I nodded, even though I hadn't felt my pain until he brought attention to it. We cut through the woods this time and were much closer to the cabin than I'd first thought. Gun was standing by a fire pit, laughing with a few other kids. After his bad dreams last night, I was fearful that he'd be damaged, but he seemed like he was okay.

Inside, I followed Gunner into the kitchen where he opened the fridge. "How about we get you some lunch?"

I nodded again. I was still quiet, but it felt good that Gunner knew where I'd been. I supposed we didn't need to get into what Enrico did to me. He found me hanging near death, so he probably had a pretty good idea.

"Ham and Cheese alright?"

"Yeah, thanks." I sat down on the stool and watched as Gunner made lunch and then set mine down on a plate and then called for Gun out the front door of the cabin. It all seemed so natural the way Gunner was with Gun.

"Knew you'd be a good dad," I said to Gunner once he returned. "I'd daydream about it. Pretend we were a family."

"We are a family," he sternly gritted out.

"Just like that?"

Gun came barreling into the cabin and raced up to us throwing his arms around my waist

and then pulled himself up on the seat next to me. He didn't wait. He just started eating, like my kid was a ravenous beast.

"Slow down. You'll give yourself a stomachache." It came out naturally for me to scold him and I think Gun appreciated it. He smirked and then looked up at me and began to take his time.

Gunner eyed us and after a few minutes began to eat. "Yeah, Mouse. Just like that."

I wanted to talk more about it, but didn't feel like it was the right time with Gun right next to us. As brave as I felt this morning, my body began screaming at me the longer I sat and ate, so after a few more bites, and once I was sure that Gun had sufficiently eaten enough food, I excused myself to lay down.

"Ma, I thought we were going to talk?"

"Kid, she's tired you can catch up after she's napped. Yeah?"

He thought about it for a few minutes and then agreed, followed by him moving to the couch and grabbing a controller.

Just then a few of Gunner's brothers walked in from the outside.

"Sleeping Beauty awakes," one of the guys said, and Gunner began making introductions.

"Charlie, this is Donnie. The fool on the couch is Reggie."

"Hey!" he flipped off Gunner, then said, "I'm awesome. Nice to meet you, Charlie."

"These two are Ace and Shane. We started this club together. Their family."

"Hi," I waved timidly.

"They were with me, when we got you back."

"Oh," I looked down, ashamed. They'd seen what I'd been through too. "Thank you. Very nice to meet you. I was just on my way to lay down." I excused myself and had hoped Gunner would stay. That was a lot. It was exhausting, and I felt disgusting knowing that they had seen what happened to me. I moved as quickly down the hall as my broken body would let me and attempted to close the door, but Gunner was right there.

"What are you doing?" I asked.

"What's it look like I'm doing?" He grabbed my hand and lead me to the bed. "Come here, Mouse." I was conflicted because I needed space, but he wasn't going to give it to me. I could tell just by the look in his eyes. I felt like he could read all of my conflicting thoughts and was right there, not allowing me to succumb to any thoughts that could hurt me. We both seemed to know that sometimes the quiet in our own minds could be one of the biggest enemies.

He pulled me in tight and tucked my body against his, "Sleep."

I would've liked to say that I fell right to sleep. His body was comforting enough. "You're thoughts are screaming at me, Mouse. It doesn't matter that they saw you, all they see is how strong you were to hold on. You were alive, when most people would've given up."

I let a tear fall, and pushed those thoughts of them finding me out of my mind. "Will you tell me about how you met them?" Gunner began telling me about the first time he met Shane, and talked for awhile until my eyes felt heavy and sleep finally took me.

Chapter Twenty-Three

Gunner

It took everything in me to keep my anger in check around Charlie. I waited until her breathing evened out, and went in search of Ace and Shane. It didn't take me long. They both had their feet propped up on the coffee table and were watching Gun take Reggie in a combat game. My kid had skills.

They caught my eyes when I walked out. I tilted my head for them to follow me. We left the cabin and once we were alone, I gripped my head in my hands. "Fuck!"

"What did you find out? Ace asked.

"The first foster home she was at, twin brothers raped her. Psycho Jesus freaks."

Shane reacted first, "I'm with you."

Ace nodded in agreement. I wasn't going to order a hit without their okay. "Good," I sneered, then hit some buttons on my phone and dialed Dmitri.

"Twice in less than twenty-four hours. You got a hard on for me, or what?" He joked in his Russian accent.

"Using that marker already. I'll be texting you an address."

He sighed, "How many?"

"Four. And Dimitri?"

"Ya?"

"Make it hurt."

I hung up the phone and we went to touch base with the guys to see if anyone had heard anything. All of our intel had been extremely quiet. No one seemed to know a thing.

"I should hear back from my Colombian contacts today," Ace informed us.

"Let me know as soon as you do."

I went back into the cabin and rejoined Charlie in the bed. She was restless tossing and turning and the moment I pulled her in close she settled. A few hours later, she began to stir and as if the two were linked, Gun bounded into the room.

"Hey, baby," she murmured, "Come here. Tell me what you've been up to since I've been gone."

"Well, Dad and I picked out stuff for my room, and I got new video games, and I started school, and it's okay, but I liked my old one better cause I miss Mr's T. But my new teacher is nice, but they make us go outside all the time, and I don't always want to go outside," he rushed out.

"Slow down. Tell me about your room. What's it look like?"

"Captain America and Iron Man. My pillow even has superheroes on it."

The two rattled on catching me up on everything, and I mean everything they'd been up too. What a difference twenty-four hours makes.

Over the next week, this became our new routine. Charlie and I would talk. She'd spend time with Gun, and she'd rest. I cooked for them and took care of my family. I enjoyed this. Sometimes, I'd get angry when I'd hear a particularly horrible story of something Charlie went through. She'd get embarrassed and that made me even angrier. I didn't want her to be embarrassed. She did nothing wrong.

It was after a grueling afternoon that I finally lost my shit. It didn't help that most of the families had left earlier in the day. We hadn't heard anything about Enrico, and after a lot of debate, they decided to leave. We were going to be on high alert, but these guys had families they needed to provide for. Their kids had to get back to school. Their wives were sick of camping, so, they packed up and left, and we stayed. Even Ace and Shane left because our business needed them. The only other people who stuck around were Reggie, Donnie, and Knuckles. Reggie, because he had a connection with my kid and Donnie and Knuckles, because they always had my back, plus I think they liked camping.

Gun was fishing with Reggie, and Charlie and I were talking. She wanted to know about my connection with Enrico. "There's shit I can't tell you. We have a code, and there are certain things that are club business, and that's one of them."

I could see that she was annoyed with my answer, but I didn't expect her to give it to me the way she did. We were in the kitchen and Charlie, who was always quiet, slammed her mug down into the sink. It surprised me.

"You don't think I have a right to know?"

I put my hands up in front of me, "Not that you don't have a right, but we don't tell our women club shit. It's to protect you. If anyone ever asked you don't know shit. It's by design. If the cops sniffed around, then you got nothing to give them. This is just how it is," I explained calmly.

Her face reddened, "I told him 'fuck you' once." I froze this wasn't a story I'd heard yet.

"You know what he said back? He told me he missed me. Missed fucking my virgin ass."

"Stop." I gritted out. I couldn't hear this. Charlie didn't stop.

"I asked him why. I always asked him why, but today he answered me. And do you know what he said? He said he got word that I was something to someone. He said he knew who I belonged too, even if I didn't, and that he got to have the best toys. Not you."

"No!" I roared. This was all because of me.

She didn't flinch. She kept on, still so maddened by what happened to her, and I couldn't fucking blame her.

"So, you don't think I get to know why he took me. It's because I loved you, Gunner."

I couldn't take it. I deserved this. All of it. It was just all so brutal. My life's big fuck you to me. Destroy the only woman I ever loved, and make it all my fault. I had no idea how Enrico could've known about Charlie, but it was clear she blamed me. How could she ever love me after the hell she'd endured? She opened her mouth to say more, but I couldn't hear it. I couldn't hear anything. My chest was pounding. My heart was pounding and all I could think was that I needed to get the fuck away from her right then and there. I felt volatile. I was becoming unhinged, and I at least had the decency to know that Charlie didn't need to see it. This was my cross to bear and she had been nailed to it for my sins. I'd never hated myself more than in that second. So, I did the only thing I could do, I left.

Chapter Twenty-Four

Charlie

He left. I was going to say I still loved him, and that It didn't matter. I didn't blame him, but it's because of what Enrico said that I felt I had the right to know. When he said I didn't get to know, it made me angry, but I shouldn't have lashed out the way I had.

I walked out of the cabin to go after him, but he was already starting his bike and driving away. I felt a deep pang in my chest. A trail of dust followed as he drove away from the cabins. Away from me.

I sighed. What could I do? It's not like I could go after him. I decided to shower in hopes that after I freshened up, he'd return. When I left the bathroom, Gun was playing with Reggie. "Do you have any kids?" I asked him as a momentary thought. He seemed like he'd make a good dad. He was young though, early twenties. But so was I.

He paused for a second. Pain flashed in his eyes. "Nope," his normal jovial demeanor was replaced with nothing. His face turned into a mask of impenetrable indifference. He didn't want to talk about whatever feeling kids evoked.

"I didn't mean to be intrusive. Gunner left, But I'm sure he'll be back soon." I explained as I sat down in the recliner. Not that he needed me to tell him. It was obvious that Gunner wasn't here.

A little while later, Donnie and Knuckles joined us in the cabin. Sometimes, the two would join us, but mostly they stuck to themselves. I was surprised to see them. Both of them looked drunk as they stumbled into the cabin.

"You got anything to eat around here?" Knuckles asked.

"Man, if you open the fridge you'll see I have a whole tenderloin marinating," Donnie answered. "Had to wait til the rest rolled out. This shit is going to be awesome."

"I'll make potatoes," Knuckles added, "You guys like steak?"

"Heck yeah," Gun replied as he threw his entire body to the left with the movement of his remote control.

"That'd be nice, thanks."

"Where'd Gunner ride out too?" Donnie asked.

I had to tell them, I didn't want too, but I knew they should know. "We were talking about something that happened, and he got ticked and left."

"How mad?" Knuckles grabbed a beer from the fridge while he waited for my response.

He waited for me to answer and he watched me closely, "Pretty mad."

"Fuck!" Donnie yelled.

Both men's happy demeanor changed immediately. They cooked and went about feeding everyone dinner, which was delicious, but they both took turns stepping outside to make calls.

Gun fell asleep on the couch and I covered him with a blanket and went to lay down in the room that I had gotten used to sharing with Gunner. Since I'd been here, there hadn't been a day that I'd fallen asleep without Gunner.

I changed my clothes into Gunner's black Bleeding Scars t-shirt. It was like a dress and had become my nightgown. As I changed, I looked at the yellow spots along my body. A few more days and my body would be mostly normal. Even my back had scabbed over pretty good. I was sure that it would scar, but it was nothing compared to the disgusting branding that Enrico left behind. I got under the covers and stayed awake listened for hours for Gunner to return. The darkness in the room began to change from pitch black to muted grays when I finally fell asleep. Gunner never returned.

I woke up late afternoon and he still wasn't back. It hurt. After the hurt wore off, fear set in. What if something happened to him? What if he left our safe hideaway because I made him think I blamed him, and Enrico found him? I hadn't seen Donnie and Knuckles today, but Reggie was being awesome Reggie.

"Mom, want to fish with us?" Gun asked.

"Yeah, I can do that." I didn't want to disappoint Gun and I'd missed him. I missed living. Besides my walks with Gunner, I'd barely left the cabin.

"Great, I dug up a bunch of night-crawlers. I can hook it for you, if you want." Gun rambled on excitedly as I walked to the lake with him and Reggie. Standing on the shore, with just a few of us left here, I could see how big this place was. When it was filled with people, I'd failed to see all of its beauty. The sun was casting a warm glow along the colorful trees.

"It's beautiful," I said to no one in particular.

Gun caught a big fish. Reggie had to help him reel it in. I didn't really fish, just sat there with my hook in the water and enjoyed how beautiful it was here.

Gun was so excited when they threw the fish in a cooler. He threw his arms around Reggie and hugged him. I wished Gunner was here.

"Thank you, Reggie," I said as I walked beside him on our way back to the cabin.

"That one was all on him. I just helped a little," He winked at Gun.

"You know what I mean," I nudged his shoulder. "Thank you for taking care of him while I get better."

"My pleasure. He's a good kid. You've done good by him."

We reached the cabin and Reggie and Gun went to clean the fish. My heart sank when I saw that Gunner's bike was still gone. I'd secretly hoped that when we returned he'd be back.

●　●　●

It was late, Gunner had been gone for two nights. It was the third night without him, and I started to wonder if he would return. I was laying in bed, staring out the window. It was an overcast day, and the night seemed even more glum. There were no stars, just a haze of darkness staring back at me.

I heard a rumble and immediately shot up to see if it was him. Even through the darkness, I could see his large frame as he dismounted his bike. He lit a smoke, the flame illuminated his face. I watched him take a few hits and then he walked towards the cabin. I wasn't going to wait for him to come to me. I needed to know where he'd been. At this point, days of not hearing from him had me scared out of my mind. I'd started to play scenario after scenario of all of the things Enrico could've done to him, and I worried that I'd never see him again.

I slipped on the Uggs and grabbed a sweater, then rushed out to meet him. "Gunner! I said racing to him. "I'm sorry. I was so scared! I'm so glad you're okay." I threw my arms around his waist and hugged him, but was surprised when I was met with a different Gunner than the one who had left. This version of Gunner was cold. He didn't seem like the man I'd known and I felt responsible. He was stiff, not hugging me back. I pulled away from him to look into his face. It looked empty. I was angry. No fucking way was I going to let Enrico take Gunner from me.

"No, dammit!" I shoved his chest. "No." He seemed startled by my outburst and then he reached into his vest and pulled out an envelope. I was lost and went to shove him again, but he caught my hand and put the envelope in it.

"This is your money from your apartment, plus some. There's a passport for you and Gun in there. New names, new identities. I'll take you to the airport tomorrow. I want you to go somewhere. Start over. Start a new life. There's enough cash in there that you can start over anywhere and do pretty well. I want to see Gun still, so once you figure out where you want to go, there's an email in there for you to email an address too. I can't promise to come often, but I want to know him." He finished his speech like he'd been rehearsing it for a while. His face still seemed impassive.

"Swear to God! Are you fucking kidding me right now, Gunner?" I was angry, but not just that. I was gearing up to fight. I'd fought some ridiculously hard battles in my time, and there was no way I was losing this fight. So I gave it my all.

"If you wouldn't have left, you would've heard me tell you that I don't blame you. I feel like I should know what's happening, so that I can protect my family, just like your trying to do, because I swear to Christ Gunner, that's what you are." My voice was raised and I was so lost in my fury that I couldn't even care if Gun woke up. "If you had stuck around, I would've told you that you're my family. I asked you if it was easy for you to say that Gun and I were your family, because I needed to know that it was the same for you, because dammit, Gunner, it's you. It's always been you. You want to know what got me through when I was in hell? It was thoughts of you being a dad. Thoughts of our first time. Thoughts of how you and I would've been if life didn't always get in our way. I swear it, I fucking swear it, Gunner Reed, you're not going to let that sick bastard and what happened to me get in the way of us, of what we should've been. Of what we have always been. I won't take this money." I threw the envelope to the ground. "You want to make me bleed? You want to hurt me, then you push me away. But know this, you'll have been the one to cut me wide open. It will be you. I'm not taking that money. You want to rip our family…"

I couldn't continue on. I couldn't say anymore because Gunner slammed his lips on mine and lifted me off the ground.. I instinctively wrapped my legs around his waist and his hands palmed my ass. His tongue pushed in and swirled against mine. He tasted of whiskey and cigarettes. I didn't care. I kissed him back with everything in me. I kissed him like I'd never kissed a man, because the truth was, I

223

hadn't. We were young the last time we really kissed, and any other kiss I'd ever had was nothing compared to the way that Gunner owned my mouth. It was hot. It was searing. It was the electricity that finally jump started my heart after all this time. I kissed him and kissed him.

Hard.

Soft.

Slow.

Fast.

We were in a battle against everything that had happened to us, and we were finally winning.

Chapter Twenty-Five

Gunner

When I left a few days ago, I did what I normally did when shit was too tough to deal with. I found an underground fight and I fought. I beat three of the largest dude's asses I've ever seen, and it still wasn't enough. So, I drank until I was good and drunk. I spent the night in a dirty rundown motel, hating that I was away from my family. I couldn't stand the thought of sleeping away from Charlie, but I did it because somehow everything that happened to her was my fault. At first, I blamed myself because I'd joined Hades Runners and left her, I was working through that guilt, but knowing everything that vile Colombian prick did to her was my fault burned me to my core.

I spent the next two days making arrangements for Charlie and Gun. They needed money and new identities, if they were going to stay clear of any danger that being associated with me could bring. I also spent that time telling myself to shut off my emotions. I needed to do that for Charlie. If I was going to be able to let them go, because Lord knows, it was going to be the hardest thing I'd ever done, but I would do it for her.

What I wasn't expecting was that when I pulled up to the cabin after being away from Charlie without a word from me that she would show me a side to her I'd never seen. She poured her heart and soul into her words. I was supposed to fight her. I was supposed to do what was best for her. But hell if the moment she shoved me and then opened her mouth to tell me no didn't crack my resolve, then as soon as she said I was her family did. If I was the fucked up reason shit happened to her, then so be it. Family hurt each other, sometimes intentionally, and sometimes by circumstance. None of it mattered, she told me so. She was my family and even though I'd hurt her, the thing that the Bleeding Scars taught me was that no matter how thick or disgusting the scar, family always had each other's back. We just get to choose who our family is.

So I kissed her. I'd wanted to kiss her from the moment I rescued her in Colombia. It never felt right. I'd been holding back so that her wounds could heal. I wanted her to be ready. But fuck it. If she wasn't, it would just be another sin she'd need to forgive me for.

The moment my lips connected to hers, there was no saying goodbye. Not for me. Not ever. It was the sweetest, hottest kiss of my life. Her lips were so tender. When I slipped my tongue inside, the kiss became almost punishing. It was that good. I lifted her and those fiercely strong thighs that I'd seen hold on to the stripper pole, clung to my waist. I didn't even really need to hold her up. I took advantage and palmed her ass. It was delicious and full, despite the fact that she still needed to put on more weight. I'd become, in that instant, an addict.

Maybe that wasn't right, maybe I'd always been and this was that first hit after years of abstinence.

I could feel the swell of her breasts against my chest. She smelled like my shampoo, even though I knew there was girly shit in the shower, she used what I used. Her nails began to press into my back as our kiss deepened. My dick raged against my jeans. It would be so easy to move aside her underwear and fuck her against a tree. I wanted too, but not tonight.

"Mmm, Mouse. You have the sweetest fucking lips." I pulled away from her lips but only so I could suck the skin on her neck. She arched into me.

"Gunner," she whimpered.

I needed more of her. I wanted to rip her clothes off of her. Her nipples were rock hard, straining under my t-shirt. I could feel her warm breath hitting my shoulder and I knew it was too cold to stay outside. I bent low with her wrapped around me, retrieved the envelope, then carried her into the cabin.

"Gun?" I silently asked.

"In the bedroom. He's on one bunk, Reggie's on the other."

"Good," I walked us into our room and closed the door behind us. Setting her on the bed, I kicked off my boots, slid my vest off, and tore my hooded sweatshirt off. She watched me with hooded eyes. I caged her in. My large arms were on each side of her body. I needed her to pay attention to what I had to say.

"This is it then? No going our separate ways?"

"I'm right here, aren't I?"

"No matter how tough shit gets?"

"No matter how tough," she mirrored my words.

I leaned into her. My nose trailed against her neck. I didn't kiss her but I was only a hair's breath away. She could feel the heat as the air left my lungs when I spoke to her. It caused tiny goosebumps to form. "This is the only time I'm going to bring up what happened to you when were together like this." I watched her throat as she gulped. "He doesn't come in here between us. When I touch your body, you think of me and you. You think of how good it feels when my cock is buried inside of you. You think of the way you feel when my dick hits the back of your throat, or the way you feel when my fingers are buried in your sweet fucking cunt, and I suck the hell out of your pussy. What you don't think about is him. He has no place in here with us. This is my body. It's always been mine, and I'm not about to be buried deep in you, if he's in here with us."

"Gunner," she sighed my name.

I reached my hand between her legs and pushed her panties aside. "Your pussy's wet for me." I slid it over her clit and swirled my fingers causing her to moan.

"Are we agreed?"

She grabbed my hand that was touching her and stilled it. "When he was hurting me, I'd go to a place in my head. I'd think of you or Gun. He didn't have me then, and he sure as shit doesn't get me now."

I sucked in a breath, "Do you know how incredibly fucking strong you are?" I didn't wait for an answer I didn't need one. "Let me see your body, Mouse."

She kicked off the Uggs and I pulled the sweater off her arms and she made quick work of pulling my t-shirt over her head. I sucked in a sharp breath. Her dark nipples on her ample breasts made my dick throb. I hadn't fucked anyone, since I'd found Charlie in the strip club. My cock swelled with the knowledge that I'd be inside of her soon.

I took her lips again kissing her so hard, they were sure to bruise. My thumb skimmed over her nipple making it bud and then my hand returned to its place between her legs. "We need to get rid of these too."

"If I'm losing mine, you should lose yours too." She looked down for a moment as if she herself was taken aback by her boldness. I sure as hell was.

I did exactly like she said and flicked the button on my jeans and then pulled down the zipper. I watched her eyes as they became hooded. There was no sign of fear. Even though I told her he had no place here, I was still concerned for her. I rid myself of my jeans and briefs and watched her lick her lips as my dick sprung free. I grabbed the edge of her white cotton underwear. She lifted her hips so I could slide them off of her. "Fuck," I hissed.

Her beautiful pussy showed a subtle glimpse of pink hiding behind her lips, gave me the overwhelming desire to beat my chest, caveman style, and shout, "mine". It was so perfect. So delicious looking. "Need to taste you."

Her eyes pleaded with me to do it.

I kissed her neck again. Her hands moved over my body exploring my expansive chest. I smirked a cocky grin as her eyes widened when she wrapped her hand around my dick. Her hands slid up and down my thick shaft as I brought her nipple into my mouth and sucked on the tight bud. She moaned, a pleasure filled moan. I loved how responsive she was to me. I moved down her body and she was forced to let go, over me. I kissed her stomach and then finally I found that sweet spot.

I spread her legs and parted her folds, letting my tongue tease around the edge, and then made it to her center. I swirled my tongue in her small hole, then began flicking her clit with my tongue and alternated between that and suction. I pushed my finger inside of her while I continued eating her tight pussy. She moaned and withered. I got no inclination from her that her head was anywhere but right here. I added another finger, curling them just right. Her hands found my hair and pushed my head down as she began thrashing back and forth. She came apart and clenched around my fingers. I lapped at her and pulled my face up, "Still the sweetest thing I ever tasted."

Her chest heaved. Her eyes were dilated and she gripped my shoulders pulling me up to kiss her. My girl, she was always so quiet until I was touching her, and then she became bold. It was one of the biggest turn-ons. The way she didn't hesitate to take my lips even though her musk was all over my tongue. I usually was the one in control, but the way she kissed me was filled with so much passion. I unleashed something within her. Something that I didn't realize until that kiss that she'd needed just as badly as I did.

"I want you," those blue doe eyes were heady and lust filled as she brazenly told me her desires.

I searched for any indication of fear. I didn't doubt that she wanted me, but the last thing I wanted to do was to sink inside of her, and have her be reminded of what happened to her.

As if sensing my reason for hesitation, she placed her palm against my face, "I'm right here with you. The only place I was ever meant to be."

That's what I needed to hear, because maybe what happened to her, happened to me too. Not in the physical pain, but her pain became my pain. I needed to heal too.

So I did.

I moved my arms around her. Her legs spread around the back of my thighs and my hard dick pressed against her soft, soaked center. She moaned before I even entered her. Just the feel of my shaft against her perfect little pussy had her grinding against me. With a quick lift of my hips, I positioned myself and then slid inside of her.

"Yes," she moaned.

She was a cocoon of warmth and tightness.

"You feel so good." I slowly moved my hips up and down getting a good rhythm. I didn't want to go too fast. I didn't need to rush it. I braced myself with both arms so our faces weren't touching and I stared at her. I was in awe. Her face was flushed with need and desire.

"God, you have a perfect pussy."

She bit her lip and gripped my ass pushing me into her more.

"Forgot my Mouse likes me deep."

"Yes," she moaned.

I pulled out and let my tip swirl around her entrance. I needed to tease her. Teasing her was a gift because the more I teased, the more she wanted, and the more she wanted, the more she gave. Her nails pressed into me, begging me to give it to her.

I moved to my knees so I was sitting on my heels and I grabbed her hips. I stopped teasing her and gave us what we both wanted.

Gripping her, I brought her whole body against my dick. It hit hard, but it hit home. "Yes, God. Yes Gunner."

"Fuck, Charlie. Nothing better. You feel that? How my dick fits perfectly in you? You feel how wet you are on my cock? How you slide against it?"

"Yes baby, I feel it."

"Grab your tits, babe."

She smirked at me, remembering how I ordered her to do the same thing the only other time we were together. She rolled her nipples.

"Fuck! Your tits. They're so fucking sexy. So big. So full."

"Your baby made them that way."

I let out a growl thinking about my seed making her tits this full. Just the thought of my seed inside of her made the primal side of me want nothing more than to claim every inch of her. I wanted my seed buried deep inside of her.

My body became possessed. I couldn't do anything but think about claiming her body in every way. I slammed in and out, hard and fast, pulling her to me at the same time. She moaned a long, throaty moan and her body, surprising her, let go. She convulsed over me, but I didn't give in. I continued on, pushing in and out until I could feel my balls pull tight, and became wilder. I lifted her body to me so her full breast bounced against my chest and came. I came so hard and so fast, as Charlie orgasmed again surprising us both.

It was bliss.

I stayed seated there. I didn't want to be separated from her. Keeping her body connected to mine, I pulled her down to the mattress. "That was so good," she murmured dazedly.

I sighed, and felt my dick twitch not nearly sated. I'd have her again tonight.

"What was that sigh for?"

"I'm finally home, Mouse."

"Yeah, you are."

Chapter Twenty-Six

Charlie

Gunner's sentiments about being home resonated so clearly with me. It was the absolute truth. You'd think that after everything that had happened to me that I wouldn't have been able to give myself so freely to him, but that was so far from the truth. Maybe I'd compartmentalized the abuse my body had been through, because the moment Gunner kissed me, all I knew was that it was right, and everything I needed to heal, I'd find from his touch. I craved it. A look from him had always been the comfort I needed to survive. A touch from him had been the spark I needed to live. And having him inside of me, well that was… it was everything. The serenity I felt after we made love soothed me in a way that nothing else could have. It didn't erase the bad, but it made me hope for the future. It made me think about going forward and my life with him was more important than anything some evil psychopath could've done to me. It was more important than a pair of twins who took something they had no right to. It was more important than neglectful foster parents, and Lord knows, my life with him was more important than where my journey began.

People talk about soul mates. Gunner wasn't my souls mate, he was the other half of me. I felt whole in a way that I'd never truly felt before. I felt powerful, and above all, I felt loved.

"I love you," I whispered as we made love for the third time that night.

"Mmm, I love you," he sleepily mumbled as he nuzzled into my hair. We embraced, holding on to each other all night. My eyes grew heavy. before I knew it, I heard, "Mom?"

"Shh, she's tired. Go on out in the living room, I'll be out in a minute."

My eyelashes fluttered open and I focused on Gun's retreating form. "Morning," I whispered to Gunner.

He kissed me on my shoulder since my back was to his front. "How are you?" he asked. "Are you sore?"

I moved my legs causing him to groan. "Sore, but in a good way." I couldn't help but shift my body into his. It became a reflex.

"I gotta get up with him, woman. If you don't want our son starving you better stop squirming."

I laughed, "I'll get up." I sat up and watched as Gunner's gaze moved to my breasts. The sheet tented in response. I threw his t-shirt on. "Stay here, I'll be right back." I walked out and smirked when I saw Gunner in front of the TV watching cartoons. "You want Fruity Pebbles, this morning?"

He was surprised that I was up and about. It felt good. It felt normal. "Reggie ate the rest yesterday."

"Nah, I hid a box for you," I said smiling as I grabbed the box I'd hidden by the pots and pans. I poured him a bowl and set the box down on the coffee table. He smirked at me, knowing that I knew how he liked to have seconds in the same colorful milk.

I made my way back to the bedroom and locked the door behind me. Gunner was still where I left him. His broad tattooed chest was exposed. He looked at me lazily with a grin on his face. I could get used to seeing him smile at me like this.

My smile widened as his eyes shifted to his still hard cock. "I want to marry you," I said shocking myself and him.

"Is that so?"

"Mmm hmm." I licked my lips. "But first I want to taste you."

"In that order?" he laughed and then groaned as I moved to straddle him on the bed.

"Something funny?"

His chest heaved up and down. His eyes grew hooded as he reached under his t-shirt I was wearing and ran his hands over my breasts.

With a devilish look in my eyes, I slid down his body, moving the sheet aside. His hard length sprung free. I licked my lips and kept my eyes fixed on Gunner.

"You gonna suck me, Mouse?"

I bent low and licked from his balls to his tip and grinned.

"Take me in your mouth."

He was big and his cock was straining with need. I took him into my mouth and hollowed out my cheeks giving him suction, and began to bob my head. I needed to use my hand on him in conjunction with my mouth due to his size. As I wrapped my hands around his cock and pumped them along with my head bobbing, Gunner moaned. It was deep and throaty, and turned into a rumble of pure pleasure.

"That's it Mouse. You know how good your lips look wrapped around my dick? I'm gonna fuck your mouth now. Are you ready for that?"

I kept my pace and wondered was I ready for that. The briefest image of waking up with that monster in my mouth flashed in my mind.

He pulled back and popped free from my mouth. "You're here with me in this room, right Mouse?" I looked at him, with all of his love and passion and all I could think was how much I wanted to give this to him and how much I wanted it for me. It was about me as much as it was about him. I wasn't pushing myself to see how far I could go, I was freeing myself from a lifetime of pain. "I want you to fuck my mouth." The seductive tone that came from my lips surprised me.

Gunner wasn't the type of man to let me lead. He moved to his knees, and I may have moaned at the pure sight of his magnificent body in the morning light. I'd seen him last night, but in the light, every inch of ink-covered skin was defined muscle and beauty.

"Lay on your side."

I propped myself up on my arm facing him.

"Open," Gunner commanded.

I opened my mouth and he pushed in deeply. I sucked and licked and he went wanton with need.

I made him wild.

He pushed in, pulling my hair and pressing in so deep he hit the back of my throat. It made my pussy clench with need. One, two, three, quick thrusts and he popped free from my mouth so I could catch my breath.

"Do you know how good you take my cock?"

"Mmm," I moaned as his cock slid back in and he continued fucking me.

"Best fucking lips. Everything you do, Mouse, is fucking perfect."

He paused for a moment, "You want to be my wife?"

I looked up at him, his cock in my mouth, all joking from earlier gone. I moaned out a throaty, "Mmm hmm."

"Good to know you'll say yes when I ask you. I like those odds." With that, he went wild, fucking my mouth vigorously."

I quickened my pace with his wild thrusts.

"Fuck," he hissed, "Keep that up babe, and I'm going to come."

I didn't let up. How could I?

He thrust harder and faster and my pussy ached so much I had to touch myself. I reached down between my legs and stroked my clit sliding my finger down to collect the moisture and using that to swirl my tight bundle of nerves.

He pumped again and then he swore so loud I'm sure everyone in a mile radius heard him, "Fuck! Fuck! Fuck!"

And then he was coming and I was swallowing, sucking up every inch of my beautiful biker's seed.

"Don't figure we'll have much time but I gotta get you off. That was one of the sexiest fucking things I've ever seen. Do you know how fucking sexy you are, Mouse? Do you know what you do to me? Sucking me off like that? You're a fucking vixen."

He reached down to my clit and took over, swirling and then moving his finger inside of me. He was quick to curl it and press exactly where I needed it. It only took seconds for him to hit the exact spot I needed and then in another moment I was shuddering and climaxing all over his large hand.

"Love you, Gunner," I murmured, and then he smacked my ass.

"Let's go. Need to get up with our boy," he grinned as he said our boy.

I whipped my t-shirt overhead and grabbed the robe. "I'm going to take a quick shower."

He pulled on some black sweatpants and a white t-shirt. "I'm going to make breakfast. Don't take too long, yeah?"

I smiled, kissed him quickly, and saw Gun still curled up on the couch like no time had passed. In the bathroom, I looked over my body. I felt different. My bruises were near gone, but that wasn't why I felt different. I felt like I was finally owning my skin. Somehow, Gunner taking my body didn't make me feel anything, but beautiful, and me giving my body to him only made me feel free.

Gunner's words settled deep inside of me. "When he asks me." Oh, how time had changed. It was just weeks ago that I'd been imprisoned by Enrico and I didn't think I would make it out alive. Now, I'd just had the most glorious night and morning with Gunner, and the idea of me spending the rest of my life with him was a real possibility.

I just wish I could shake this sense of foreboding that something bad was coming.

Chapter Twenty-Seven

Gunner

The next several weeks were what I could only describe as a dream. Charlie, Gun and I were a family. We'd eat together, go fishing, hike around the property, and yes, Gun and I would play video-games together. I continued teaching Gun how to fight. He loved it as much as I did. There was no way my son was ever going to let anyone push him around. We talked with the school and Charlie had enrolled him in homeschooling for the time being, just until things settled down. She would work with him for several hours on school work, he never complained. I loved that about him. He wasn't a whiner. He never got upset about moving, at least not anymore since his mom was back. In fact, he seemed to be flourishing. If it wasn't for the fact that we were hiding here, then I'd say life was about as close to perfect as it could be.

As for Charlie, she was becoming more and more sure of herself. We'd talk, and make love, and when we could occupy Gun without him knowing what was going on, we'd sneak off for a quickie. She was always so ready for me. Damn, this woman! She had no idea how mesmerized I was by her. She got stronger every day, whether she knew it or not.

Reggie and the guys started to come and go more frequently. Shane and Ace came up on the weekends. I talked to them often. We hadn't heard anything on Enrico, and we weren't sure if we would. The radio silence was unusual, and everyone was still on high alert.

I heard the roar of motorcycles and smiled. Thank fuck. The weather had been unseasonably warm, and they were still able to ride out. I'd asked my brothers for a few favors, and I knew when this shit settled, I'd owe them, but that was the thing about brotherhood, you'd do what you could if you could do it for each other. You'd have each other's backs, and judging by the smile on Shane's face as he threw up his kickstand on his Dyna, he had mine. Even Ace seemed to be in a good mood. I greeted them with a slap of the hands and then a quick hug. I couldn't help, but grin. I was excited. "You got everything I asked for?"

"You know it," Shane said. I heard more bikes approach. "Reggie, Knuckles, Donnie, Lachlan, Anthony and his old lady." Shane motioned his head to the guys as they approached.

Gun and Charlie came out of the cabin, and Gun ran to Reggie before he could even shut his bike off.

"Little dude, how's it going?" I lifted my brow to Ace and Shane.

"There's a reason they're a few minutes behind us," Ace grumbled. He was never one for smoking pot.

"At least he didn't do it here," Shane laughed. This was true and I didn't give a fuck if my brothers smoked.

"Well, did you bring it?" Gun asked Reggie just as Charlie found her place next to my side.

"Bring what?" she asked knowing that those two were thick as thieves.

He grinned opened his backpack and pulled out a gun.

"The fuck is wrong with you? You're not giving my kid a gun."

"Relax, bro. It's a BB gun. I promised him we'd shoot."

Mouse laughed. She must've already known about this because she joked so casually, "A BB gun! You'll shoot your eye out."

Ace's head snapped towards Charlie. He looked at her like he'd never seen her before.

"You know what? A little target practice is a great fucking idea," I said kissing Charlie's temple.

"You know, I did shoot a gun before." Charlie looked at me like I was completely ridiculous for teaching her to shoot. "Yeah, and you got lucky. So, the basics. This is the magazine. Your bullets go here. You release it by pressing this." I showed her the release and the bullets that I had in the chamber and pointed. "Barrel. This one's easy, it's the trigger. Now, this is your sight, and this right here is your safety." I pushed my jean clad leg in between her black yoga pant covered legs and moved her legs apart with mine. I adjusted her arms so that she was holding the gun correctly and noticed the smaller goosebumps break out over her skin. "It'll have some kickback and it'll be loud. Don't let it scare you. When it's in your hands, it's an extension of you. You have control of it and there is nothing to be afraid of. Now, I want you to focus on the tree. When you feel comfortable pull back and squeeze."

She focused for a few seconds staring through the scope then she squeezed the trigger. "Did I get it?" she asked not fazed by the blow back of the gun.

"No, completely missed. Don't worry. Let's try this again. Your hips were in front of your shoulders. Try to move your shoulders forward, like this." I adjusted her body by grabbing her hips and pulling them back into me. I had to restrain myself from pressing my half erect dick into her ass. This wasn't the time for that. I don't know why I didn't think of it sooner, but Reggie wanting to teach Gun how to shoot made a light switch go off in my head. For Charlie and for myself, I needed to teach her how to protect herself. I planned on always being with her, but I didn't want to take any chances. After moving her into the correct position and placing her hands on each side of the gun, I ordered again, "Aim, and shoot."

She did and this time, I'll be damned, she nailed it!

"Again," I commanded. We did this over and over again until it was the most natural thing to her. When we were finished, I taught her to clean the gun and take it apart. There was nothing to be afraid of when it came to guns as long as you knew what the fuck you were doing, and you didn't leave one where a kid could play cops and robbers with it.

"Your kid's a great shot! Check this out!" Shane slapped a hand on my shoulder, and Charlie and I followed him to where Gun was shooting his BB gun with Reggie. The rest of my brothers all stood around cheering him on as he aimed at a row of pop cans that were set up fifteen feet in front of him.

Pop. Pop. Pop.

He took out all of the cans, knocking each one over with precision.

"Damn, kid," Shane ruffled his hair.

"Son," I called.

He gave me a chin lift. Seven years old and he's giving chin lifts. Ace saw this and grinned at me.

"Yeah, Dad?" I'd never get over that word, *dad.*

"Great shot."

He smiled, "This was fun, can we practice sometimes together?" I nodded. His hazel eyes caught the light, looking almost golden as he smiled hugely at me. Charlie kissed him on the top of his head and whispered something in his ear.

"You're a lucky man," Ace said for my ears only.

Didn't I know it.

'You got any grub on?" Donnie asked. That man was always thinking with his stomach.

"I already checked, man. They got shit," Knuckles said joining the group. I hadn't even realized he was gone.

"Good thing, I brought extra," Donnie laughed and pulled a small cooler from his side bag. I shook my head. He always had something cooking.

A few hours past and we were all very full and content. Charlie was sitting with Anthony's old lady and Gun's head was in her lap, where she lovingly stroked the side of his head.

Ace caught my eye. I kissed Charlie on her forehead, "I'll be back."

"Everything alright?"

"It's fine, Mouse. Just need to talk with the guys about a few things."

I followed Ace into the early evening air. Shane was already sitting by the recently lit fire pit. "You got it?"

Shane grinned while Ace retrieved something from his bike. He reached in his pocket and handed me a box. "You sure about this, man?"

"As long as you've known me, you ever know me not to be sure about this?"

"Relax, he's just pissed 'cause you're the first of us," Ace said handing me a bag.

"Keep an eye on Gun?"

"Jesus, we got it," Shane said waving me off.

I made my way back into the cabin and Charlie's head was thrown back, laughing at a story Donnie was telling about me.

"He didn't," she said wiping a tear from under her eye.

"He did too, he was so drunk…"

I cleared my throat and shot Donnie a look that said, "I'm going to kill you if you don't shut your fucking mouth."

Charlie looked at me and grinned.

"Mouse, come with me. We're staying in cabin two tonight."

"But… what about Gun" She asked visibly confused.

"We got him, sweet heart. Don't worry about a thing," Mary, Anthony's old lady, said.

"You sure?" she looked around and could tell everyone in the room pretty much knew what was going on. Gun had been asleep on her lap so she moved carefully to free herself so as not to wake him.

I took her hand and led her towards cabin two. On the short walk, she looked at me curiously, but I kept a steady pace anxious for what came next.

Inside, I'd lit a few candles. There wasn't much to this cabin. A queen bed, small couch, tiny kitchenette and an old box television was the sum of it. The room had a soft glow. She squeezed my hand and whispered, "Gun."

"Got you something that I wish I could've given to you years ago."

"Is that so?" she smiled and sat down on the edge of the bed. I moved across the room grabbing what I came here to give her. I handed her a bag and her eyes sparkled with curiosity.

I knelt in front of her balancing on my toes but closer to her level. "Open it."

She cautiously opened the bag.

"It's not going to bite you, babe."

She pulled out the leather vest with the Bleeding Scars logo on the back and read out loud, "Bleeding Scars Motorcycle Club, Property of Gunner," her breath hitched.

"You know what that means, Mouse?"

"Maybe?" she asked tucking her hair behind her ear nervously.

"It means that if you choose to wear that, you're declaring to everyone that you're mine, and will always be. It's the biker version of 'I do.'"

"Gunner," she sighed, "Like it's even a choice. It hasn't been a choice since I was eight years old."

"Take off your shirt. The first time I see my vest on you I want to see it against your skin." She stared at me long and hard. I don't know if she was daring me to change my mind, because there wasn't an ounce of uncertainty. It was more like her look was saying this better be it for us. I watched her throat as she swallowed then whipped her shirt overhead and then slid each arm out of her bra, finally freeing her beautiful, full breasts. I would've taken them in my mouth right then and there, if I didn't need to see that leather wrapped around her. Without breaking eye contact she slipped her arms into the leather vest. She was making me wild with want.

"Do you know how sexy you look with my patch on your back and your tits peeking out? Now, reach into the pocket."

She did like I told her. Her lips parted in awe, when she felt the little box. She pulled it out and I grabbed it from her. I moved to my knee. I might've been a biker, I might've been a badass, but my Mouse deserved one knee.

"Mouse, do you know the first time I talked to you wasn't the first time I noticed you? First time I saw you, you took my breath away. I wasn't even really into girls yet, but I saw you and there was something about you. I'd look for you, and sometimes you'd already be watching for me, but if I was lucky, sometimes I'd spot you before you'd see me. Watching you was like finding this treasure that I didn't want anyone to ever find out about. I felt like if I talked to you, it might take away from that, until one day you just looked so sad that I had too. I couldn't stand seeing you sad. God, then the first time I kissed you, Mouse? It was like heaven. You know my dad died and my life was shit, but there you always were, and then those lips of yours, I swear to Christ, brought me more happiness in a single minute than anything had in years. Life dealt us some serious blows. But you? You protected my kid. You held on and you fought. And then, after all of this shit, you've let me love you. After everything, you've never doubted my love. And I can't tell you how thankful I am for that, because if I'm honest, I've always loved you. You're wearing my patch, Mouse. Now wear my ring. Be my wife."

She was crying and I wanted to wipe away her tears, but she hadn't said anything yet. "Charlie," I prompted.

"Yes. Yes to all of it. I'll be your old lady. I'll be your wife. I'll be it all. I love you."

I slid the diamond ring on her finger, my hand trembling with nervousness. "I love you." I kissed her hard and long. She smelled so good. Her scent was like me, but fresher, prettier. My buckle clinked against the ground as my jeans hit the floor.

"Need you," she whimpered my exact sentiments. I tore my lips from hers and pulled her leggings off of her. Her slick pussy glistened. I licked my lips wanting to taste her, but my need to be inside of her was greater. In another quick movement, I tore my shirt over my shoulders and moved on top of her. Her legs dangled over the edge. None of that mattered. I was mad with lust. All I knew was I needed to be buried inside of her.

"Charlie," I gasped out her name as I pushed inside of her in one quick thrust. She was tight. She always felt tight. "Love this pussy. You're so wet for me."

I slammed in and out relentlessly. I wasn't careful. She wasn't the same woman as she was weeks ago, when we first made love. Now, she was just as hungry for me as I was for her.

"Give it to me. Give it to me hard," she begged, and I was lost in desire. I lifted her legs and fucked her deep, and when that wasn't enough I flipped her onto her stomach taking her from behind. She came hard for me the moment I took her this way. It wasn't enough for me. I bent over her, marveling at how my patch looked covering her back, while I fucked her senseless. She cried out, her hands gripping the sheet in front of her. My balls slapped against her perfectly round ass. I slapped it. "Want to fuck you here soon."

"Mmm," she moaned and I knew she wasn't opposed to it, but I wasn't going to take it tonight. I didn't want anything to mess up tonight. As much as that appealed to me, I couldn't risk something new for us tonight. I needed it to only be about what the two of us have. She pushed back into me and began to meet my thrusts.

"Yes, Gunner. Again." I smacked her ass again and I swear she purred. Yes, she would do just fine with that. She met me thrust for thrust and that tingle tight in my balls began. I wrapped my arm around her and flicked her clit over and over again. Another moment, and we were both exploding. "Jesus," I panted.

She collapsed on the mattress and my body landed next to her. Out of nowhere, she began to giggle. "What's funny?"

"I'm going to be your wife."

"Yeah?" I asked trying to find out what was funny about that.

"Yeah, nothing. I'm just happy."

I held her in my arms and it wasn't long until our gentle strokes turned into more and before long, we making love, slow and sweet. After she ran her hands over her vest, we slipped it off. Her fingers traced the Bleeding Scars insignia.

"What's this mean?" she sleepily asked.

"It's something Ace said to me. When I met him, I was in a bad place. I hated Hades. I couldn't find you. I felt so lost, and then Shane was there. I was wasted one night and he said something to me that I'll never forget. I was telling him to just let me be. I was too fucked up, had too many scars, and he said we all have scars, some scars bled brighter than others. It made so much sense to me. When we met Ace and decided to start our own club, Ace had his own set of demons he was running from. One day, he takes off his shirt and I see this scar he has running down his chest. The thing is angry,Jagged. He's never said what happened, but I know it was bad and that's when I was reminded of what Shane said about some scars bleeding brighter than others, and so that's what we were, Bleeding Scars."

"I like that." her eyes turned downward, and I know she was reminded of her own scars.

I tilted her chin upwards. "Don't hide from me. We all got scars, Mouse and you're one of us now." I kissed her tenderly, and held her close until exhaustion took us both. It was only hours later, when the phone rang and the voice on the other end completely burst our happy bubble.

"Hello," I answered.

"Help," the raspy voice begged.

"Mom?"

251

Chapter Twenty-Eight

Charlie

I heard a ringing phone and I blinked. I didn't think I was asleep for long. Gunner got up and fished his phone from his jean pocket. "Hello," he said and his body visibly tensed up. I sat up behind him and put my hands on his shoulders. The tenseness in his rigid back told me that whoever was on the phone, it was not good.

"Right. Where are you?" he clipped, paused and then said, "Stay there. Keep your head down, and I'll send some guys." He hung up the phone and immediately started dialing.

"I need you to pick up my mom. She needs a cage and a doctor. Use caution. I don't trust her. Bring guys. Bring back-up, but don't make 'em known. She's hiding out at a gas station on Decanter Street." He disconnected the call and sat with his head in his hands. I gave him a few minutes to collect his thoughts.

"Gunner?" I picked up on some of the conversation, but I needed him to fill in the blanks. "What's happened with your mom?"

He sucked in a breath and then slowly released it.

"She's hurt. She said she got sober and tried to leave Hades, but he didn't take to that so kindly, so he beat the fuck out of her. She's sitting in a gas station with no one. Fuck! Part of me wants to leave her there like she left me when those fucking Hades bastards beat the shit out of me. The other part of me, can't do it. Deep down, she's my mom, you know? My club's going to get her, and bring her here. I don't trust her, but I can't let them find her and kill her if she's telling the truth, that is. Fuck! This is so messed up. Let's get dressed, go to the main cabin, and fill Shane and Ace in."

"You okay?" I asked.

His eyes left mine and looked at the door, "I really don't know, Mouse."

I quickly dressed as did Gunner, and as we were about to walk out of the cabin, Gunner handed me my new patch, as he called the vest. "You wear this, when you're outside. You wear this, when we're around my brothers. You wear this pretty much always unless we're fucking and even then I might still want to see it on you. Got it?"

I smiled at him, and wagged my fingers, showing off my new engagement ring. "And this too," I said meaning I'd wear that always, as well. Then, I pulled him down to kiss me.

Inside the main cabin, Knuckles, Donnie, Anthony, Lachlan, and Mary were still up quietly playing cards and drinking beer. Gun was nowhere to be seen, and I surmised that he was in our room, since Ace and Shane were taking the other room. Reggie was asleep on the couch.

Taking in the scene only lasted a few seconds before Knuckles leapt up and clapped Gunner on his shoulder, hollered like it was the most exciting thing ever and then picked me up in a huge bear hug saying, "Welcome to the family."

Reggie woke up from the noise and sat up abruptly, He rubbed his eyes then said, "What the fuck? You ain't supposed to be back 'til the morning."

The room's jovial congratulations stopped, when they realized that Reggie was right. Gunners face said how pissed off he was. "The guys in there?" he nodded to the other room.

"Yeah, Shane's been asleep for a few hours, and Ace just went to bed a little while ago," Lachlan said.

"Be right back, babe," Gunner kissed me.

As he walked away, Mary walked up to me. "Congrats. I know something's going on, but that doesn't mean we're not all excited and happy for you. I've known Gunner a long time, and I used to hear whispers about him looking for some lost love. I'm glad he found you."

I smiled at her. She was older than me, by at least fifteen years. She had gray streaks in her long signature biker braid and she wore a patch similar to mine. She had on black jeans with small jewels over the pockets and some kick ass black boots.

"Thank you," I said smiling through the uneasiness in my belly over Gunner's mom's return to our life.

Both Ace and Shane had pissed off looks on their face as they followed Gunner out. I got it, no one liked to be woken up. Ace spotted me with the patch on first and quickly came over to me, gave me a hug, then whispered quietly, "Thank you. He needed you."

As Ace moved away, Shane loudly exclaimed, "Looks even sexier in our colors." Then, he swooped me up in a big hug, and Gunner shot him a dirty look. Shane set me down. I couldn't help but grin at the boys. I was glad Gunner had them.

Shane changed again. His mood suddenly much more serious. "Alright, now what the fuck is going on that you had to wake us up?"

"I got a call from my mom," Gunner explained everything he knew and that he sent some of his brothers to go and get her. Just as he was finishing, his phone rang again. He took the call and I silently waited for him to finish and let us know what happened. "It was Briggs. They have her. Everything went smoothly. They'll be here in an hour and a half."

"I don't trust her." Gunner said, "I can't stand that Hades put his hands on her, but we need to be on alert around her too. We don't leave Gun alone with her."

Everyone nodded sensing what they needed to do.

"I'll call Doc," Shane said.

"Do you want us here, or do you want some space?" Donnie asked.

"Why don't you guys get that fire going," Gunner told everyone at the table.

"I'll check the perimeter. I know they'll make sure they don't have a trail, but I want to be sure we're secured." Ace said as he began shrugging on warmer clothes and checked the clips in his gun. What did they think his mom was capable of?"

Reggie and Shane stayed in the cabin with us. Time seemed to go slowly. "Go to bed, Mouse. I got this."

I shook my head. "I'm not doing that. This isn't going to be easy for you, and there's no way I'm letting you face her alone." I kissed him quickly and held his hand in the silent cabin until we heard gravel crunch followed by motorcycles.

"Stay here," Gunner shot me a look. I wanted to argue, but the look he gave me left me little room. "Reggie, stay with her."

A minute later, he carried his mom inside. She was bloody and banged up, but she wasn't as bad off as I imagined. I grabbed a first aid kit and followed Gun into the tiny bathroom.

"Mom," he sighed as he took a look at her in the bathroom light. She didn't look anything like I remembered. I used to think she was beautiful and full of life. Now, she looked weathered, used even. Her hair was dirty and stringy. She didn't smell good. Her face was swollen, and it reminded me of Enrico, and how he hit me in the face. Blood was dried from her nose and her lip was split wide open. I looked at her clothes. She had on a long sleeve t-shirt and jeans that I noticed had vomit on them. That's what that smell was.

"I'm sorry, Gunner. I'm so sorry. I was so stupid." She began crying and I momentarily felt sorry for her. Then, I remembered how she let those men hurt Gunner, and I'd lost any sympathy I felt. I grabbed a washcloth, ran warm water over it and began to gently wipe her face. Once the blood was gone, it didn't look so bad, but I had a feeling that the puke on her jeans meant something worse.

"Gunner, check her ribs," I said quietly, and it was then that his mom really seemed to notice me.

He sucked in a breath as he lifted her shirt. In her raspy, teary voice she said to me, "You were always staring at my boy. Wasn't sure what he saw in you. You turned out to be a looker." She flinched as his hand touched her skin. Her skin was already beginning to change colors.

"Doc's on his way, but I'm guessing you have a few broken ribs."

"Gunner, why don't you let me help get her cleaned up?" I met his eyes and motioned my eyes to the puke on her.

"Not leaving you alone with her." He made it perfectly clear to her with that simple statement that he didn't trust her.

"Can you lift your arms?" I asked and she nodded. Gunner hissed as I helped her lift her shirt off completely and the extent of damage to her torso was revealed. Gunner started the shower and I helped her out of her jeans.

She stood in her bra and panties and I helped her in the shower while Gunner stood there. He was on guard, it was like he was waiting for her to strike. It was so very clear that he didn't buy her apology. I had her wrapped in a towel and her hair washed when a knock at the bathroom door came.

"Yeah?" Gunner asked.

"Doc's here," Shane said from the other side.

We let Doc in and I sat on the couch until Doc came out and told us, "I got her ribs wrapped. They look worse than they are. I think they're probably bruised. I just gave her a shot of something to help her sleep. But she'll need help walking for now.

Gunner nodded and a minute later came back with his mom in his arms and brought her to the spare room. He closed her inside and came back out. "I want you in with Gunner for the rest of the night. I'm going to watch her." The way he said watch her didn't make me think it was for her benefit, but for mine.

"Alright," I said stepping on my tiptoes and meeting his lips half way as he bent forward. "Love you."

"Love you, too."

Gun stirred beside me. The morning light filtered in through the room. I yawned and stretched my arms, thinking about last night. I'm going to be Gunner's wife! I'll also have my future mother-in-law to contend with today. With that thought, I dressed for the day. Gun woke up as I'm about to go grab coffee.

"Hey, honey." I leaned forward and kissed him on his head. "How did you sleep?"

He rubbed his eyes. "Good," he said with yawn.

I plopped down beside him. "Dad and I have some news."

"Did he get me the new Turbo Racing game?"

"Nope, better than that."

"What could be better than Turbo Racing?"

"Well, your dad and I are going to get married?"

"You are?"

I wiggled my finger showing off my new diamond ring. Seeing it in the light only made me smile more. It was beautiful. It was a princess cut diamond set on a twisted, diamond, platinum band. It rocked.

"Kick ass," he shouted and before I had a chance to scold him on his language, he bolted out of the room in search for Gunner.

I followed him and saw Gunner drinking a cup of coffee just as Gun threw his arms around his waist. "Dad! Mom says you're getting married."

"We are. That cool with you, kid?"

"Gun, you watch your mouth," I scolded. I could tell he was about to use the same language.

He gulped and answered, "Yeah, Dad. We'll be a real family."

"Already are, kid. Just making it official." He ruffled Gun's hair and Gun broke free, grabbed a bowl for cereal, then he opened his arms for me. I immediately stepped into them putting my arms around his waist and he dipped his head for a kiss.

"Missed sleeping next to you."

"Where is she?" I asked.

"Still sleeping. I imagine she'll be out for a while. Her body needs to heal."

I nodded my head in understanding. "You mad I told Gun without you? I was just so excited."

"'Course not. Glad you're happy. What was up with the watch your mouth comment?"

"As soon as I told him, he said, 'kick ass' and ran out to you."

"Gun."

At the sound of his father's voice, our son looked up from his bowl of cereal.

"What?" he asked with a mouthful.

"Watch your mouth around your Mom."

"Just around me, huh? He's spending too much time with Reggie."

Reggie's head popped up from the couch and he grinned at us, "Heard that."

"Wasn't whispering."

Gunner's arms tightened around me, "You shine, Mouse."

"Hmm?" I asked distracted by the feel of his body wrapped around mine.

"Never saw you shine so much. My mom's in the next room, beaten. But you're not letting that get you down. Nope, instead you're smiling and wearing my ring. Like I said, you fucking shine."

I leaned up on my tiptoes, because what else could I do with that declaration, and kissed him.

"Eww," Gun said and started coughing. We pulled apart and Gunner glared at Gun making him halt his dramatics. I laughed and reached for a coffee cup.

The door opened, and Ace and Shane walked in. They both poured themselves coffee, and I immediately started brewing more. A pot didn't go far with these guys.

"Be back, babe. If she wakes up, get me. I'll be just outside," Gunner said leaving me in the kitchen. Reggie followed the guys outside, and it was just Gun and me.

"Something else happened last night, Gun." I grabbed his attention before he pressed play on the video-game.

"Gunner's mom, your Grandma's, here. Your dad hasn't seen her before last night and they don't have the best relationship so I want you to be cautious around her. Follow your dad's lead." He gave me a chin lift, and I was reminded that my boy needed to spend more time with kids his own age and less time with these grown bikers.

Several hours later, my boys and I were taking a walk around the lake, when Lachlan walked up. "She's up."

Gunner gave Lachlan a chin lift, and we headed back into the cabin.

We walked inside. His mom sat on the couch slowly sipping coffee. She was black and blue, but her face wasn't as swollen as I would have thought that it would be. I momentarily thought about how beautiful I used to think that she was, and how she really wasn't anymore. Life hadn't been kind to her.

When she saw us, she gasped. "Gunner," his name fell off of her lips in a whisper, but it wasn't Gunner she was looking at. She was staring directly at Gun.

"Fuck," she hissed. "You got a kid."

He glared at her, and placed his hand on Gun's shoulder.

"I didn't know," she stuttered out. "I had no idea."

I walked in front of her, "Hi Cathy. How are you today?"

Her eyes left my son and flashed to me like she was just now noticing that I'd moved in front of her.

"Fine," she spat, a little too annoyed by my presence. She'd been through a lot, I needed to cut her some slack. I never really knew her growing up. We'd see each other in passing mostly. She was never rude to me, but never quite acknowledged me either.

"Cathy, this my son, Gun. Gun say hello to your Grandma."

He waved shyly.

"Son, why don't you go find Reggie, and hang with him for a little while." Gunner squeezed Gun's shoulder. Sensing some tension, he didn't hesitate to hightail it out of the cabin. He was followed out by the rest of Gunner's brothers that were lingering in the cabin.

"Ma, we need to talk."

I sat on the edge of the table in front of her and Gunner sat beside her. He grabbed me by the hand and deposited me on his lap. "Need you next to me," he whispered for my ears only.

Cathy watched us cautiously.

"Go on, Ma. Let me hear, how after seven years, why you think coming to me for help would be okay."

She flinched. It was barely noticeable, but his words stung her.

I watched as she pulled in a deep breath, and she began her story, and it wasn't anything like I would've expected.

"I was with Hades before I met your dad."

Gunner's entire body went stiff, and I linked my fingers with his.

"I met him when I was young. My parents hated him. Thought he was no good for me, but you have to understand what it was like for me growing up. Grandpa, before he retired, he worked out of town a lot, and more often than not, it was just my mom and me, and she was a cold woman. She never hugged. She didn't hurt me, or anything but it was like I wasn't hers. Like she felt no connection to me. You know? So, when I met Billy, that's what he was called before he became Hades, I craved the attention he showed me. He was older than me by five years, and I met him when I was fifteen. No surprise, my dad lost his shit, when he found out. He tried everything he could to keep me away from Hades. He'd lock me in the house. Ground me. Anything he could think of, but he had to work, and Mom was not really there, so I'd always find away to see him. I was sixteen when I found out I was pregnant."

My eyes found Gunner's. I hoped like hell she wasn't telling us that Hades was Gunner's real dad.

He squeezed my leg, interrupting Cathy's story. "She was nineteen when I was born."

I let out the breath I was holding and whispered, "Thank God."

"No, he's not your Dad, but he's your sister's."

"What the fuck!" Gunner bellowed, yes bellowed. I felt like the walls of the cabin were ready to implode with his fury. "Say what, Ma?"

"I was a kid. Hades was a man. My Dad didn't want me to raise a kid at sixteen, so he made me sign over custody to Hades. It was horrible. I hated Hades then. I never saw her, I held her in the hospital, and after that, nothing. He said he sent her off to live with family, and that she'd have a good life, but I resented him. I couldn't understand how he could side with my dad, and send my baby away. I withdrew. I didn't talk to Hades anymore. He wouldn't give me my baby, so I wanted nothing to do with him. It was too much. Grandpa's and my relationship never really recovered."

"I need a drink. You need something?" I interrupted. I didn't really need a drink, but I could tell Gunner was ready to combust from the news that he had a sister. Not only did he just find out about the having a son that was kept from him, but now he was finding out that he had a sister too.

"Get me whiskey, babe."

"I'll have one too," she added.

"Thought you were getting clean, Ma?" Gunner gave her an irritated look.

"From the powder," she said quietly.

"Well, you're not drinking on my watch either, so if you want to be here, you're clean for real."

I got up and poured Gunner a small tumbler of Jameson for him, grabbed myself a beer, then returned to my spot on his lap where he needed me.

Gunner took a large swig from the tumbler and said, "Go on."

"Alright, where was I? So, I avoided Hades. My mom got sick and Grandpa moved us. I always wondered what happened to my little girl, but I was a kid myself, you know? Then, I met your dad and we started a life here. He was a good dad to you. Everything seemed good and then one day your dad and I were out, and we ran into Hades. Your dad did his best to get me away from him as quickly as he could, but I wanted to know about my daughter, so I ended up going to their clubhouse sometimes. Then, your dad had the accident, and Hades started coming around more. He kept hanging the promise of my girl over my head, and so we spent more and more time together. Then, he told me about her accident and I lost it. I guess that's when I started to use with him. It was all about getting high, and well, you know the rest. One day, I overheard Hades talking about you, and how Enrico wanted you dead, and I knew I needed to clean myself up. I couldn't be with a man who'd let that happen, but I knew I was useless using. I'd been doing a pretty good job of getting sober. I told him I was leaving, and he beat the shit out of me. I got away from him, called you. And here we are."

"There is so much fucking there, I don't even know where to start, so how about you tell me about this accident."

I was so frustrated with his mom's account of things.

"He told me there was an accident, and she didn't make it. I never even got to meet her."

"Fuck," Gunner hissed out. "What'd you hear Hades say about Enrico?"

"Not much, just that Enrico Santos was after you, and he'd be on the look out, and would report back."

I flashed Gunner a look. That was our first real confirmation that Enrico was alive. My stomach turned at that news. Gunners hand squeezed my waist. "I'm not letting anything happen to you again, Babe."

I was shaken. I heard his promise that I'd be safe, but something about all of this felt off.

Chapter Twenty-Nine

Gunner

I didn't trust my mom. Something about the entire thing felt off. It might have been the slight tremble in her hand, when she watched me sip my whiskey, or the way she licked her lips at the drink. She wasn't a sober woman, no matter what she said. I also failed to feel like she was truly sorry. It felt disjointed. I told my brothers this, and we were on high alert.

I wasn't letting on to her that I didn't trust her. I let her sit with Gun. He spent a few minutes asking her about her life, and once he saw that she wasn't that interested in him, he quickly went about his business of hanging out with the guys.

Charlie stayed by my side until much later when she yawned, and I told her to get some rest and that I'd be in soon.

She grabbed Gun, "Want you with me, baby," she told him and he didn't argue. He gave his momma what she needed without any questions.

I knew hearing Enrico's name shook her. I had the guys take shifts watching my mom sleep in the other bedroom. The longer the day went on, the more she seemed to be getting antsy. I figured it was more withdraw than anything. She said it was the pain that was making her irritable and she needed sleep. That might've been true, but my gut said it was more than that.

After she went to bed, I found my woman and son curled up. I paused and watched how Charlie clung to him and I wondered if that's what it was like before I found them. I changed into sweats, laid on my side and threw my arm over both of them, holding them in their sleep. Her body relaxed. She didn't need to hold on anymore. I was there, and I vowed that I'd always be there.

* * *

My phone vibrating on the nightstand woke me. It was dark and the red glowing numbers on the alarm clock flashed one-thirty-six. I didn't recognize the number, but I wondered who the fuck could be calling at this hour.

"Yeah," I answered.

"Uh, uh, Mr. Gunner?" a young guy's voice wobbled on the other end.

"Who's this?"

"It's me. Joshua." I had no idea who the fuck Joshua was.

"You told me to call if I saw any other bikers with cuts on heading your way." The light bulb went off in my head, the geeky kid from the gas station.

"Good job, kid. How many?"

"Maybe ten, but there was also a bunch of Black SUV's with them. I was taking a piss. Almost missed them. I did good, right?"

"Yeah, kid. Real fucking good. You catch their colors?"

"You mean, were they white or black?"

"No, I mean, you catch what their patch said?" He didn't answer me. I was getting frustrated. "Did their vest tell you the name of their motorcycle club?"

"Oh, yeah. Sorry. Something about Hell or Hades. I don't know. It was pretty quick."

"Were they heading East or West?"

"East, for sure."

"Good job, kid." I hung up and gently shook Charlie's shoulder. "Babe."

She sat up abruptly, looked at Gun to make sure he was safe, and then to me. Sliding out of bed, I quickly put a shirt and boots on. She followed my lead and I watched her eyes move as I grabbed my gun, checked my clip, and left the room. She followed a second later.

"What's going on?"

"What's going on is Mom, tipped 'em off to where we are. I don't know how or when, but I know it was her."

"Oh, God. He's coming for me."

"No, babe. We're ending this shit. That's what's happening. Go to the cabins. Wake 'em up." Charlie headed towards the door when I handed her my gun, "Take this." I knew we had time, but I wasn't taking any chances. Besides, I had more guns, and I didn't want her to witness me waking up my mom, because fuck that bitch.

Reggie who was on the couch already began stirring as Charlie quickly moved out of the cabin. "Got company coming. ETA maybe thirty minutes; maybe more, maybe less."

"Fuck. Ace is on the perimeter. I'll let him know."

Shane was watching my mom sleep when I threw open the door. "Get up you, lying fucking cunt."

Shane sat up straight and gave me a look that said what the fuck. She moved groggily and I grabbed her and shook her by the shoulders. I'd never hit a woman before, but I was so damn close. "What the fuck did you do?"

"You don't understand."

"No? Enlighten me. How come there's a convoy of bikers and SUVs heading this way?"

She began to cry. "I'm sorry. I'm so sorry."

Just as I was about to interrogate her further, I heard a sound I'd never forget. Charlie screamed in the distance.

"Shane," I said about to bark orders as I ran for the door.

"Got it," he said aiming a gun on my Mom.

"Gun," I shouted at Reggie as I ran out. We'd already talked about in case of anything happening that he was to take care of Gun above everything else. My brothers had all started to exit their cabins with their guns raised, but what I saw made my blood boil.

Enrico-motherfucking-Santos had a gun on Charlie. Her chest was rising and falling abruptly. "Let her go," I shouted.

He looked out of place. He was wearing a tailored suit, that even in the darkness, I could tell cost a mint, and his shoes were expensive too. What he did not look like was a man who was prepared to be in the woods in the fall. Everything was slick from an earlier rain. He spoke in his thick accent, "You know, I never intended to meet with you, but when I met Hades at the strip club, and I laid eyes on Charlotte, I knew she'd be mine. When he recognized her as someone you'd been looking for, well you see, that made everything even fucking sweeter."

"Again, let her go, and I'll make it quick." I saw Lachlan move in from behind and Enrico shouted, "Tell your man, he moves again, she gets a bullet."

"Please," she whimpered.

"You shouldn't have come after what was mine," Enrico said.

My girl in all her fierceness said, "I was never yours."

He pressed the gun into her side, "I said tell him to back down." I watched as he gripped her side. In one hand I held a gun, in the other my balled fist. I spotted my gun on the ground not far from where Charlie stood. He must've disarmed her. Fuck.

"Gunner, no?" My mom shouted, panic lacing her voice as she joined the party while Shane held a gun to her.

"You promised. You fucking promised, if I led you here that you'd tell me where to find her and Gunner would be safe," she cried.

I shot her a look, and in that quick second my eyes moved from Enrico to my mom, he somehow pulled a second gun, aimed it at my mom and fired. He hit her in the stomach and she dropped at the same time, two simultaneous explosions went off in the not so far off distance. That was Ace. I didn't have time to dwell on the fact that my mom was shot, she just lied to me again, and I really couldn't say how I felt. All I knew was that I needed to get my family safe. I used the distraction from the explosion, and fired a shot at Enrico. He ducked, but in doing so let go of Charlie. She scrambled for the gun on the ground. I shot off another round, but Enrico ducked behind a large tree. Lachlan, who had been approaching shot towards Enrico and I couldn't be certain if he hit him or not.

Motorcycles roared through the trees. Ace didn't get 'em all apparently. They began firing shots off at us, and suddenly we were in an all-out war. Bullets blazed in every direction, and all I thought about was, I had to get to Charlie. She moved like there wasn't a gun battle blazing around her. I ducked to miss a bullet. A Hades Runner aimed at Charlie. I fired taking him out, before he could pull the trigger. She grabbed the gun and moved. She was going after Enrico. Hades pulled his bike into the mayhem, a bullet nearly missed him. I fired, grazing his shoulder. A small explosion went off to my right, and then I lost sight of Charlie. Hades saw my mom on the ground, her body shaking as she spat up blood. He looked wrecked. I'd never thought he'd actually give a fuck about her. Seeing her on the ground, I wasn't sure how I felt. One thing I knew is we wouldn't be in this situation, if it wasn't for her.

"Fuck! Fuck, fuck fuck!" I heard Donnie yell and watched as he dropped to his knees. He was shot and I hoped like fuck it wasn't too bad. Two Hades also dropped in rapid succession as Knuckles moved in to get Donnie clear from any more danger. Shane had my back shooting men as I moved to where Charlie had gone.

It was dark, the smoke from gunfire made everything hazier. There was a red glow in the sky. I assumed it was from the SUVs that Ace had no doubt set fire to. It helped me see Charlie's form running towards our cabin, right towards Gun. She didn't know that I'd already given Reggie strict instructions that no matter what, the first sign of danger, he was to get Gun as far away from here as possible. I trusted that he'd done just that, but when Charlie threw open the cabin door, I was afraid. He could be inside waiting for her. I ran as fast as I could.

I moved to the door of the cabin with stealth speed, and breathed a sigh of relief, when I saw that Charlie had the gun aimed at Enrico.

"I'm not yours, you sick fuck," she said holding the gun exactly like we practiced.

"You can't kill me."

"No? Watch me, motherfucker." Her finger was about to pull the trigger when he said, "If you kill me, your old man's sister will suffer a fate far worse than you ever did."

"She said she was dead," I said coming up beside Charlie.

"She lied to get you to trust her. You stupid moron."

"You fucking killed her," Hades shouted from the doorway, "You're my brother, we had a fucking deal, and you killed her." Before we could do anything else, his gun went off in a burst of rapid shots. Holy shit, they were brothers!

"No!" Charlie shouted.

Enrico's body slumped to the ground. Blood pooled. He was dead.

I grabbed Charlie, pulling her to me trying, and failing to shield her from the bloody mess in front of us. I aimed a gun in Hades' direction, not sure of the danger we were still in, but he was gone. Too many bombshells dropped in his wake. He was brother's with Enrico. I had a sister and my mom was now dead. Motorcycles roared to life, and I knew the war was over, at least for tonight.

Chapter Thirty

Charlie

"I feel cheated."

I was back in Ohio, lying in our bed, and by ours, I meant Gunner's and mine. We had been back for about a week, and we were cuddling after we'd just finished making sweet love. Gunner wouldn't call it that. He'd say we were fucking hard, but it didn't matter what he called it, or how rough it was, it was always love to me, and no matter how hard it was, it was always sweet.

My back was to his front. He had a leg thrown over mine and he was lightly kissing the scars on my back. It was something I found he did quite often, but I wasn't sure if it was for him, or if it was for me. Nonetheless, anytime his lips were on me, it was good.

'Why do you feel cheated? You got yours a few times, babe."

I sighed. I wasn't talking about that. I turned to face him, not sure why my mind went here, but it did. "I wish Hades hadn't shot him. I wish it was me. I feel like he robbed me of that, and I deserved to get to do it after everything he put me through."

Gunner studied my face, "I'm not sorry."

I looked at him questioningly.

"You kill a man, that stays with you. You hold on to it, even when it's deserved, some part of your soul knows you took that from someone. I don't wish that on you. Glad it was Hades and not you, babe. Saying that though, I wish it was me I also wish we knew what the hell happened to my sister."

"I'm sorry. Now, I feel bad. You're right. I shouldn't be glad he's dead, knowing you have a sister out there, and not knowing what she's been through. I've been thinking about my time there."

"Mouse," he said exasperatedly because he hated when I thought about my time there. I couldn't help it though, it happened and I was still working through it. Knowing Enrico was dead helped.

"I know, but hear me out. That day that he took me to a restaurant," Gunner growled, he knew which day I was talking about. I placed my hand on his chest to calm him down. "I remembered something." This peaked his interest and he raised a brow. "We were walking down a hall. I wasn't allowed to lift my head, but I remember that there was a woman who banged on her door and asked him to let her out. He ignored her, but the more I think about it, what if she was your sister? She was upstairs, not in the dungeons with me, and the woman spoke to him with more familiarity than he'd ever allow me to have."

"That's good info, babe. Maybe you're right. Maybe it's her. Ace has been searching some sex-ring internet sites and has been reaching out to contacts, but I'll tell him this. Maybe it will lead to her. It's good, Mouse."

I knew how this weighed on Gunner. We'd talked about everything from that night and what we concluded, after finding out that Hades and Enrico were actually brothers, was that Gunner's sister had been living with Enrico. We didn't know for how long or why, but we were going to find out.

He cupped my cheeks and kissed me, then said, "I've been thinking about this revenge thing."

"It's not a revenge thing. You act like I want to go all vigilante," I laughed.

"I'm thinking one of the strippers you used to work with set you up. Past shit's been rolling through my head too, and I'm pretty sure that I remember Enrico handing a blonde money the night you were drugged."

"Skye," I whispered her name. She was such a bitch. I shook my head, "No, Gunner. I want to move on from that place. I don't think we can move on from the past, if we keep looking back. As fucked up as it is that she had something to do with it, she couldn't have really known how dangerous he was."

"You're too nice."

"No, I just know that we've got much more to look forward to then all the shit we've got behind us.

"God, I fucking love you." He kissed me hard.

I kissed him back with such ferocity. That's how it was with us. Sometimes, it was soft, and other times, it was like, even though we just had each other, we were desperate to have one another.

"I was just inside of you, but you make me so goddamn hard every fucking time you kiss me."

"Gunner," I sighed his name as his fingers found my already wet clit and began circling.

"Turn around." I did as he said and quickly rolled away from him. "Grab your tits." I did that too. "Good. now play with those fucking perfect nips."

"So bossy," I laughed.

"You love it," he said and pushed inside of me from behind. Oh, but I did love it. His long thick cock slid deeply inside of me and I was already so sensitive from cumming from our last bout that I let out a loud moan.

"That's right. Take my cock." He pushed in with such vigor and then pulled out again. One hand of his was placed over my back and he did this every time he saw me from this position. My skin was too fragile to be tattooed on, but as soon as I could, I knew I'd be getting the Bleeding Scars MC tat on me. I let go of my nipples. I was already becoming lost in us. I grabbed the sheets in front of me in a tight fist as he continued to pump in and out of me.

He gave me a few hard strokes, slid out of me, moved me to my stomach, then grabbed my hips so they were raised slightly and began fucking me so deeply from behind, I felt it to my very core.

"Fuck," I panted, "Yes!"

He slowed and rubbed my asshole with his fingers, then pushed one in. He began fucking my ass with his finger and fucking my pussy with his beautiful dick, and it was marvelous.

I came, and then once I was done, he added another finger, and fucked me even harder until I came again. I could feel his hard body slapping against mine as his speed increased and I knew he was close.

"Yes, baby. Give it to me," I shouted, loving the way he felt when he came inside of me.

A full minute later, he removed his fingers, flexed his arms on each side of my body and rode me until he came so hard, he too roared out in pleasure.

He collapsed on top of me, then pulled me back to the position we started in; my back to his front. "Marry me," he whispered.

I laughed, "I already said yes."

"I mean today. Let's not wait. I don't want to wake up another morning with you not being my wife."

I again turned towards him, searching his eyes. In those beautiful amber eyes with flecks of greens and browns, I saw the boy I used to watch from my window. With his tattooed arms wrapped around me, I saw the man he had become, the man who I knew would do anything to make me happy and keep me safe.

"Alright, let's do it."

"Yeah?" he asked.

"Yeah."

He kissed me again, smacked me on the ass, and said, "Let's go."

I laughed again, and did exactly like he wanted and got up.

* * *

Several hours later, we stood in front of a judge. I had on a white sundress that I bought a local department store. It was strapless, fitted around my breasts and flowed to the floor. My hair was twisted up in a french twist with loose curled tendrils hanging around my face. I went darker on my make-up, making my eyes pop. Gun wanted to wear his new Captain America shirt. Gunner wanted him to dress up. Gun looked at him pointedly and asked, "Are you?" Needless to say, Gun won that round and I didn't really care what he wore.

Gunner did buy a new pair of jeans that he paired with a black button down shirt. The top two buttons were undone showing off some of his ink. He had his patch on top of it and the sleeves on his shirt were rolled up to his elbows. Next to Gunner to bear witness, stood Ace and Shane, neither of them dressed up, but I didn't care about that either. The only thing that really mattered was that Gunner Reed and I were getting married.

The judge began his very efficient vows when Gunner shockingly cut him off. "You don't mind, got something I'd like to say."

"By all means," the judge said clearly uncomfortable in the presence of bikers.

"You used to watch me. I knew. You watched me for so fucking long." The judge cleared his throat obviously displeased with his language. I just smiled as Gunner shot him a look. "Thing is, I loved your eyes on me. Once I saw you staring, I hoped your eyes would never leave me. Well, we know how that went, but I got some promises I been making, and in front of you, our boy and the rest of these fools, I want you to promise me that your eyes will always be on me. Do you promise?"

"I promise."

"You promise to never leave me. To not let me do anything stupid, and to love me forever?"

I laughed, "I thought you said you had promises?"

"I do, but I gotta hear yours first."

"Then, yeah baby, I promise I'll love you forever. I'll never leave you."

"Thank fuck, and I promise, that as long as air is coming from my lungs, I'll be right there for your eyes to watch me. I'll be with you so much you'll get sick of me, and then when you need space, I promise to give it to you, but that I won't be happy because we wasted too much fucking time apart. I promise to love you. I promise to fucking cherish you, and mostly Mouse, I promise I'll never let anything hurt you again. It's me, you and Gun. You're my family, and I promise to do right by you."

"I love you, Gunner."

I couldn't wait. I reached up and kissed Gunner, hard. The judge cleared his throat again and then declared, "Alrighty, by the power invested in me, by the State of Ohio, I now pronounce you husband and wife."

I kissed my husband again, telling him how much I loved him in between kisses. After a minute, we broke apart. He grabbed my hand, and we left the courthouse. Outside, Donnie, who thankfully ended up being okay, handed me my patch, and I put it on over of my dress. The rest of his brothers, their old ladies and a few of the girlfriends, if that's what you could call them, all shouted, whistled and hugged or slapped each other's backs.

Reggie took Gun in his truck, and I found my place behind Gunner. It was exactly where I wanted to be.

We rode away from the courthouse with as many of The Bleeding Scars MC that could be present on such short notice. I was chilly being that it was fall and I had a sundress on, so I clung tightly to Gunner hoping we'd get back to the clubhouse soon. We stopped at an intersection and directly across from us at the opposing light was Hades surrounded by several Hades Runners. My breath caught and I was so afraid that today, my happiest day, was going to be ruined.

I squeezed Gunner letting him know I was afraid. He shot Hades a glance who lifted his chin and we rode away without any problems. I knew we had a pass for the day, but it wasn't over. How could it be? Today, we were okay. No, not just okay. Today, we were more than okay. Today, we didn't let those scars bleed into our future. Today we moved forward.

I didn't look back to see where they went. Neither of us let them seep any further into today. What we did do was go back to his clubhouse, party hard and when we were done, we went home, made love, and I never woke up another day where I wasn't Charlie Reed in my husband's arms.

The End

Gunner

Us

We're in your studio. A few boxes are stacked next to the wall of mirrors and six stripper poles extend down the center of the studio. I'm sitting in the chair your note requested I sit in. I look around and smile. It's so genuine. My life with you makes me really fucking happy, and watching you fulfill your dream? Priceless. You really out did yourself. When you told me your dream was to open a studio to teach housewives how to strip, I have to admit, I thought you were a little nuts, but after seeing it? Damn. Well, I'm just reminded of how smart you are.

The room goes dark and then blue and purple lights flash. You are there on the pole. You're wearing a black, silk robe, cinched tightly at the waist, black, thigh high, silk stockings, and black, spiked heels.

"Goddamn, my wife is sexy," I murmur. No one is here to hear me and I know you can't over the music, but you're beyond enticing.

Awolnation's 'Sail' starts to thrum through the room. The bass is loud and I watch you. Your body moves slowly at first, one hand grabbing the pole. You move around it in a circle.

I'm mesmerized.

Never have I felt my heart thrum more through my veins than in this moment.

You bend at the waist and flip back up as they sing "*sail*". Your hair flips. Your hands roam over your body, moving seductively over your silk, covered breast. The urge to move to you, grab you and fuck you silly is strong. You're a drug. I know your potency will only get stronger, if I wait. You smile at me as your eyes glance down to see my cock straining against my jeans. You sway your hips. You tease me.

Hand over hand, you raise your body on the pole. Your ankle is hooked around it, and I admire the shape of your legs. They're toned and tan, and right now, look longer than I've ever seen them. You begin to spin on the pole. Your body is a work of art. I want to rip the robe off of you, and see all you have to bare, but this is your show. One you are giving to me quite nicely.

You're at the top of the pole again and you flip backward. Your body arches with the pole and your robe slips up. I can see a small black thong. The curves of your ass are driving me crazy. Then, you near the end of the pole,and you spread your legs. The barest hint of your perfect pussy peeks out at me. You reach the ground, move your body, and mimic fucking. I shift in my seat, adjusting my dick. You're making me fucking wild. I feel like a fucking beast ready to claim you.

You move to your hands and knees and crawl to me.

"Jesus," I hiss.

You move around me touching my shoulders as you sway your hips. I put my hand on your tie attempting to rid you of the robe; The stupid robe that's obstructing my view. My, how you taunt me and I wonder, not for the first time, how I got so lucky.

You slap my hand away, "No touching." You throw a leg over my lap and you give me the best fucking lap dance of my life. Your pussy grinds against me. You're not even shy about the moan you make. You turn your back to me, making me suck in a breath as the curve of your ass grinds against me. Your hair flips smacking me in the face.

"God, I want you." I groan. Your hands move over my thighs, then you grab my hands and you guide me to the tie holding your robe closed. I untie it and you let it fall from your shoulders exposing your back.

I hiss. There on your back is everything. You tattooed the MC's logo on your back, and right where the brand was, it says, "Property of Gunner."

I'm out of control with need. I don't care if the song is still blaring, or if you had another song in mind, I need to be inside of you.

I unzip my pants and pull my cock free. Then, in a fast movement, not even waiting for you to give me anything else, I move your panties aside and thrust into you.

"Gunner, are you even listening to me?"

No, I fucking wasn't. Shane and I were at The Select Club. Some unimpressive dancer was on stage, and I was daydreaming about my wife and the dance she gave me just yesterday in her new studio. It beat anything these dancers could do. We'd been sitting at the bar waiting for Skye to get in for her shift. I'd already beat the fuck out of Dick which ended with him pissing his pants, and truthfully, Shane held me back from doing far worse to him.

Shane nudged my shoulder. I turned my head and saw the blonde, Skye. She must've slipped in while my thoughts were on Charlie. She looked ragged, not that I paid much attention to her the last time I was here, but I could barely believe that this lady could dance, she could barely walk. She moved down the hallway that led to the dressing rooms. I got up to follow, and Shane mumbled, "Keep your cool, man."

Yes, part of the reason I brought him here was to make sure I kept my cool. Not that I'd hit a woman, but I was still pretty fucking pissed, If it wasn't for this broad, Santos wouldn't have gotten a drop on Charlie.

We passed Frank, and he gave us a chin lift. He knew I married Charlie, and I actually liked the guy. Skye wasn't in the dressing room, which surprised me. We looked around, she only had a minute on us. Where the fuck could she have gone? There was a small bathroom that I hadn't noticed at first, because it was behind rows and rows of clothes on freestanding rolling clothes racks. I opened the door with Shane was close by. Inside, sitting on the toilet seat was Skye. Her head lulled to the side and a needle stuck out of her arm.

"Jesus," I muttered. There was no way I was going to have a talk with her in this condition. I wasn't even sure she was conscious.

"Looks like she might be OD-ing, Shane said.

I lifted her head and smacked her face, not hard, but enough. She opened her eyes and smiled at me. "Are you here to end it?" Her eyes lazily moved to Shane, "Are you my angel here to make it all stop?"

"No, we're not fucking angels," I snapped.

She looked at me again, "You. I know you. You're the one that hell guy was talking about. They think I'm so stupid, because I'm a stripper." She smiled as if her own words amused her. "They probably didn't even think I paid attention to them. You know it was all a set up, right? They didn't take her because that guy wanted to fuck her, they took her because they wanted you distracted. Said you'd be so caught up in finding her, you wouldn't even notice what was going on right under your own nose." She looked on dreamily and her eyes moved back to Shane. She reached her hand up for him, her needle falling to the ground, "Take me, angel. I'm ready."

Thank you

Hey, you guys! (said in my Goonies voice) Thank you! Thank you for reading this book and I would love for you to please leave a review on Goodreads and Amazon.

After writing Tainted by Crazy, which had it's own dark elements but Maple didn't cuss, I needed to go darker. I love writing MC's, so here we are. I do plan on writing more from this story. For sure Ace and Reggie, and most likely Shane too.

Books are not born alone, so I need to thank some wonderful people. Thank you Kevin. I love you honey. Thank you Misty, who at nine months pregnant took my kids so I could go write. Thank you Nicole, you are a wonderful editor and friend and you help make every book possible. Thank you Louisa for managing Blushing Babes are Up All Night and for being such an awesome friend. Thank you, Stephanie, Tera, Jade, Kerry and Dawn, you ladies rock! Thank you Emily with Social Butterfly. I don't know how I got lucky enough to have you in my corner, but each and every book I'm so dang grateful. Thank You Lisa Hines, Chrissy Weston, Renee McKinney and Cheryl Wilkins. Thank you Hang Le, for making me one hell of a sexy cover. Thank you Shana and Jessica, yeah I know I thank you every book, and even Jess who doesn't read my shit, I still love you. You ladies are the fucking shit. Both of you help me smile on a daily basis. Hey, Katie and Melissa, thanks for reading my books, giving me feedback and just being awesome sisters. Thank you a million times to all of the blogs who have shared, read or helped support this book. Being a blogger myself, I know how much time and effort goes into it and you matter to us authors more than you know.

ABOUT THE AUTHOR

Website, order signed books here!

http://abbymccarthyauthor.com/

Twitter

abbyemccarthy

Facebook

Facebook http://www.facebook.com/abbymccarthyauthor

Abby McCarthy is reader and a lover of words. She is a blogger turned author and released her first novel in May 2014. She is a mother of three, a wife and a dog person. She has always written, sometimes poetry, sometimes just to vent about failed relationships, however in parenthood she has found her voice to help keep her sanity. Words have flowed from her, to review and with the support of amazing friends in the Indie community she has decided to pursue her dream of writing! She loves to write and read romance, because isn't that something we all yearn for? Whether it be flowers and hand holding or just the right tug on your hair. Isn't that what life is about? The human connection?

Other books by Abby McCarthy

Standalones

Series

The Wrecked Series

Made in the USA
Middletown, DE
17 October 2022

12888547R00163